Full Figured 18:

Carl Weber Presents

Full Figured 18:

Carl Weber Presents

Monica Walters

and

Treasure Hernandez

www.urbanbooks.net

Urban Books, LLC
300 Farmingdale Road, NY-Route 109
Farmingdale, NY 11735

ISBN 13: 978-1-64556-451-5
ISBN 10: 1-64556-451-7

First Trade Paperback Printing March 2023
Printed in the United States of America

10 9 8 7 6 5 4 3 2 1

Distributed by Kensington Publishing Corp.
Submit Orders to:
Customer Service
400 Hahn Road
Westminster, MD 21157-4627
Phone: 1-800-733-3000
Fax: 1-800-659-2436

Full Figured 18:

Carl Weber Presents

Monica Walters

and

Treasure Hernandez

Love Won't Let Me Wait

by

Monica Walters

Prologue

Giánni

"You know, it's really pitiful that you're so insecure. You already a big bitch. You should be happy anybody wants to be with you at all."

My eyebrows shot up in shock as Jermaine spit his words of venom. I'd just accused him of fucking around on me, but it wasn't without evidence. I almost let the tears fall from my eyes. Instead, I allowed my anger to step to the forefront and take control of the situation. I grabbed his phone from the countertop and threw it right at his head. He quickly ducked to avoid impact.

"You are a pitiful excuse for a man. I mirrored your phone, Maine. I've seen *every* text message you've sent *every* slut for the past few days. Why do you think I've been at my parents' house instead of coming home?"

This was all my fault. The signs had been there from the beginning. However, the words he spit at me hurt because they were my own thoughts that he was mirroring. I'd told myself countless times, *at least you have a man.* That was the most toxic shit I could have ever said to myself. Toxicity wasn't just someone making excuses for their fraud attitude and actions. It was also downing yourself to believe you didn't deserve better.

We'd been together for a little over a year, and I allowed him to move in with me three months ago—like a dummy. In my mind, I thought I could be there for him more if we lived together. Despite my parents' warnings, I let him persuade me to do all sorts of things, starting with taking out a personal loan for five grand. He needed a new transmission for his truck and didn't have all the money. I was stuck paying the loan back because he had no intentions of *ever* paying the monthly note, knowing that it could ruin *my* credit and put *my* job at Community Bank at risk.

And still, I accepted him and his toxic behaviors . . .

As I walked to our bedroom, he grabbed my arm and slung me against the wall. "Don't you *ever* in your life do no shit like that again. If that had hit me, I would've beat yo' ass in here."

That was one thing he had never done before. Jermaine had never put his hands on me. This was escalating into dangerous territory. I needed to get him out of my house. If nothing else had moved me toward that decision, this did. I refused to let a man hit me. My dad and my brother would murder to protect and defend me.

I continued to our bedroom as I mouthed off, "You have to go. I can't take any more. You've sucked me dry of all my confidence, self-worth, and self-esteem. I can do so much better than you."

He chuckled as he stared at me. "Girl, I don't know who lied to you."

I wanted to cry, but again, I'd brought this on myself. We rarely went anywhere in public together. We'd go to a matinee at the movie theater every now and then, but that was about it. He refused to go to dinner with me because he said I ate like a pig. He made it seem like I was sloppy and unhealthily large. I was a healthy size twenty-two. Granted, I could probably stand to lose a few pounds since I was starting to have pain in my knees, but other than that, I didn't have any medical issues. Plus, I was always fly when I stepped out. There was nothing sloppy about me.

I began pulling his clothes out of the drawer, showing him I meant business. There was only so much a person could take, and I was at my limit. I pulled my phone from my pocket and stared at him. "I need you to leave. Take all yo' shit and get out of my house. You can do that voluntarily or involuntarily. I can *definitely* call for reinforcement."

I unlocked my screen, ready to hit the emergency call button, then looked up at him as he fumed. "You have five seconds to decide which scenario is gonna play out. Five . . . four . . . three . . . two—"

"A'ight, bitch, a'ight. I'm leaving. You ain't shit anyway. Big ass can barely fuck. I don't even know why I was here."

"I know why, nigga. Because no woman who values herself will put up wit' yo' broke ass! You bring nothing to the table but mediocre dick. But I loved the hell out of you, and I was good to you. What did I get in return? Disrespect and chlamydia."

I slowly shook my head as my lip quivered. I couldn't believe I'd let myself sink this low. My parents didn't raise me to accept this type of abuse from a man. I was so much better than this. I *deserved* better than this shit, and as soon as he was out of my life, I would pamper my-damn-self and restore my confidence in just who the fuck I was . . . a beautiful, black queen.

Chapter 1

Giánni

Two years later . . .

I yawned so hard it felt like my mouth was about to come unhinged from my face. I wiped the tears that accumulated in the corners of my eyes, then rested my cheek on my hand. Today had been extremely slow, and had I not had a glass office, I would have taken a power nap. The tellers seemed busy today, but as a loan specialist, I only worked if people came in to apply for a loan or someone applied online. Commercial loans were my specialty.

I worked my ass off to get people approved. That made the bank more money and laced my pockets quite nicely as well. I'd gotten an $11 million loan approved for a megachurch here in Beaumont, and the bonus I received for that had paid off my Toyota Camry two years early. However, I haven't had a significant loan approval since then, and that was almost a year ago. If I could get another million-dollar approval, that would help me *really* enjoy my vacation to Jamaica in August.

Since I'd left the toxic situation with Jermaine's ass, I'd tried to cater to myself more. Besides this solo trip to Jamaica, I'd enrolled in a pole-dancing class and began taking vocal lessons. I loved singing. It gave me such peace, and the lessons taught me breathing techniques that were great for stress relief. The pole-dancing class was my form of exercise. I'd lost a few pounds and had gone down a size in my waist. Instead of a twenty-two, I was now a twenty.

That may not have seemed like a big difference, but I felt just how significant it was in my knees. I felt lighter on my feet. I was healthier because my BMI had gone down as well. That pole-dancing class had me building muscle, and I loved every minute of it. *Now, if only I had a man to show my skills to.*

Jermaine had ruined me on relationships for a while. However, my family was over the moon happy that I'd finally dropped his loser ass, but now they were worried that I'd sworn off men altogether. It wasn't that, but the right man would have to find *me* because I surely wasn't looking. I was content with enjoying life alone for now. If a man worth my time came along, I would go for the test ride, but this time, I refused to settle for less than everything I wanted.

My desires were simple. He had to have a job and live on his own . . . be stable but still on his grind to improve his life . . . and sweet but rough around the edges. I wasn't superficial about material possessions or about how he looked. I would be happy if he was clean, smelled good, and I could stand to look him in the face. I mean . . . he couldn't look like a gremlin.

As I yawned again, my friend Tucora, who I affection- ately called CoCo, knocked on the door to my office. "Hey, CoCo. Y'all finally slowed down out there, huh?"

"Yep, but you need to walk around the branch a little more. Get out of this office. Ford came in today to make a deposit, and his eyes darted over to you a few times."

I rolled my eyes as I pushed my curls over my shoulder. She was always trying to hook me up with somebody. It seemed she'd been on this Ford guy kick for a couple of months. "Girl, whatever."

"Whatever, nothing. He asked for your name today."

My eyebrows rose. Then I frowned. "Besides my name, what other information did you volunteer?"

"Who, me?" she asked as she laid her hand on her chest and looked around my office like it was full of people.

I chuckled. "You make me sick. I'm not chasing no nigga, so I hope you volunteered *that* shit."

She laughed. "I told him you had a major attitude because you needed to get fucked. This drought has lasted long enough, pooh."

I discreetly shot her the finger as I rolled my eyes yet again. "Shut up, CoCo. Don't you have some work to do?"

She chuckled and said, "I must be telling the truth. Are we still going to our pole-dancing session tonight?"

"I don't know. I need to visit my people. I haven't been there all week, and you know that's saying a lot. My daddy is going to put out an APB on me in a little bit if I don't show up."

"Gi, it's only been two days."

"Okay, and you know I normally swing by their house every day after work. It depends on what time it is when I can get away. Don't hate how much my family loves me. I'm a daddy's girl 'til the day I die. Period."

"And on that note, I'm going back to work. Call me and let me know one way or the other."

"Okay."

As she sashayed out of my office, I stood from my desk to be nosy and see who was signing in at the help desk and why. CoCo was right. I needed to get out of my office and mingle. That would also help rid me of the sleepiness that had been plaguing me all day.

As I made my way to the gentleman, he spun around and smiled. *Jesus Lamont Christ*. It was Ford. I'd never really seen him so up close, and I was regretting every moment of missed opportunities.

His gorgeous, white smile had my insides melting under his gaze. I smiled back as I got closer. "Hello. I left my office before I could see whose services you needed today."

"I think you're the woman I'm supposed to see, Ms. Giánni."

Aaah. He'd asked for my name because he needed to handle business. I glanced over at CoCo and visualized myself kicking her in her damn mouth. "The handle isn't necessary. Giánni is fine, Misteerrr . . ." I questioned, allowing my voice to trail off as I extended my hand.

"Ford. No handle necessary on my name either."

I nodded, then quickly turned on my heels as I said, "Follow me, please."

My face was heating up, and I refused to allow this man to see me blushing. Once we'd gotten to my office, I extended my hand toward the chair in front of my desk. "Have a seat, Mr. Ford. Unlike you, I'm at work, and they require me to be professional."

He smiled as I closed the door, but he didn't respond to my statement. When I sat behind my desk, I pulled up the login information to mark his name off. *Ford Ajani Noel*. That was a unique but beautiful name. "Okay, Mr. Noel, I see you wanted to inquire about a business loan. Is this for an existing company, or will it be a start-up?"

"It's existing. I've already paid off my first loan."

"Great. That gives us something to work with. Let me look at your information."

As I worked, I could feel his gaze on me. That shit was making me so nervous. Usually, while waiting, people played on their phones. This man was staring at me like he was in a daze. *Shit.* I was starting to sweat under my breasts, and my scalp was sizzling under this damn wig. When I lifted my eyes to him, he met my gaze. There was no smile this time. It felt like he was looking through to my soul and taking my clothes off simultaneously.

I cleared my throat. His stare made me nervous as hell. "I'm sorry for staring, Ms. Giánni. You're just so beautiful."

I wanted to huff. Hopefully, he wasn't one of "those" guys. The ones that flirted to get in a woman's panties, then pretended she didn't exist. Although something told me he wasn't that guy, I couldn't stop my mind from going there.

"Thank you, Mr. Noel."

As if sensing my slight attitude, he voiced, "I apologize again. I'm extremely forward, and it's something my father once told me could get me in a world of trouble. But I figured it was better to let someone know how I felt. It could make their day or knock them down a peg, whichever was needed. Please, don't let me take up too much of your day. What do I need to do?"

"No apology needed. I just need to put in your financials and more information on how much money you're trying to borrow."

He proceeded to explain to me how he was trying to expand his trucking business. He owned an eighteen-wheeler and a dump truck and was trying to purchase another one of each. He set a business proposal on my desk along with his financial records. I was thoroughly impressed. He was way more prepared than a lot of people. "This looks great. Let me input some of the information. How did you get into driving trucks?"

He smiled. "Honestly? I didn't want to go to school, and a friend told me about classes he was taking to get his CDL to drive trucks. It was only a six-week course. My parents told me I had three choices: school, the military, or getting a job. I didn't know why they gave me choices because they ultimately wanted me to go to a university to get a four-year degree like my brother. So instead, I went to truck driving school and got my CDL to enter the workforce. While the job has little prestige, I make a decent living."

Yes, you do. He was right about that. He profited nearly three hundred grand last year. His total earnings before taxes and expenses were almost twice as much. "Well, they're probably proud of you."

"Naw. They hate that I drive trucks. My dad is a retired attorney, and my mother is a retired nurse. My older brother is the mayor of San Antonio. So I was the rebellious, spoiled one."

I gave him a soft smile, then turned my attention back to the computer. My parents were the total opposite. They didn't care what we did as long as it was legal and provided us with an income that would be sufficient for us to take care of ourselves. But of course, our happiness mattered to them as well.

As I continued to process his loan request, I had to also factor in his monthly bills to calculate his debt-to-income ratio and pull his credit score. He finally looked away from me and began playing on his phone. I took that opportunity to scan his vanilla latte complexion. His bald head and beard were sexy as hell, but his dimples when he smiled were warm and inviting. However, he frowned while he stared at his phone, and I nearly creamed my panties.

His rough side could be seen in that frown, and I was mesmerized. I started sweating when he looked up from his phone and caught me staring at him. He smiled slightly as his head tilted. I quickly averted my gaze to my computer. "Ms. Giánni, I have some business to handle. How much longer will this take?"

"I apologize. Only another five minutes or so. I'll have you sign your paperwork, and then we can call or inform you by email to let you know if your request is approved."

"Okay."

His brows furrowed once again as he stared at me and nodded in acceptance. After taking a deep breath, I hurriedly inputted the rest of his information instead of stealing glances at him. That shit was so unprofessional. I turned the screen to him and handed him the stylus from the electronic device so he could initial and sign. Once I went over the details, and he confirmed them by initialing them, he signed the final document.

"Thank you, Mr. Noel. You should have an answer by tomorrow. If not tomorrow, then Friday."

He stood from his seat, and I did as well. He extended his hand to me, so I placed my hand in his. He gently shook it and said, "Thank you. I would prefer that you be the one to call me."

I smiled somewhat and nodded. "I will be since I'm the officer on the paperwork. Enjoy the rest of your day, Mr. Noel, and thank you for doing business with Community Bank."

He tucked his bottom lip into his mouth as his thumb caressed the top of my hand. "Thank you for giving me a reason to do my business here."

He winked at me, then exited my office, leaving me with conflicted feelings. CoCo was practically running in my direction when he exited the bank. "Girl," she whispered harshly when she reached my doorway.

I licked my lips and tried to gather my composure. His aura was still in my office, suffocating the hell out of me.

She walked inside and closed the door behind her, and the lingering scent of his cologne wafted its way to my nose. Closing my eyes and taking a deep breath, I said, "That man is dangerous."

"What? What are you talking about?"

"He could have me acting like the dumb bitch I was with Jermaine. If I'm not careful, that man could have me losing myself again. But he's just that fine . . . and charming. Jesus."

CoCo sat in the seat he once occupied. "Well . . . I mean . . . shit. I don't know what I want to say to that. Losing yourself is never good, but fireworks were in this office when he was here. I couldn't quite make out your facial expressions, but I could clearly see his. His eyes barely left you, girl."

I huffed and leaned back in my chair for a moment as I stared at his request for five hundred grand. His loan history was short, and he'd only borrowed one hundred grand the first time. He had excellent credit and the income to cover it, though. "I could see him staring at me. I'm wet all underneath my titties. I gotta go clean myself up."

CoCo laughed, then made her way back to her station as I headed to the bathroom. It had been a long time since a man affected me that way. I'd seen some attractive men, but Ford Ajani Noel could get it all. I couldn't be a fool again . . . I *refused* to be a fool again. Going into the stall, I silently cursed myself because I knew I would have to put toilet paper in my panties or forego wearing them altogether. They were soaked.

I only had an hour left of work, but I knew I would be thinking about him almost the entire time. Opting to use toilet paper, I stuffed it in my panties, then pulled my pants back up. After washing my hands and wetting a paper towel, I dabbed under my breasts, sighing at the coolness I felt. I slowly shook my head, condemning myself to hell for my devilish thoughts, then headed back to my office.

I was sure of one thing: I would do everything I could to ensure his loan request would be approved.

Chapter 2

Ford

"You had one job, my dude. Pick up a load of 60/40 dirt and bring it to a residence. Where the hell are you?"

I was beyond pissed. My reputation preceded me in my business, and people expected professionalism when they called F.A.N. Transport Service. Chris was MIA, and I couldn't understand why. He should have delivered this load two hours ago.

"I'm sorry, boss man. I'm on my way."

"Naw. Where are you?"

"I stopped to get something to eat."

"Bring it back to the yard."

I ended the call. Now I would have to deliver this load of dirt to the customer for free. Losing money always puts me in a fucked-up mood. Had it not been for fine-ass Giánni Judice, I would have called him right then and fucking went off. I'd been watching her beautiful ass for months, not wanting to approach her for fear of how she would receive me.

I really had to control my mouth in her presence. I was overly forward, and everything in me wanted to tell her how fine she was and how I'd fantasized about making love to all her curves. Her thickness caught my attention and wouldn't let it go. Whenever I was in the bank, I looked for her. I could have easily done what I needed to do from the drive-thru, but I couldn't see her if I didn't go inside.

When I looked at the bank's website and saw she was in commercial lending, I knew I would see her soon. I was trying to expand my business, but with workers like Chris, that would be damn near impossible. I still drove the eighteen-wheeler, but I took off today to handle business. Chris had been driving my dump truck for a month, and he'd already missed two delivery times. Today would be his last day working for F.A.N.

I felt like twenty-three dollars an hour was decent pay for a new employee with little experience. His insurance would have gone into effect next week, but oh well. He missed out on that *and* the five hundred thousand dollar sign-on bonus. He would have been eligible for the bonus after working without incident for ninety days. *Five grand.* How does a person fuck up an easy five grand over stupidness like this?

Allowing my mind to go back to my thoughts of Giánni, I couldn't help but bite my bottom lip. I knew she was feeling me as much as I was feeling her. I'd caught her teller friend eyeing me several times, then calling her. Giánni was the perfect representation of the word "woman." When God took the rib from Adam, that was who he came up with. She was so beautiful, and her smile somewhat mirrored mine. She had dimples just like me.

Her round face, thick lips, big titties, and phat ass called out to my soul. When she wore a shorter skirt, and I saw those thick-ass legs, I knew I was all in. She would have to be able to maintain a serious rejection of me for me to stop trying to be with her . . . like threaten to file a restraining order on a nigga. She didn't overdo the makeup, either. I could tell I wouldn't discover a different person once she wiped it off.

I closed my eyes for a moment, visualizing how intense her gaze was when she thought I wasn't paying attention to her. She'd soon learn that whenever she was near where I was, my attention would always be on her, even when she thought it wasn't. I tried to remain professional, but looking at her fine ass wouldn't allow me to. I had to verbalize *something*. While it seemed to turn her off initially, she soon recovered.

I was never one to play games or waste time on something I wanted. I suppose I was impatient in a way. A relationship of some kind was what I desired, and I wanted to believe that Giánni was the woman to fill the position. I was 32 years old and ready to start a family. As I sat in my truck, fantasizing about spending time with her, Chris drove into the driveway. There wasn't an ounce of dirt in sight.

It was gonna take everything in me not to strangle the fuck out of him. I hopped out of my truck and headed to where he was parking. As soon as he got out of the truck, he said, "My bad, boss man. I lost track of time."

"Where's the dirt, Chris?" I asked calmly.

"I brought it to the customer."

I took a deep breath, trying to calm the adrenaline that I felt coursing through my body. "What did I say for you to do when I talked to you?"

"Bring it to the yard."

"What about that is hard to understand? Hand me the keys."

I extended my hand, and he hesitantly dropped them in my palm. I brushed past him, heading to the truck. I could smell the scent of weed all over him. It was seeping from his fucking pores. When I got to the truck, he was right behind me. I frowned hard at him before I opened the door. The smell slapped me in the face before I could even get in.

"Yo, this shit ain't cool, man. Get yo' shit out of here. You gotta go."

Glancing in the truck, I could see the rolling papers in the console and fucking seeds and roaches on the damn floor. I was so angry I could have slammed his ass in the door of the truck.

"Ford, please give me another chance. I fucked up."

"My name is Mr. Noel, and your chances have run the fuck out."

I stepped back and watched him get his shit, because the last thing I needed him to do was further destroy my property. I'd made it to 32 years old without getting arrested, and I would like to keep it that way. Once he finished, he turned to me. "I apologize, Mr. Noel."

I didn't respond to him. He walked off, and I couldn't help but think about where he would go from here. These kids didn't give a damn about anything, and they grew up to be adults who didn't know how to be responsible. Chris was young, 22 years old, and still behaved like a teenager. I could only shake my head in disgust. I wished him the best and that he would grow the hell up. In the meantime, I would have to find someone else to drive this truck. I couldn't have it down too long. That was money I would be losing.

After going to the office and hanging the key on the hook, I called someone to come and clean it for me, then headed home to shower and get ready for dinner at my parents' house. I dreaded it, but every Wednesday, we had a family dinner. My big brother, Ducati Roman Noel, had gotten away from here and was no longer subjected to it. They didn't give him as hard a time as they did me since he'd gone to school and majored in political science.

Whenever he rolled through, the visit was always pleasant. However, for me, most times, it turned into a "bash Ford" session. I made more money than Mayor

Roman Noel made. He refused to run on the name Ducati. My dad loved Ducati motorcycles and even owned one, so he named his first son after it. The same goes for my name. Fords were his trucks of choice, so that became my name. My mother was in charge of our middle names. My brother feared he wouldn't be taken seriously with his first name. I thought that he just figured it sounded ghetto.

Whatever the real reason, it didn't change the fact that he'd gotten the hell out of here and left me to deal with them alone. Unbeknownst to him, his name came up every time I was there. They were either bragging about something he'd done or condemning me for not following in his footsteps by attending school and attaining at least a four-year degree.

It wouldn't bother me as much if they never acknowledged my accomplishments, but it irritated the hell out of me that they constantly downed my career choice, like I was borrowing money from them all the time or something. Ducati and I were pretty close and talked almost daily, even if it was just for a few minutes. He had a busy life. Besides his job, he had a family: a wife and three kids. That was something else that they found to talk about . . . how I needed to settle down. I didn't know why I subjected myself to the shit. I could call to find out how they were doing and be done with the whole thing.

However, the grown man in me knew that despite how they treated me, I needed to treat them with respect. How they treated me was their problem, but how I responded to them would be my problem. I knew that one of the reasons why I was blessed beyond measure was because of the way they handled me. I wasn't the most religious man, but there was a part of the Bible that my pastor was teaching that was in Matthew 5:44. I was successful and had more than my heart desired because of how I blessed them . . . the very ones that persecuted me.

I was still a work in progress, and I knew there would only be so much I could take, but my way of getting back at them would be to continue proving them wrong. There would come a day when they would need me and my "little" trucking business to be of service to them, and just as Joseph in Egypt helped the brothers that sold him into slavery, I would help them, without a doubt.

After I'd gotten home and showered, I thought about Giánni and wondered what she was doing at this very moment. I should have asked her for her number. *No, I shouldn't have.* Then again, she probably would have turned me down. She would have crushed a nigga's spirit. But that was okay because she was going to be mine whether or not she wanted to be.

Once I got dressed and splashed on a bit of cologne, I locked up and took the ten-minute drive to my parents' house. The drive over went by in a haze because my mind had transitioned from thoughts of Giánni to the loan I hoped I got approved for. I was ready to take F.A.N. to the next level. I had already taken out an ad for a full-time mechanic, and the moment I found out the loan was approved, I'd put out ads for drivers. I needed four full-timers and one part-timer.

I got out of my truck and headed to the back door. I could see my mama in the kitchen, putting the finishing touches on dinner, and my dad standing behind her, holding her close. One thing I admired about them was how strong their love was. Dad always catered to my mom's every need, and she did the same with him. I wanted a love to rival theirs. Arguments and fights were few and far between, and until this "issue" with my career choice, I would have said I grew up in the perfect, loving home.

I suppose I could still say that. My childhood was amazing. They were firm but loving, and I couldn't have asked for better parents back then. But the side of them they'd shown me since my venture into truck driving wasn't the same parents I grew up knowing. I was still baffled at just how long they'd kept this going . . . well, mainly my dad. My mom just cosigned nearly everything he said like his word was golden. She'd done that my entire life. I'd been driving for almost eleven years. I thought when I started my own business three years ago, they would eventually get over it. Not so.

I knocked on the door, then entered. My mama smiled at me as I made my way to her and kissed her cheek. "Hey, Mom."

"Hi, baby."

I shook my father's hand and nodded as I said, "Hey, Dad."

"Hello, son," he responded.

He kissed my mom's neck, causing her to giggle, then walked away to the family room. I followed behind him as I always did. After sitting in his recliner, he said, "Your mom is cooking your favorite tonight."

I frowned slightly. How I hadn't noticed that when I walked in was beyond me. I loved the hell out of her meat loaf and potatoes. "Really? I wasn't even paying attention to what was in the pot."

"How can you miss the smell of smothered pork chops?"

I wanted to roll my eyes. My mouth had started watering as I anticipated sinking my teeth into that meat loaf. "Dad, my favorite is meat loaf."

"Huh? I could have sworn it was smothered pork chops."

He looked perplexed. It wasn't like him to forget details. He was an attorney. Ducati and I couldn't pay him to forget anything when we were younger. "It's okay, Dad. I like smothered pork chops too. It won't go to waste."

He chuckled. "I know your greedy ass won't let it. Your mom's cooking is all our weakness. Ducati called earlier and said he plans to be in town in a couple of weeks. He wanted to plan an outing. He said he would be calling you to talk about it."

"Okay."

He stopped there. He didn't talk about how proud he was of him or what family stuff he had going on. Something was definitely up with him. I hadn't visited since last week, but he seemed to be his usual self. Making an excuse to go and talk to my mama, I said, "Let me see if Mama needs any help."

"Okay."

I quickly went to the kitchen to find her pulling corn bread from the oven. She smiled at me as she brought it to the countertop. I glanced back toward the family room to make sure my dad hadn't decided to follow me. "Mama?"

"Yes, baby?"

"What's going on with Dad?"

"What do you mean?"

"I don't know. He seems different. He didn't remember what my favorite meal was. Dad never forgets anything."

I didn't even want to bring up Ducati because I didn't want her to get started on how I should be more like him.

"Well, we are getting older, son." She chuckled softly. "However, there are some things we need to speak to you about."

That shit had made me nervous immediately after she said it. That could only mean bad news. If it were good news, she would have said so already. "Okay. Will that happen before or after dinner? Well, let me rephrase. I hope it happens before dinner because now you have me on edge."

"As soon as I turn the fire off on these greens, we'll talk to you. We wanted to wait until Ducati was here so we could talk to you both at the same time, but he can't get away for a couple of weeks."

"Well, do you need any help with anything?"

"No. Go keep your father company."

"Okay."

I returned to the family room to see Dad looking at pictures of my brother's kids on his phone. He had a slight smile on his face. As I sat, he said, "I can't wait until you give us a daughter-in-law and grandkids. Then we'll have some grandbabies that we could spend more time with. When you gon' get a girlfriend?"

I chuckled as I slowly shook my head. "I'm working on it, Dad."

"So you have someone in mind?"

"I do. Her name is Giánni Judice. She works at my bank."

"Hmm. I need a front-row seat to see how this plays out."

I laughed audibly. "Thankfully, that's impossible. If she knew my father was that involved, she might run in the opposite direction."

He laughed along with me as my mama joined us. My nerves heightened once again as she sat next to him. They glanced at each other, then my dad grabbed her hand and kissed it. He nodded at her, and she turned to me. I could see the sudden sadness that clouded her face. Her eyes watered, and the corners of her lips turned down. "Your dad has Alzheimer's disease. He's in the middle stage and is rapidly progressing to the late stage. He has good days and bad days. We found out a while ago, but your father didn't want to worry y'all until the time came that we had to tell you."

I was stunned into silence. The once invincible Horace Noel was declining. Only 60 years old, and he had to deal with dementia. Maybe now he would forget to demean me and my accomplishments and learn to accept who and what I did for a living with the love and support of the great father I knew he could be.

Chapter 3

Giánni

"You know I'm gon' whoop yo' ass, right? I don't care how good you *think* you are with numbers. That won't master strategy," my dad said as he pulled out the dominoes.

"Listen, old man. I don't know who you think you playing with, but your baby girl ain't here right now. Giánni is gone. Gi is here, and she finna put a whoopin' on you like you ain't ever seen. This ain't me talking noise. This straight facts, my nigga."

My dad laughed so hard at my response that he could barely walk back to the table. I couldn't help but join him. It was the same thing every time we played dominoes. I hated that I'd missed my pole-dancing class, but I'd miss any day for my dad. I was his baby, and he was my baby too. My older sister always did her own thing, and my brother was a mama's boy. So I was the only one that spent time with him.

He dumped the dominoes on the table. "Okay. You better back up all that shit you talkin', or I'm gon' clown you about it for months to come."

I laughed because I knew he wasn't lying. He never let me live down much of anything. But, of course, serious matters were different. He was the one who babied me and held me close when I needed it. If I could be with a man like my daddy, I would be set for life. He was the best example of a husband and father. I was determined to follow the blueprint this time around. Jermaine was an imposter, and I refused to let anyone dupe me that way again.

After washing the dominoes and we pulled our nine, I slammed the big six on the table. "I'm in charge of the rock and I have a control fetish."

My dad rolled his eyes and hit me with fifteen, causing me to pipe down and focus on the task. Finally, my mama entered the room with food, and we both put our bones down to see what she'd brought us.

"You two are two peas in a pod, I swear. Gi, I hope you whoop his ass because he's been on me all day, cracking jokes and working my nerves."

I chuckled as he playfully swatted her ass. She set paninis on the table and said, "I made potato soup, but I didn't know if y'all wanted to fool with that while you were playing."

"Bring that soup in here, woman. Ain't nothing gon' stop me from handling Gi's ass."

I laughed loudly, then thanked my mama for the food. She always catered to the two of us and my brother Jules when he was here. When my mama walked away, I said, "Looka here, Lloyd. I'm about to shut you up in just a minute. This ten I'm 'bout to get is just the beginning."

I dropped my domino to the table as he nodded repeatedly. He got so tickled when I called him by his name. That let him know that I meant business. This relationship was the healthiest one I'd ever had. I had a wonderful family and couldn't have been more blessed. My mind drifted to Ford and how he said his parents weren't happy for him. I couldn't imagine my parents not being there for me or celebrating my wins with me.

Once my mama brought our soup, she joined us at the table to watch the competition. Right after I played, my phone vibrated, alerting me of an email. I checked it because I was logged into my work email. I was anxious to see the decision for Ford's application. Sure enough, there was an email requesting a meeting with me. Unfortunately, they only wanted to approve him for three hundred grand. After getting the needed vehicles, I knew he would need more for operating expenses.

I responded to the email, letting my supervisor know that I would meet him first thing in the morning, then watched my dad rack up twenty points on me. He stood from his chair and did a body roll, causing me to roll my eyes. "Nigga, sit down and take this twenty-five."

My mom hollered as she watched our theatrics. Good times were bound to happen whenever I came over, and I loved every minute of it. "Morgan, don't be cheering for *Giánni*. Gi ain't showed up yet. She playing all that offense and forgot all about the D," my dad said to my mama.

He slammed his bone on the table, getting thirty points. I had no choice but to admit that he'd spanked me this round, but I would come back with a vengeance.

I was nervous as I made my way to the conference room. I could barely sleep, worrying about how this meeting would go. Ford was plaguing my thoughts. If nothing else, I wanted to see him succeed. Something about seeing a Black man own his own shit and making it work was sexy as hell. It also proved the opposite of what society thought about them as Black men. Ford seemed so sure of himself and determined to make this business work. I couldn't let him down.

When I walked in, Mr. Hammon was sitting there waiting for me. He smiled, then stood from his seat as his secretary walked in behind me. We shook hands, and I took a seat. He immediately got right to it. "I know you need to get to your office, so I'm going to get right to it. Mr. Noel seems to have all his ducks in a row except his credit history with us. He only has that hundred-thousand-dollar loan that he paid off last year."

"I think he's worth the risk. As you said, he looks good on everything else. He's building a business, and the fact that he wants to expand speaks of how well his business is prospering. I mean, we can see it in his financial records. His records are detailed and concise at the same time. His profit margins are amazing. Let's show a little trust. He has never defaulted on any loan. We should help him build. Please, Mr. Hammon."

He looked through more papers, then looked back up at me. I knew there was only so much begging I could do. I wasn't willing to put my job on the line for a man I didn't know. But technically . . . that was precisely what I was doing. Mr. Hammon looked away again, reading more paperwork. He took a deep breath, then intertwined his fingers and closed his eyes like he was praying. When he reopened them, he grabbed his ink pen and wrote on the top sheet of the loan application.

I was practically holding my breath as I awaited the verdict. Finally, without looking up at me, he said, "Judging by his predictions and budget, he's cutting himself short. Offer him seven hundred fifty thousand to assure he has enough to cover any overhead. He's approved up to seven-fifty."

He finally looked up at me and offered me a smile as I beamed about giving Ford the good news. "I'm trusting you, Ms. Judice. You haven't disappointed us in the past five years that you've been a loan officer, so I'm going to trust that you know what you're doing. I can't trust Mr. Noel just yet because I don't know him, but he's got the loan because I trust you."

I beamed with excitement and shook his hand again. "Thank you. I can't wait to give him the good news."

I stood from the table and grabbed all the paperwork to take back to my office to begin processing it. I would process it for the seven-fifty. He could always apply it back to the loan's principal balance if he didn't need it. I practically skipped back to my office. Before I could get there, CoCo stopped me. "Hey, Gi. Why you all happy and shit this early in the morning?"

"I got Mr. Noel's loan approved and more than he asked for. I can't wait to call him in to sign the paperwork."

"Who is Mr. Noel?"

"Ford."

"Oh, shit!" She quickly covered her mouth as she looked around to see if anyone had heard her. Thankfully, no customers were inside yet. "You *better* get your man that money."

I rolled my eyes as the smile fell from my face. "Shut up, fool. You have no sense at all. Ugh."

I walked away from her as she laughed. I'd catch up with her later about class and if she went without me. But now, I was anxious to call Ford. As soon as my ass touched the chair, I logged into my computer to see if my supervisor had added the details to his account yet, and he had. So instead of processing the seven-fifty as I had planned, I decided to call him first.

My hand trembled as I picked up the receiver. I didn't know whether it was my nerves or the excitement of being the bearer of great news. The phone rang twice, and he answered. "This is Ford Noel. How may I help you?"

I was stuck for a second. His baritone voice was so damned powerful and smooth at the same damn time.

The sweet nothings he could whisper in my ear would have me on overflow. Clearing my throat, I quickly said, "Hello, Mr. Noel. This is Giánni Judice of Community Bank and Trust. Your loan has been approved for up to $750,000 dollars. I didn't know if you wanted to take the increase or stay at the five hundred you originally requested. We'll need you to come in to sign the paperwork."

The line was quiet, and I thought I had lost him for a moment. Then as I listened carefully, I could hear the background noise. "Ms. Judice . . . wow. Thank you so much. I'll take the seven-fifty. If I don't need it, I'll decide what to do with it later. I'm on a job right now, but I can be there by two thirty. Is that okay?"

"That's perfect. I'll have your paperwork ready, and we'll deposit the money into your business checking account. Then you can allocate it however you want to in your app."

"I really appreciate this. I know you did something. I just don't know what. Getting a loan is like pulling teeth for someone like me. So, thank you so much."

"Your work and records spoke for you, Mr. Noel. See you at two thirty."

"Okay."

I ended the call and sat back in my chair. This would be a nice bonus, over seven grand. This was why I loved Community Bank. They appreciated their employees. Even the tellers got yearly bonuses. While they didn't contribute to the bank's income, they kept the big machine moving, and the owners valued that. That yearly incentive was the shit when I was a teller. It was ten percent of my annual income.

I sat up in my seat and began processing his paperwork, preparing it for him to sign. I didn't know what the day would bring, so I'd better get this done while I had time.

Soon, my office phone began ringing, and I noticed it was Mr. Noel's number. It was the number I'd just called. I picked it up. "Community Bank and Trust. This is Giánni speaking. How may I help you?"

"Ms. Judice, this is Ford Noel. I wanted to call back and ask if I could take you to dinner tonight. Would you attend a celebratory dinner with me at Larry's French Market?"

I love that damn place! My stomach had the nerve to growl at the mention of one of my favorite seafood spots. There was usually a live zydeco band on the weekends, and people danced and just had a good time. "Umm . . . I don't know about that, Mr. Noel. It would be a conflict of interest because I just got your loan done."

"It would have been a conflict of interest had I asked you last night. But now, the loan is done. No conflict. However, I'll understand if you still don't want to go. Just . . . think about it and let me know when I get there."

"I will. Thank you."

He ended the call, and I wanted to melt in my seat. *Good Lord, this man's voice is everything!* I could barely focus on his paperwork now. Did I want to go to dinner with him? Larry's was way in Groves. That was a thirty-minute drive that I would have to take alone. There was no way I would ride with him. I fanned myself with some papers on my desk as I contemplated what I would do. *What is wrong with you, Gi? I had* to go. How could I turn down a chance to get to know this gorgeous specimen God had created?

Once I'd finished getting all his paperwork together, I pulled up my computer screen to see who was waiting. Just that little while I was working, the lobby waiting area had filled like everyone had come in at once. I had two customers waiting, but the first name immediately pissed me off. However, because I didn't want to make a scene at work, I went to the lobby area and called his name. "Jermaine Brown?"

The smirk that graced his face made me want to curse his ass. When he stood, I said, "Come on in."

Although I felt anger on the inside, I would pretend that his presence meant nothing to me. He came here to start shit. There were a ton of other banks he could have gone to, but he chose the one where *I* worked. There were also several branches of Community Bank he could have patronized if he just had to choose this bank. When I walked into the office, I offered him a seat. "I'm Giánna Judice. How can I help you today?"

"What's up, Ms. Judice?" he asked slowly.

What in the fuck was I thinking when I was with this slow-ass nigga? I smiled politely, waiting for him to say what the hell he wanted with me. When he finally realized that I wasn't going to respond to him, he cleared his throat. "I came because I want to make things right with you. I know it's been two years, but it took me that long to get myself together."

"Mr. Brown, that's a service that is no longer offered. So unless you're here to inquire about Community Bank's services for its customers, we have nothing further to discuss."

"Please, Gi. Hear me out. Let me take you to dinner tonight."

"I have a dinner date already," I blurted. My face heated up tremendously. Why was I trying to make this fool jealous? "If there's nothing else, Mr. Brown, I have customers waiting." *Legit customers.*

He huffed, then stood from his seat. "I won't stop trying. I need you to see that I'm a different man now."

I nearly rolled my eyes. I wanted to say, *Nigga, if you don't carry yo' ass on . . .*

If this foreshadowed how the rest of my day would go, I should have just called in sick. Instead, as I called my next customer, I thought about how I blurted out my dinner plans. I suppose I will be driving to Groves tonight. I had to know Ford if he was plaguing my thoughts like this. No doubt about it.

Chapter 4

Ford

When I walked into the bank, it seemed all eyes were on me. I'd gone home to shower after I finished my load at the refinery. There was no way I would come here smelling like sodium thiosulfate, a harmless chemical used to treat cyanide poisoning, chlorine removal in pools, and so many other things. Anyway. I'd splashed a little cologne on and made sure my skin was good and moisturized. I wanted to be at my best, so it would be hard for Giánni to turn me down again.

As I signed in, I could feel a presence behind me. Turning around slowly, being sure not to startle whoever it was, I caught a glimpse of the most beautiful woman on this side of heaven. Licking my lips in her presence seemed like a natural reaction because everything about her looked tasty as hell. She wore a skirt with a split up the side that revealed her thick, beautiful legs. She knew what she was doing, just like I did.

She smiled brightly and said, "There was no need to sign in, Mr. Noel. How are you?"

"I'm great. How about you?"

"I'm great as well. Right this way, please."

I followed behind her watching her ass jiggle slightly. Of course, my mind went straight to hell after that as I imagined fucking her from behind and seeing all that ass jiggle while I glided in and out of her. My mind needed to come back from the flames, though, before my hose exposed itself. Bringing my gaze up to her hair as it slightly swung across her back only made matters worse because then, I imagined her riding me in reverse cowgirl. When she looked at me over her shoulder, I could have fired off in my pants.

We got to her office, and she smiled, then closed the door behind me. Her smile was bright, and I could see she was extremely happy. *Or is she just happy to see me?* I smiled at her and asked, "So what did you do to get me approved?"

"I didn't do anything but talk to my supervisor about how I believed in you. Your records and credit history spoke for themselves. You're practically perfect on paper."

She glanced up at me and blushed. Apparently, she was thinking about more than what she said for her to be blushing. I sat up in my chair and leaned across her desk. I grabbed her hand and held it between my large ones. The way it heated up only confirmed that what I felt between us wasn't imagined. "Why do you believe in me?"

She stared into my eyes unashamedly. I liked that. "Something about you tells me that you are about your business, even if it's only to prove your parents wrong. However, I do believe it's more than that. I can sense your hunger. You want to succeed and climb the ladder to the top. I wanted to be sure that Community Bank would be the financial institution to help you do so."

I closed my eyes for a moment while still holding her hand. To have someone believe in me this way touched my heart. No one has ever encouraged me the way she has, not even my family. Sure, they thought I was smart, but they always accompanied that acknowledgment with something negative. *You're so smart, Ford, but you can do better than this. You're too smart to settle for being a truck driver.*

When I opened my eyes, I stared right into her slanted brown ones. "Thank you, Ms. Judice. That means so much to me. Please tell me you'll join me for dinner tonight."

She was going to be mine. The faith she had in me without even knowing me just proved that she was wifey material. She was already a wife, just waiting to be scooped up by her groom. I was finally here to whisk her away to paradise. A woman like her deserved to be catered to, appreciated publicly, and worshipped privately.

She bit her bottom lip, revealing her dimples, and slowly slid her hand from mine. That gesture made me think she was about to turn me down, but she said, "I would love to join you."

I smiled and released the tension that was building in my chest. This beautiful woman would be accompanying me to dinner. I was going to invite my parents to come along, but after what she said to me just now, I knew I needed to know everything about her. I wouldn't be able to do that with my parents in attendance. "Is Larry's okay with you? We can change it up if you want to go somewhere else."

"Larry's is perfect. Besides, this is *your* celebration. Why would we go where *I* want to go? This is about you and your business moving to the next level. I'll go wherever you want to go, even McDonald's."

I chuckled at her admission. *Damn.* "Seems like you're perfect too, Ms. Judice."

She blushed again. "Please call me Giánni."

"Please call me Ford."

"Deal."

She began explaining the terms of my loan, interest rates, and consequences if I defaulted, including her credibility with her company. I stared at her the entire time she spoke. I hadn't seen a word on the computer screen or the paperwork she had set in front of me. Instead, I'd begun memorizing every detail about her, from the small mole on her right cheek to her slightly rounded chin. As smooth as her voice was, she had to be a singer. The richness of it was just as sexy as she was.

She wasn't wearing much makeup besides lashes, eyeshadow, and lipstick. Giánni was just a natural beauty. I'd never before dated a full-figured woman, but I wasn't a shallow individual where her body type mattered. She was beautiful in my eyes, which was all that was important.

"Do you have any questions, Mr. Noel? If not, sign here."

"Ms. Judice, my name is Ford. Call me Ford."

"I'm sorry. I forgot that quickly. Do you have any questions, Ford?" she asked as she tilted her head to the side.

Jesus. I had plenty of questions, but none of them pertained to the loan or the business. I would read over the loan documents in my free time. I didn't know this woman, but I trusted her already. She was genuine, and I could feel that in my spirit. "Giánni, I have a lot of questions. All of them are about you, though. So, I'll wait until tonight. Is six too early?"

Her cheeks reddened a bit as she smiled. "Six is perfect. I'll meet you there."

I frowned slightly. Then I thought about it from her perspective. I was a stranger. I nodded in acceptance. "So, listen. I like to eat off the buffet. I need you to be about that life. If I get the buffet, you have to get that too."

"What else is there to get at Larry's?" she asked with a playful frown.

"My kind of woman," I mumbled.

She slid my paperwork to me as she blushed again. This wasn't a damn celebratory dinner. This was a date. I had a feeling that she knew that too. Once I signed my paperwork, I slid them back to her. "Is that it?"

"Yes, sir. You're all set. The money has been deposited into your business account. Here is your receipt for that."

"This process seemed so easy. Thank you for that. I'll be sure to write a review on the website. You're gifted at what you do. I can't wait to spend more time with you away from here, so you won't have to be so professional."

She chuckled. "You may not like me too much after that. I can be loud sometimes, a li'l ratchet, and bossy."

I chuckled too. "You sound fun. Again, I can't wait."

She smiled at me, and I had to reciprocate.

"I can't wait either, Ford. You seem extremely charming."

I lowered my head as I stared at her. One day, charming would be the last word she thought to use to describe me. But when she cleared her throat, I realized I had gotten caught up in her beauty. "I apologize. You are just so beautiful. I can't stop staring at you."

I stood from my seat, towering over her. She couldn't be any taller than five foot seven, which was no match for my six-foot-four-inch frame. Thoughts of what I could do to lift her to my level of elevation were running through my mind, nearly causing me to lose focus again. "See you in a couple of hours, gorgeous."

She smiled and mumbled. "Mmm-hmm."

That shit sounded dangerous, and I was down for every minute of that. I moved fast when shit just felt right, and everything about Giánni felt right for me. When I exited her office, I went to the teller line to withdraw some ends. One of my classmates had a floral shop, and I wanted to swing by and place an order before it got too late. I'd already reserved our table at Larry's since they accepted reservations during the week.

When I got to the front, her friend ended up waiting on me. Somehow, I always ended up at her station. "Hello, Mr. Ford. How are you?"

"I'm good. How about you, Tucora?" I asked as I read her name tag.

"I'm great. What can I do for you?"

"Can you tell me what Giánni's favorite flower is?"

"She loves magnolias. The purple ones. If you can find them, she'll fall in love." She giggled. "Gi loves flowers, but magnolias and lotus flowers are her absolute favorite."

I glanced back at her office to see the huge lotus flower on the wall behind her desk. *Duh, Ford.* "Thank you. I also need to make a withdrawal from my account."

"She's going to know that I told you about her flower. Not many people know that about her. She's somewhat private. So I suggest getting a mixed bouquet, but if they have a purple magnolia, make sure they throw it in."

I gave her a slight smile as I said, "Noted. Thank you."

Hopefully, she'd let her hair down with me. After Tucora had given me my money, I turned to see a man entering her office, and her face didn't look too happy that he was there. As much as I studied her face, I could tell her smile wasn't genuine. The guy had flowers, and she refused them. I decided to make my way back over. I felt extremely territorial now.

When she caught a glimpse of me, her face reddened, and she stood from her desk, but the guy remained seated. As I got to her door, I knocked on it, mainly to get his attention because I already had hers. "Thanks again for everything. See you tonight."

"See you later, Ford."

I winked at her, then glanced at the nigga sitting there. He stood from his seat and followed me as I walked toward the exit. I was very aware of his presence. My mind was wondering why he was giving her such a hard time. Then it dawned on me that I had never asked if she had a man. I thought she wouldn't have accepted my dinner offer if she had been involved with someone.

As soon as we exited the bank, he said, "I guess you her new nigga. Don't mess up because I'm gon' claim what's mine."

I turned to him with a frown on my face. However, I didn't bother correcting him about my status in Giánni's life. She wasn't mine, but she would be eventually. He gave me a slight smirk and walked off. I didn't know who the fuck he took me for, though. I was trying to do right and love my enemies, but I wasn't the type of nigga that would let people walk all over him. I had a feeling we would see each other again.

Before I walked off to head to my vehicle, I turned back toward the bank, wondering if I should check on Giánni. Looking at the card on my paperwork, I decided that I would just call her. When I got to my truck, I pulled the card from the paperwork and dialed her direct number to her office. Flipping the card over in my hand, I realized she'd written her cell number on the back.

The smile that graced my face was unstoppable. There was nothing I could do to keep it from shining through. I hadn't even thought of asking for her number just now, knowing that I could need it. She had all my info, but the only thing I knew about her was her name and where she worked.

When her voicemail picked up, I left a message. "Hey, Giánni, This is Ford. I just wanted to check on you. Call me on my cell phone when you get the message."

I ended the call. She probably had another customer or had left her office. This fool had to be an ex that was still in his feelings. He was pitiful for harassing her on her job.

He could have had those flowers delivered with a note attached saying everything he needed to say. Instead, his presence had only irritated her. I could see that shit in her eyes. Hopefully, tonight, I could rectify all that and make her forget about the interruption of her day.

Giánni Judice would be mine because she was made specifically for me. My past had only prepared me for her, so I appreciated every ex-girlfriend and sour date I'd been on. They all shaped me into the man I am today. The man I was today was ready for the love I could see Giánni was prepared to offer to the right person. I could only pray that God would show her that her Boaz was here.

Chapter 5

Giánni

My nerves skyrocketed when I turned into the parking lot across the street from Larry's. It had taken a lot for me to even show up from the embarrassment of what I knew Jermaine probably did. When he walked out behind Ford, I knew he'd said something to him because that was just the type of fuck nigga he was. Ford had seen that I was irritated for him to come back to my office in the first place.

While this wasn't a date, it felt like one, and I didn't feel like that interaction had worked in my favor. Seeing that I had drama could be a turnoff for him. Jermaine was going to make me get my father and brother involved, which was the last thing I wanted to do. I tried to keep my personal affairs just what they were . . . personal. Jermaine was making that shit hard.

He'd been MIA for the past two years. Now he wanted to pop back up like I'd been pining or even thinking of his ass all that time. Obviously, he didn't get the message earlier. When he said he wouldn't give up, I wasn't expecting to see him again so soon. He was going to force me to file harassment charges against him. I'd threatened him with that before Ford peeked in.

I looked around the parking lot to see if I saw him anywhere. I didn't think to ask what type of vehicle he would be driving. Then taking a deep breath to calm my nerves, I got out of my car. It was only five forty-five, so I was early. I was always early when I went somewhere. I hated being late. Nothing peeved me more than someone who didn't take my time seriously. As I made my way to the street to cross, I saw Ford with a lovely bouquet.

My heart melted with every step I took in his direction. I *love* flowers. The fact that no one had ever taken the time to buy them for me had me wondering if I deserved them at times. The ones Jermaine had bought earlier didn't even count to me. That was a bribery tactic he was using. As I got closer, I noticed a couple of purple magnolias in the bouquet. *That* had my middle pulsating. Purple magnolias were my absolute favorite, but people rarely had them in Beaumont. I had to go to Houston one time to get a bouquet. I'd kept those flowers alive as long as humanly possible.

Once I made it across the street, Ford smiled as he scanned me from my red, four-inch platforms to my off-the-shoulder, red shirt with a train to die for. He licked his lips, and I swore I wanted to give him something to savor every time he did that.

"Hey, Giánni. You look beautiful."

"Hey, Ford. Thank you. You look handsome."

He looked delectable. *God.* This perfectly sculpted man was clad in black pants and a black, short-sleeved shirt that failed to hide the definition his body flaunted. I wanted to slide my hands over his chest and pull him to me by his neck. That bald head and beard combination just did something to me. It had my inner freak wanting to show out prematurely. He extended the flowers to me and said, "These are for you."

"They are so beautiful. I love flowers. Thank you."

He gave me a small smile, then grabbed my hand and kissed it. His lips were so damned soft. "Let's head inside."

I nodded in response because he'd taken my breath away. Being treated like a woman worth chasing was new to me, and that was a sad admission. He intertwined his fingers with mine and led me inside the restaurant. He went to the hostess desk to let them know we'd arrived for our reservation, and we took a seat to wait since we were a little early.

I got a whiff of his cologne as he sat next to me. Just him being so close to me had me nervous as hell. I didn't trust myself to be cool. My body wanted to move faster than my mind wanted to, and his cologne was enticing both. I smelled my flowers as he stared at me. Finally, Ford eased his hand into mine and said, "I feel like this is a date."

"I kind of got that vibe when you handed me the flowers." I stared into his eyes and continued. "You have this aura about you that's extremely magnetic. It sort of puts me in a trance if I'm not careful."

He slid his fingertips down my arm, and I knew he left goosebumps in their wake. Before he could respond to me, the hostess called his name to escort us to our table. "Will the two of you be enjoying our buffet tonight?"

"Yes, ma'am," Ford answered.

I didn't know if I would be able to even eat with the way this man was looking. My time would be spent staring at him and ogling his body, something I couldn't fully commit to doing while at work. Then the hostess placed paper bracelets on our wrists to indicate our buffet purchases, took our drink orders, and told us to enjoy ourselves. The moment she walked away, Ford said, "Come on here. I'm hungry as hell."

I chuckled because those were my sentiments exactly. I skipped out on lunch just to eat like a damn fool when I got here. I would get my money's worth for sure. As we headed to the line, Ford grabbed my hand, gently pulling me in front of him. "Damn," he mumbled.

I glanced back at him, and our eyes met. Without a doubt, he would definitely get kissed if things kept going the way they were. After filling my plate with fried shrimp, crab cakes, and fish, I got a bowl of crawfish étouffée and then returned to our table. When Ford joined me, I noticed he'd gotten a bowl of the gumbo. So that was next on my list.

After setting his food down, he quickly made his way to me and pulled out my chair. Everything this man did had me feeling like I was on top of the world. I just hoped this was real. Once he sat across from me, he grabbed my hands and blessed the food. *Lord, take me now.* He prays too? I was on the verge of sliding right out of my seat.

The moment he was done, he said, "I hope you don't think my manners went on hiatus once I start eating, but I'm finna tear this shit up."

I laughed and quickly covered my mouth. He laughed too. "Why are you covering that beautiful smile? Let loose. Let me see the *real* Giánni Judice."

"You sure you want all that action on the first date?"

He set his gumbo spoon down and gave me a serious stare, showing that he meant business. Then he bit his bottom lip, setting my soul on fire. "I want *all* the action. So don't hold anything back because I won't."

I smiled softly. "I just didn't want to be too loud in here."

"I know you hear all this noise. These folks don't give a damn about nobody else in this establishment. Join them."

He winked at me, and I could have levitated. Instead, I immediately dug into my étouffée and allowed my eyes to roll to the back of my head. I hadn't been to Larry's in at least a year, and it only seemed like the food had improved during my absence. Before I could even filter myself, I released a hum that sounded more like a moan from my lips. My eyes darted up to his, and he was doing his best to bite back a smile.

I narrowed my eyes at him as I swallowed my food. "So, first, you tell me to let loose. Then when I do, you laugh at me?"

He wiped his hand down his mouth, then lifted them in the air. "Hol' on. I'm just trying to keep my slick-ass comments to myself because I don't want to make you uncomfortable. I'm just saying. I wish I could enjoy my food like that. That shit was sexy as hell."

I rolled my eyes at him and continued eating while he laughed. "I gotcha. One for Ford, zero for Gi. Oh, but wait. I'm on offense now."

He laughed more and finished off his gumbo. "I'm not tripping. I can handle it. I can take whatever I dish out."

I repeatedly nodded as I licked my lips. We continued eating and enjoying each other's company, and the moment I was dreading or hoped he'd forgotten about came up. "So, was that your ex that showed up at the bank today? I never bothered to ask you if you were seeing anyone."

"I'm as single as the day I was born. I wouldn't be here if I weren't. Yes, that was my ex," I said as I rolled my eyes. "We broke up two years ago, and he had the audacity to show up at my job today . . . twice! As small as Beaumont is, that was my first time seeing him since I put him out of my house."

"He came back after I left?"

"No. That was his *second* visit. Next time, I'll call the police on his ass."

"Well, he seems hell-bent on getting you back. Told me not to mess up because he was coming back for what was his."

"In his fucking dreams," I mumbled. "He was a user. I provided the whole damn table, and all he had to bring to it was love and loyalty. He couldn't even do that. I set myself up for failure. Had I—"

"Hold it right there. Don't blame yourself for him being a punk-ass boy. It was a hard lesson, and you learned it. But the guilt? That shit is on him. You suffered enough by enduring his pathetic ass."

Damn. I wasn't blaming myself anymore, but I thought I had to prove that I'd definitely learned from that situation. The truth was, it seemed I had to remind myself that I'd learned. However, I was happy that Ford didn't immediately jump to conclusions. I could only hope that he didn't think that I was a dumb broad. I only nodded in acceptance as I watched him eat crumbs off his shirt. I bit my bottom lip, trying to stifle my laughter, then said, "You know there's an entire buffet line of food if you're still hungry. You shouldn't have to eat the crumbs off your shirt."

He looked at me as a smirk found its way to his lips. I'd caught him off guard, but I wanted to change the subject to anything but Jermaine's ass. I laughed at his turned-up lip and his head nod. "You got me, champ. You caught me slipping. So, I guess we even."

"Naw. I don't go for even. I'm extremely competitive."

"Hmm. Sounds like being around you will be interesting. I'm competitive as well. I just hope you have enough grace to accept your whooping like a woman."

"Only if you can accept yours like a man."

"Mmm-hmm. You trash talk, too, I see. It's gon' be on. Let me go get some more food before I snatch your piece of fish off your plate."

I laughed more and realized I was having the time of my life with a man for the first time in years. I ate my piece of fish, enjoying the music that I finally had a chance to pay attention to. As I danced a bit in my seat, Ford appeared next to me with a bowl of gumbo. "See how nice and thoughtful I am? Even when I'm starving, I'm thinking of you."

I laughed and clapped my hands. "You're so sweet. Acts of service will get you *everywhere*."

"Word? What can this bowl of gumbo get me?"

I curled my finger, beckoning him to come closer. He leaned over to me, and I kissed his cheek. He smiled as he reddened a bit. I knew he wasn't expecting a kiss. That wasn't the kiss I *really* wanted to give him, but it would have to do for now. Before walking away, he asked, "So what I get if I bring another plate of food? What about boiled crawfish?"

I laughed and damn near choked myself. "Get away from me before you have me choking to death."

He laughed, then grabbed my hand and kissed it. Public shows of affection were everything, and it was truly something I wasn't used to. When he returned to the table, he said, "This gon' be it. My food done had time to digest, and now I'm getting full."

I chuckled. "Yeah, me too."

"So, what do you like to do in your spare time? I feel like our night is winding down, and I'm not liking that at all."

I gave him a soft smile. "I'm having such a great time. I'm glad I came. I like to sing, spend time with my dad playing dominoes or spades, and I, umm . . ." I glanced to the side and said quickly, "pole dance."

When I looked back at him, his eyes were low. "Damn. I thought you had a smooth-talking voice. I would love to hear you sing. I would also love to see you . . . umm . . ." He turned his head like how I had done and said just as quickly, "pole dance."

"Who knows? Maybe one day you can."

We continued eating, not saying much in between. I suppose both of us were thinking about that pole dance.

I'd never had an audience, but there was nothing I would love more than to perform for him. As I finished my gumbo, Ford asked, "Do you eat oysters?"

"Only if they're fried."

He picked one up from his plate and held it to my mouth. I gave him a one-cheeked smile and opened my mouth, accepting the food from his hand, never taking my eyes off him. I closed my eyes as I chewed. When I opened them, I said, "It's delicious."

He nodded. "I was kind of hoping to get another one of those moans."

I laughed as I rolled my eyes and brought my hand to my forehead. "You are not going to let me live that down, are you?"

"Not in this lifetime."

The waitress appeared with the check, and just as he was about to reach for it, I snatched it from the table. He frowned hard. "What are you doing?"

"Celebrating and congratulating you on the expansion of your business."

"Naw, Giánni. That ain't cool. I invited you."

"So I can't take care of the tab to celebrate you? I promise, if you ask me out again, you can pick up the tab."

He shook his head. "I don't feel comfortable with that. Please hand me the check."

I set it on the table and looked away. I went from one extreme to the next: a man that took everything I had to offer and now one who couldn't accept a gift. When he touched my hand, I looked up at him. He gently rubbed his thumb across the top of it. "I wasn't raised that way. I'm always going to pick up the tab. I'm always going to provide, protect, and offer comfort. *That's* how I was built. I feel like it's my job as a man. So while you aren't my woman, when the time comes that you are, I want you to think about this moment and what I just said. I'm preparing to take care of you for the rest of your life . . . starting now."

I frowned slightly. He was taking this a bit too far. It was only our first date. While I thought I wanted there to be another one, I wasn't so sure now. It seemed like he wanted to move a lot faster than I was comfortable with. I slid my hand away from his and nodded. I remained quiet as the waitress returned and took the check and his card.

As I people-watched, I could feel him staring at me, no doubt trying to figure out where my head was. Honestly, I didn't know where it was at this moment. So while I was flattered, I was somewhat nervous. He seemed to be jumping the gun, and I didn't have the heart to tell him so. So instead, I said, "Thank you for dinner, Ford. I really enjoyed myself."

Until this awkward moment.

"I enjoyed myself as well. I didn't mean to offend you. Hopefully, you won't hold that against me. I'm a fast mover, but I'm willing to move at your pace. I won't try to speed up yours. I just know what I feel and don't spend much time doubting my intuitions. I'm more than willing to wait for you to catch up and figure out what I already know."

I smiled slightly. The mood was way too serious now. So to break it up, I mumbled, "Cocky ass."

Chapter 6

Ford

As I walked out of Peterbilt, I couldn't help but feel a sense of accomplishment. They'd had a sale, and I could purchase two used rigs for under $100,000 with all the warranties necessary to give me peace of mind. Because of this sale, I could also purchase two trailers instead of just one. The dump truck would be the one to cost the most money. The best deal I'd found so far was a 2015 Kenworth for eighty-five thousand.

I wasn't in a huge hurry. I needed drivers for these trucks. I'd had two interviews Monday, and one was a no-go. The other I wasn't totally sure about. I'd also placed an ad for an experienced human resource person to handle all the new hire paperwork and insurance information. Expansion would cost me, but it would pay off in the end. Besides my profits from last year, I saved up quite a bit of money. I knew this would be an uphill battle, but I was ready.

As I got in my pickup, I couldn't help but think about Giánni and our date a few nights ago. When we left Larry's, she'd given me a sweet peck on the lips, but I could also feel I'd scared her off. Sometimes, it was best to keep your visions to yourself because not everyone would understand where you were being led. I knew without a shadow of a doubt that she was the woman for me. She'd given me the silent treatment all weekend and yesterday, even after my good-morning texts.

I wished I had gotten to know more about her past situation with her ex, but since she quickly steered the conversation in a different direction, I knew she didn't want to talk about it. I wasn't the type of man that let a woman take care of me or do anything for me financially. Maybe I should have just let her pay for dinner if it was that crucial to her, but I didn't want to send out the wrong message. I was an alpha in every sense of the word and didn't tend to bend on things I believed in.

However, I felt like I was losing it, and the last thing I wanted to do was go to her job. I wasn't that nigga. So, calling my classmate, I placed an order for those purple magnolias. I even paid her extra to go to Houston to pick them up so Giánni would have them today before her day ended. It had been five days since I heard her sweet, melodic voice, and I was having serious withdrawals already. I couldn't believe she was willing to throw the entire night away because of me not letting her pick up the check.

I slid my hand down my face as I huffed, then headed back to my office to check my messages. My desktop served me better when looking at the online applications and résumés. I needed at least four drivers as soon as possible. I also needed a dispatcher. My job as the owner was to supervise the flow of things. While I knew I would have to get my hands dirty at first, I was trying to set myself up for my future.

When I got to the office, my phone started ringing. I got excited, thinking it could possibly be Giánni. I was disappointed when it wasn't. I answered my brother's call. "What's up, Cati?"

From the time I was a kid learning to talk, I'd short-ened his name to Cati instead of Ducati. It was easier to say, and it stuck. "What's up, bruh? How's everything go-ing?"

"Good. I've been waiting to hear from you. You're supposed to be coming to town soon, right?"

"Yeah. Not this weekend but the next. You think you can have a date for our formal dinner outing?"

"I don't know. What's this formal outing about?" I asked, trying to take the focus off having a date.

"I wanted to tell all of you at once, but since you asked . . . I'm going to run for governor. I'm meeting with the state representative in Beaumont."

"Damn. That's good. I'm happy for you."

"Thanks, man. So how's business going?"

"Good. I've expanded. Just purchased two more rigs, and I'm looking for another dump truck."

"Damn, Ford, that's great news! Why don't you sound excited about it?"

I took a deep breath, then decided to tell him about Giánni. She'd gotten the loan for me, shown me the best time of my life, then ghosted me. After telling him all about her, he said, "I've never known you to be so hurt about something like that. You must really like her."

"Yeah, I do. I've been watching her for a long time. While I don't know her, I've been imagining her as being mine for some months. Ugh, I'm tripping, though. I'm sending her flowers today. If she doesn't respond after this, I'm done. Hopefully, I'll be able to find a date that I can stand long enough for the dinner."

"Maybe she'll come around after she gets the flowers, and I'm sure a personal message."

"Yeah. I think I scared her off. You know how I talk when it comes to something I want."

"Yeah. You like Joseph in the Bible with his li'l coat of many colors. You sound arrogant as hell sometimes."

I chuckled. "She called me cocky when I told her she would be mine and I was preparing to take care of her for the rest of her life."

"Damn, nigga. You said all that?"

"Yeah. I see it, but she doesn't. So, she ain't fucking with me. Anyway, I don't wanna talk about her no more. How's Kelsey and the kids?"

"They're good. The kids are excited about seeing their uncle and grandparents."

"It's been a while. I miss them too."

We continued catching up for another ten minutes, then ended the call, promising to talk again soon. I wanted to tell him about Dad's issue so he wouldn't be surprised at this formal dinner. That way, the shock of it wouldn't completely knock him off his game. Since the dinner was so important, I knew I needed to tell him before Mom and Dad did.

When I talked to my parents yesterday, Dad couldn't remember me even being there for dinner last week. It seemed his mind was slamming into that latter stage quickly as hell. While it pained me, it also gave me a reprieve from the constant ridicule he threw my way. I'd told him of the expansion of my business. While he didn't exactly congratulate me, he didn't criticize me either. He asked a few questions about it concerning payroll and equipment, and that was about it.

After reading over applications and résumés, I called some potential hires for interviews, then hopped in my eighteen-wheeler to transport a hazardous load of sodium bisulfate. As I drove to Calabrian, a refinery in Port Neches, I wished I had declined this job. They took forever and a year to load. Sometimes, I could wait five hours to be loaded and sent on my way. It was ridiculous, but what else did I have to do?

I didn't have many hobbies. I worked to live and lived to work. The only close friend I had was my brother. My work ethic was insane, and it only worsened over the years. I hadn't had a girlfriend in years, and I'd only been in love once. She was a whole slut, though . . . tried to pin a baby on me and everything. After that, I threw myself into work and saving money to buy my rig. I was only twenty-three at the time. Now that I was trying to slow down, I regretted those choices. This life was lonely as hell.

My brother had lived life and gotten a family out of it. He worked hard, but not nearly as hard as I did. So when I wasn't sleeping, I was working. I'd chosen the tough route, but I'd done a hell of a job at making a successful career for myself.

When I got to Calabrian and had gotten checked in, surprisingly, they didn't waste any time getting me to the back to get loaded. I only had to deliver this load to GE Betz back in Beaumont. That was only a twenty-minute drive, if that. My phone rang as I sat in my truck, waiting for them to finish. It was my classmate, Denishia. "Hello?"

"Hey, Ford. I'm heading back from Houston with your flowers. This bouquet is going to be so beautiful. Whoever this woman is, she's extremely blessed to have your attention 'cause, baby, listen. I know of a few women that wanna stake claim to you."

I slightly rolled my eyes. "Denishia, you full of shit. The only reason I got attention back in high school was that I played basketball. Y'all wasn't checking for a nigga with braces and shit back then."

She died laughing, and I couldn't help but chuckle. I looked like a whole-ass nerd, and I was goofy as hell. Once she stopped laughing, she said, "What that got to do with right now? You don't realize that you're getting noticed, boo. You nice . . . *real* nice."

"Uh-huh. That's why the woman I want is ignoring me. How long before you get back?"

"About an hour. Call the office and tell them what you want the card to say."

"A'ight. Let me know when you deliver it," I said as I looked at the time.

It was only ten. Giánni should have her bouquet before four for sure. That was what time she got off work.

"Okay, Ford. Hold your head up. If she doesn't bite after this, maybe she isn't for you."

"Thanks, D. Talk to you later."

I ended the call. I didn't want to hear that Giánni wasn't for me, but maybe the timing was off. After dialing the number to the floral shop, I quickly thought of something short that I wanted to say that would pack a powerful message. After Dawn answered the phone and gave the spiel, I informed her of what I wanted the card to say.

It's hard for me to take things slow because I know our potential. . . . Love won't let me wait. Please call me.

"Aww, that's so sweet. She *has* to call after that. Let me read it back to you just to make sure I got it correct."

She read the words, and I couldn't stop my eyes from closing. I visualized Giánni's face and imagined what her expression would look like when those flowers arrived. I could only hope my words would have the same effect the flowers did. "That's correct, Dawn. Thank you."

"You're welcome, Mr. Noel."

I ended the call and thought about moving on from here. If her reception wasn't something I desired, I would have to find a date for the dinner. Unfortunately, I would have to put a time limit on when that would happen. I wanted to give a potential date at least a week in advance notice. Maybe I would ask Denishia to go. She wasn't married, but I didn't know much about her love life. Whether she was involved with someone was a mystery to me.

They'd gotten me loaded within an hour and sent me on my way. I was shocked beyond belief. Usually, their asses took forever. Maybe they'd gone through some major revamping. I hadn't been here in a while because of their load times. Nevertheless, my day would be done a lot sooner than I thought it would be. Had I known, I would have taken two loads today.

Once I'd gotten to GE and had unloaded the product, I made my way to the tank wash to get my trailer washed out. Afterward, I went back to the yard to get my pickup and head home. It was only two o'clock, so I had the rest of the day to do absolutely nothing. I'd probably go outside and shoot hoops once I got there. Every now and then, the teenagers in the neighborhood would venture over when they heard my ball bouncing on that concrete. They liked challenging me, not realizing I was a whole-ass movement on that court in high school.

I turned down a basketball scholarship at Florida State, and my parents nearly choked the shit out of me when they found out. I hid the mail and deleted the messages, but somehow, the one about me denying the scholarship got to my dad, and he beat my ass within an inch of my life. I'd never seen my parents so angry.

"You have to be a damn fool if you think there will be no consequence for this! I can't believe you turned down a full scholarship for one second. Growing up in this house has taught you nothing, and there is no way any son of mine will grow up and be a bum!"

He pushed me against the wall and slid the belt from his waist. I was 18 years old, and he was finna beat me? What the fuck? I took a step in the other direction as he said, "If you run, you won't be able to walk for a week when I catch you."

"I don't wanna go to school. So would you rather me accept the scholarship and flunk out for not attending class? College isn't for everybody. I'd rather just learn a trade and do something hands-on . . . something where I can enter the workforce and make a decent living for myself."

He swung the belt like a whip and hit me across the chest. "Well, I can't make you go, but I can take my disappointment, anger, and frustrations out on the direct source. You wanna be a man and make your own decisions? You finna take this ass whooping like a man."

My mama watched and nodded in agreement. She hadn't said a word, but I could see she was just as angry. I tried my best to endure the licks from that belt, but after a while, I couldn't hold it in any longer. He finally stopped when I fell to the floor and balled up in the fetal position, screaming and cursing. I believed it was just a coincidence. He was winded. That was the real reason he stopped.

"You get six months after graduation, and then you have to get out of my house."

There were times when I questioned if I had made the right decision, but I knew that this was the path I was destined to take in life.

Just as I had changed into some basketball shorts, my cell rang. When I saw Denishia's number, I knew she was confirming delivery. "Hello?"

"Foooord, I delivered these myself because I needed to see this woman's reaction to these flowers. I just sent you a picture of what they looked like before I delivered them. When she saw me with that bouquet, she froze. I mean, like, for a minute, she didn't move or say a word. Then she burst into tears. Man, you need to go get your woman. When she accepted the flowers from me, she set them on her desk, closed her door, then sat in her chair and just stared at them."

I bit my bottom lip as I listened to Denishia go on and on about how much Giánni loved the flowers. I could only hope she felt the same way about the message attached to it. When I ended the call, I headed to the shower to make it to the bank before they closed.

Chapter 7

Giánni

"Do you need help carrying your flowers out?" one of my coworkers asked me.

"No. Thank you."

I'd gotten so emotional when I saw them. Purposely avoiding Ford had caused him to break out the big guns. I ran from him because I let my fear ruin me. My brain wanted to tell me he could be controlling and run in the opposite direction, but my heart had me depressed as hell. My heart could be way too kind and soft . . . at least in the past. I didn't trust myself to make the right decisions regarding love.

However, when I saw that note, it really took me down. A man who knew exactly what he wanted wasn't controlling. He was just sure . . . he was confident. I hated that everyone here saw my breakdown. My personal life was never on display at work, not even when I was going through the bullshit with Jermaine. Today, *everyone* was in my business. I'd closed myself in my office for the rest of the day. Thankfully, I didn't have any more customers or wear makeup. It would have been all over my face.

I didn't want even to know what he'd gone through to get two dozen purple magnolias delivered to me. His effort meant the world to me. Today, I would choose him as he'd chosen me. As soon as I could get home, I would call him. I remotely started my car and unlocked the doors since it was outside my office window. But I'd have to walk through the front door and around the side of the building to get to it.

After putting my crossbody on, I grabbed the vase and made my way to the exit. One of the new accounts representatives opened the door for me and made sure that I made it down the steps safely. When I looked up to thank her, my eyes met Ford's. My emotions fell from me once again as he took the bouquet from me. The look of sincerity on his face touched my heart, and I couldn't hide how he made me feel just by being here.

I didn't try to say a word, and neither did he. I continued to my car, and he quietly followed me. I opened the trunk, took out the empty box I kept in there, and put it in my front seat so he could set the vase in it. Once he did, he turned to me and gently swiped my cheek with his thumb. I closed my eyes briefly, then opened them and stared up at him. "Can you follow me to my house?" I asked softly.

"Yeah."

Before walking away, he lowered his head and gently kissed my forehead. I couldn't stop the steady stream of tears that left my eyes. After helping me in the car, he went to his. I wiped my cheeks, then headed home, not knowing what I would say to him, but knowing that I needed to say something. The flowers were so special to me. Besides Jermaine's pathetic effort last week, Ford was the only one who'd ever taken the time to buy them for me. My love for them was so intense I was surprised I'd never wanted to own a flower shop.

When I noticed Ford was behind me in his truck, I left the parking lot and headed home. I hated missing another pole-dancing class, but I could practice at home once Ford left. I had a pole installed in my bedroom. My house was only ten minutes from my job, but I couldn't help but constantly check my rearview mirror to be sure he was still following me.

It seemed that my old self was making a return, and I didn't like her ass one bit. I'd become the woman that Jermaine had halfway destroyed, thinking that there was no way that Ford wanted me as badly as he said he did. That there was some ulterior motive for his wanting to be with me.

When I turned in the driveway, my nerves heightened once again. My stomach was turning somersaults, and my mouth was as dry as cotton. Once I pulled into the garage, I went to the passenger side to get the flowers. But before I could pick them up, Ford had met me inside the garage and said, "I'll get them."

I nodded, then allowed him to hoist them from the box. I closed the passenger door, then headed to the back door of my home to unlock it. After walking inside, I silently instructed Ford to put the flowers on the countertop by moving items out of the way for him to set them down. Once he did, I grabbed his hand and led him to the couch. He surely felt my hand trembling because the moment we sat, he brought it to his lips and kissed it. Finally finding my voice, I said, "Thank you for the flowers. I'm sorry for ignoring you."

"You don't owe me an apology. I can sense that this is hard for you. I apologize for being so forward and not considering your feelings."

"You don't owe me an apology, Ford. I actually like that you're forward. I don't have to guess how you feel because you're gonna voice it. I'm just not used to that. In my last relationship, I was controlled and manipulated into believing that he loved me as much as I loved him, but he didn't love me at all. Being with me was all a game to him. He used me to get what he wanted out of me.

Because of me, he had somewhere to live and always had money in his pocket."

As I shook my head, he brought his hand to my face and stroked my cheek with his thumb. His tenderness was precisely what I needed. I leaned into his touch, closed my eyes, and enjoyed its feel. "I've grown so much since then, but you made me realize just how fearful I am of loving someone . . . of being intimately involved with anyone. I'm afraid of being used again. It even made me start questioning your motives. What could you possibly see in me? Why me?"

He gently slid his pointer finger over my lips as he stared into my eyes. "You are the most beautiful woman I've ever laid eyes on. Giánni, I'm honored that you even feel as attracted to me as I am to you. I've admired you for a while, but what really sealed the deal for me was how you looked out for me and spoke for me in places I couldn't reach. You don't even know me, and you cared that much. That's unheard of. You put your neck on the line for me. Why wouldn't I want a woman like you to be mine? I would benefit from having you because I would be the most blessed man alive. Knowing that you would choose me is an honor."

Ford's baritone voice had given me chills, and his words had touched my soul. I lowered my head briefly, then lifted my eyes to his. "You are such a handsome man. I felt like you could have any woman you wanted."

"Have you looked in the mirror lately? I can't help but be in awe of your beauty. You're gorgeous, Giánni. Being a part of your life would be renewing mine. I see my future with you. I want you to be a part of everything I accomplish in life, and I want to see where you will go in your career. I don't feel like you will stop where you are. God has destined you for greater. So we can fulfill our purposes together."

I could no longer contain myself. The way this reflection of God was speaking life into me was overwhelming. I leaned into him and softly kissed his lips. Allowing it to linger caused my insides to heat up like a car with a busted radiator. Sliding my hand to his face, I threaded my fingers through his beard. When our lips parted, he lowered his head to mine. "Can I take you to dinner? I mean . . . I'll let you pay if you want to."

I chuckled, then pulled away from him. "I would love to go, but you can pay. I will allow you to cater to me as often as you like. But when I decide to cater to you, there should be no reason why you would want to stop me. Just like you desire to do for me, I have a desire to do for you, despite my past. Your admissions of how you felt scared the hell out of me. I didn't really care about you not wanting me to pay for the food. It wasn't that serious. It was the shit my mind was trying to make it out to be."

I stood from the couch, and he did as well, then pulled me into his arms. "It feels good to hold you, Giánni. You got me soft as hell. That's how I know you're the one. I can be stubborn as hell, but for you, I'm willing to compromise on just about anything."

I smiled at him, then glanced over at the flowers. "It had to be extremely hard to find those."

"My classmate owns a flower shop. She drove to Houston to pick those up for me."

"Wow. All that trouble for little ol' me, huh?"

"Nothing for you is trouble. You're worth that and so much more. Now, let's go get something to eat."

"Can we just pick up something and come back here?"

"Whatever you want. I would love to learn more about the woman that's gonna be mine. I can't be telling my parents that I met my forever if I don't even know her middle name."

I had to be blushing. To meet a man that spoke so freely about his feelings was rare. I chuckled. "Lecrae."

"Like the rapper?" he asked as his brows furrowed.

"Exactly like that, Mr. Ajani. I love your middle name."

"Thank you. I love yours too. I'd never heard anyone named Lecrae other than the rapper, so it's quite unique."

"That it is. Well, let's go so we can come back and continue our conversation."

We made it back to the kitchen, and when I turned to him, he smiled at me, but I could see the intensity in his eyes. There were things he wanted to do and say, but I had him walking on eggshells because of how I received what he had to say last week. Before he could pull away, I stepped closer to him. "Ford, you don't have to be reserved around me. I'm sorry I made you feel that way. I can tell there's more that you want to say."

He bit his bottom lip, and his dimples winked at me. Then bringing my hand to his cheek, I slid my fingers over one of them as he gazed into my eyes. "There's not much I want to say. I just don't want to offend you."

I pressed my body against his and said, "Try me."

I immediately felt his erection against me. *Good Lord.* All the stereotypes about tall men packing around blessings some didn't have room to receive proved accurate at this moment. Ford licked his lips, and my eyes followed his tongue every step of the way. "Giánni, I don't want to move too fast. We've only been around each other a couple of times before this. We don't know a whole lot about each other."

"We know that we're insanely attracted to each other, and we also know that we want to have a great relationship. So say what you want to say, Ford . . . Ajani . . . Noel."

"Mmm . . . Don't say my name like that. You making my resolve weak as shit."

Sliding my hand to the back of his neck, I pulled him to me. I knew he wanted to kiss me because I wanted the same thing. But this time, I wanted more than just a peck. I needed to feel how potent the passion within him was. I knew he was thoughtful and attentive, but I didn't want my exploration to stop there. He rested his forehead against mine, then shocked the shit out of me when he lifted me and set me on the countertop next to my flowers.

I figured he was strong but damn . . . two hundred forty pounds compacted into a five-foot-six-inch frame wasn't an easy lift. He did that shit like it was nothing. He slid his hands over the tops of my thighs, then gently spread them so he could step closer between them. The heat around my ears and the rapid beating of my heart seemed to block out all sounds because his lips moved, and I didn't hear a word.

However, when I moaned softly, he brought his lips to mine as he wrapped one arm around my waist. The way his soft lips moved against mine had me wanting to wrap these thick-ass legs around him and give him a sample of the temperature below, although I was almost sure he could feel it through my pants. When his tongue breached my mouth, I couldn't stop myself from moaning again. My hands slid up his neck to the back of his bald head as I allowed my tongue to dance with his.

This was everything I thought it would be . . . and more. His passion could completely devour me, and I wanted it to possess that type of power over me. I wanted it to have me lose focus on everything around me. So when he slowly pulled away, I literally followed him for a couple of inches. "Damn, I been wanting to do that shit for a long time. Your lips been calling me for months now."

"Don't hold back any longer. If I'm ever uncomfortable, I'll slow you down."

I didn't give him a chance to respond. Instead, pulling his face back to mine, I pressed my lips against his again and slid my tongue to his. These two years of celibacy were about to be torn to shreds because my shit was twitching in excitement, hoping that something would soon fill the space within its walls.

Ford pulled away again and kissed my cheek, gradually making his way to my neck. When his hand gripped my thigh, he said in a low voice near my ear, "I'm not taking it this far until I know for sure that you're willing to give in to me totally. Once I dip into you, ain't no going back. I have a feeling this pussy gon' have its way with me, and I'm not ashamed to say so. If that's the case, it's gonna have me wanting it all the time and jumping into commitments you may not be ready for, so let me take my time with you, baby."

He licked my neck, then nibbled on my earlobe. I couldn't move or speak. I was already on my way to euphoria and didn't want to come back. "Ford . . . Please don't stop," I whispered.

My body was in starvation mode and wanted to suck Ford dry of all the nutrients he had to offer. I slid my leg up to his waist and curled it, pulling him closer to me.

"Giánni . . . You gon' make me fuck you up right here in this kitchen. Stop before you have a nigga going too far," he said.

He sounded so damn rough, and I *loved* that shit. His words didn't threaten me. They only propelled me forward as I whispered in his ear, "Please . . . please, Ford."

He swiftly grabbed me by the neck, tilting my head backward, causing it to hit the cabinet behind me, as his other hand slid up my body. No apologies were offered, and I didn't expect any. That act alone had my panties overflowing. He took his time on my breast, gently flicking my hard nipple through my bra. It felt like my body had gone up in flames. I picked up my other leg and curled it around him as well. I was probably coming off as thirsty, but I didn't give a damn at this point.

He grabbed my ass, lifted me from the counter, then walked to the couch and sat with me. Feeling all his inches pressed against my center had me leaking like a faucet. I was willing to ride him to heaven right here. As I began rolling my hips against him, he popped the shit out of my ass. I hissed in excitement.

"Listen, Giánni. I want every inch of you, and I'm beyond ready to tear you apart in the most pleasing way, but no. We not taking it here yet. I want you so fucking bad, but we have to wait. I promise it will be more than worth it."

I poked out my lip as he slid me to the couch next to him. Then he slid his hand down his face and huffed. "You so fucking sexy," he mumbled. "Stop pouting."

I frowned at him. I understood him perfectly, but I wanted to be difficult. It was my fault he wanted to slow down. My actions evoked this behavior in him because last week, he was on some full steam ahead type shit. *Ugh.* Sucking up my feelings, I said, "I understand. How do you feel about Chinese food?"

"Love it. Let's get it." He stood, then assisted me from the couch. As he led me to the door, he added, "I promise, when I get to that pussy, I'm taking all nine lives at once."

Just those words had killed it, so I could only imagine the devastation his dick would bring.

Chapter 8

Ford

No one could have told me I would have had to fight Giánni off me with a damned stick. That was the hardest shit I ever had to do. When I got home that night, I had to jack off twice before my dick even acted like it wanted to get soft. After we got back and ate dinner, we talked for hours. It was like we forgot we both had responsibilities to handle the next day.

We talked about our families, jobs, and dreams. We even talked about what we expected out of a relationship with each other. It was the most enlightening conversation I have ever had. I didn't want there to be much guesswork when it came to us. I knew that sometimes, some critical thinking would be required, but if we were open with each other from the beginning, that would be minimal. I appreciated that she could be so honest with me about what she wanted from me.

I learned that our wants were somewhat the same. We both wanted someone who would be considerate, loving, and kind. She said she liked my rough side, and I could tell it turned her on when I grabbed her by the neck earlier that day. Just the fact that it turned her on had turned me on even more. I wanted to be everything she desired me to be. Loving her would be easy, and I couldn't wait to free-fall in every facet of our relationship.

Since that day, we'd gone to lunch a couple of times and had dinner three nights in a row this past weekend. She put us on restriction this week because she said I would have her gaining weight and missing all her pole-dancing classes. I had yet to see that shit. However, I knew the moment I witnessed it would be when I had my way with her. She would experience everything I had to offer all in one session.

Her body was everything. The way her waistline curved into her wide hips gave me chills whenever I stared too long. She had those perfect childbearing hips too. I could envision putting a couple of babies in her. I couldn't wait for her to meet my family this weekend. At the immediate thought of that, I realized that I hadn't told my brother about my dad's diagnosis. Tonight, I would be going to their house for our Wednesday night family dinner. Thankfully, I wouldn't miss any time with Giánni since she was going to her class.

After conducting a couple of interviews, I called Ducati to fill him in, but he didn't answer. Hopefully, he would call before they came to town on Saturday, or dinner could be a major event. So after I set my phone on the desk, I got ready for my next interview. Once that was done, I could go home, shower, and get ready for dinner. This was my fourth interview for drivers. My mechanic was already on staff, and I'd hired one driver. They'd accompanied me to get the two eighteen-wheelers I'd purchased.

Someone knocked on the door, so I yelled for them to come in. When the woman walked in with heels on, a face full of makeup, and her hair hanging down her back, I was confused about who she was exactly. The name of the person I was supposed to be interviewing was Charli. *I guess that's a unisex name.* I stood from my seat as she approached and said, "Hello. How can I help you?"

"Hello. I'm Charli Daniels, and I'm here for my interview."

"Oh. Okay. I'm Ford Noel, the owner. Have a seat," I said as I pulled the chair out. "Let's see what we have here," I continued when I got to my seat and looked over the paperwork I'd printed out.

Sure enough, she had ten years of experience as a truck driver . . . no accidents, tickets, or bad referrals. Most of the women I ran into that were truck drivers weren't as feminine or put together as she was. I supposed I was adhering to stereotypes a bit, but I was truly caught off guard.

"So, Ms. Daniels, what makes you want to be a part of this company? It's newly formed, whereas the company you're with now has been in existence for nearly twenty years."

"Rumors are circulating about the company folding. They come from very reputable sources. I'm just trying to get ahead of it. I don't want to be without a job because I wasn't prepared."

She crossed her leg as she averted her gaze. She seemed tense or nervous. I suppose that was normal when interviewing for a new job.

"Okay. I'm glad you thought enough of my company to give me a shot. You already know the pay. I'm willing to match what you're making at your current place of employment because of your experience. I have yearly evaluations in place for raises and bonuses. All you need to do is take the road test and a drug test. If all that checks out, you have the job if you want it."

She smiled and nodded. A load seemed to lift from her. Her shoulders relaxed somewhat. "I'm sorry if I seem nervous. It's just that I have four children that I'm taking care of, and I can*not* miss a paycheck. Do you offer overtime?"

"If the work is there, I sure do. If you know of any other good workers who will need a job, please send them my way. I'm going to need three more full-time drivers and a dispatcher."

"Oh, okay. I have two friends that are also coworkers that are looking for something. One is our dispatcher. He's great."

"A'ight. Well, you don't seem to be ready for a road test today, but if you—"

"Oh no, I'm ready. I have my boots in my car. I didn't know if you would want to do the road test right away. I'm always prepared, Mr. Noel. I work until I need to rest. Those kids don't understand not being able to do certain things because we don't have the money. My mama helps me by watching them while I'm at work, but I need to keep a roof over our heads. She lives with me."

"Okay. I understand. Being a single mother of four must be hell."

"It is at times, but it's rewarding. Only two of them are kids I birthed." She looked away for a moment, then turned back to me. "The other two are my deceased husband's children. Their mother fell victim to drug addiction and is in no shape to take care of them. So I did what I knew Keenan would do. He loved his babies. We only have one child together . . . my youngest. All four of them are between the ages of six and fifteen."

My heart went out to her. "I'm so sorry for your loss. How long ago did that happen?"

"He died three years ago. We were team drivers. Now that he's gone, I don't care much about being on the road without him. That was when I started working for ITW . . . after he died. That massive heart attack caught me so off guard. It was hard being without him . . . It still is, but I'm managing."

I nodded. She was a beautiful sister and didn't look to be older than thirty-five. I stood from the desk, and she did the same. "Well, I hope that you can continue excelling. I want to create a family atmosphere here once everyone is comfortable in their positions. What I mean by that is that we all look out for one another . . . even if it's just a listening ear. In my opinion, that makes work more pleasurable."

She nodded. "Let me get my boots."

"Okay."

I followed her, grabbed the key to the freight liner she would be driving, then locked the office door. I couldn't wait to have my team up and running. Charli seemed like she would be an excellent asset to my company, and I could only pray that the others I chose for employment would be as well.

"Sometimes, I think you forget that you're the son and I'm the father," my dad spat.

I'd gotten to their house for our family dinner and had joined him in the family room like I always did. Unfortunately, mentioning that he should probably tell Ducati about his diagnosis before the dinner had fallen on deaf ears. I just didn't want Ducati to be blindsided at this formal dinner in front of his colleagues. Even after explaining to my dad how important this dinner would be for my brother, he refused to listen.

"Dad, I was just making a suggestion. That's all. That doesn't mean I'm disrespecting you. We won't be having dinner with Ducati, your son and my big brother. We will be dining with Mayor Roman Noel. Huge difference. I'm almost sure news outlets will be present as well. Giving him that type of information during that dinner won't be what's best."

"Says the boy that decided to be a truck driver. Your decision-making capabilities are nonexistent. You don't have the good sense God gave you. So why would I listen to anything you have to say? That's my fault for naming you Ford. I should have named you Bentley or McLaren. Maybe you would have met our expectations of you. Instead, you've been a disappointment your entire adult life."

I stood from my seat and walked away, leaving him in the family room alone. The high I was on after Charli had finished her road test was gone. He was having a bad day, but I wasn't sure if that was him or the disease speaking. He'd always given me a hard time about my career choice, but he'd never been this ugly about it. I was on the verge of cursing my father if I didn't get away from him.

Ducati still hadn't called me back, and no matter what Dad said, I knew that he needed to know ahead of time just in case Dad was having a day like he was now. I would much rather sit in the back of Giánni's pole-dancing class. But that would be a form of torture too. Then as I thought of her, she texted. Hey, baby. I'm on a water break. I can't wait to talk to you later.

I smiled slightly. Whenever she sent a text, it always brought a smile to my face, no matter what kind of mood I was in. She could make me forget all about my issues, struggles, and depressive moments. So I sat on the front porch and texted her back. Hey, baby. I miss you.

I rolled my eyes when the door opened, knowing it would be my father. I wasn't disappointed as he poked his head out. "How dare you leave the room while I'm talking, Ford. Dinner is canceled. Just go home. You don't want to be here anyway."

He slammed the door, and I wanted to go in there and shake the hell out of him. This was going to be difficult, but I suppose if I'd tolerated his hateful ways all these years, I could continue to put up with it. After huffing, I stood from my seat to go back inside. When I tried to open the door, I realized he had locked it. Hard wasn't an accurate description of how this experience would be. Even though I knew his illness was affecting his behavior, it didn't stop me from becoming angry.

I walked down the stairs and went to the back of the house. When I opened the door and stepped inside, I saw my mama putting food on the table. She frowned slightly as she stared at me. "When did you go back outside? I never saw you walk out."

"I'd gone out the front door to get air, but somebody locked me out."

She chuckled like the shit was funny. However, when she turned to look at me, I could clearly see she was probably laughing to keep from crying. Her eyes were glossy, and her hands trembled as she fixed the tablecloth. I walked over to her and pulled her into my arms. She lay her head against me as her body shook from silent tears. Then after only a few seconds, she pulled away like nothing had happened and continued getting ready for dinner.

I followed her to the kitchen. "Mama, Ducati needs to know about Dad's condition before dinner. This is a business dinner. He's meeting with the state representative. He plans to run for governor. It was supposed to be a surprise for y'all, but if Dad is having a day like he is now, there's no telling how that dinner will turn out."

"He doesn't want to tell Ducati until dinner. I can't dishonor his wishes."

I frowned at her, not believing what I was hearing. "So you're willing to take a chance and sacrifice Ducati's career by doing this in front of his dinner guests and possibly the *entire state of Texas?*"

"I'll try to talk to your father, but if he doesn't want to do it, I can't force him to."

"Mama, even if he didn't have dinner guests, I don't think a public setting is the best place to do this. Like y'all told me here, I think y'all should tell him here also. That's not fair to him. I can't believe y'all want to do this to your favorite son."

My mama turned to me, her eyes wide. But before she could say anything, my dad walked into the kitchen. "I thought I told you to leave. Get out of here, Ford. When you learn to respect us, you can come back here."

I glanced at my mother. This wasn't my father. No matter how much he hated my career path, he never kicked me out of their house. When my mother didn't open her mouth in my defense, I nodded and grabbed my keys. My father wrapped his arm around my mother, and they watched me walk out the door. I knew there was such a thing as being old-fashioned, but my mother going along with what he was saying now, knowing that he wasn't in his right mind, was crazy as hell to me.

When I got in my truck, I sent a text to Ducati. I need you to text or call me ASAP.

After backing out of the driveway, I headed home, still shocked about what had just transpired at my parents' house. If Ducati didn't get back to me before Saturday, this shit would be wild, especially if Dad behaved the way he did today. I could only pray that he didn't get violent. I knew that happened with some Alzheimer's patients.

Instead of going home, I ended up at McAlister's to get something to eat for dinner. This wasn't what I had in mind, and my stomach was utterly disappointed with leaving the kitchen, which smelled like some good Southern cooking, to come here and smell lunch meat. I ordered a small sandwich, just something to curb my appetite, then headed home to wait for a call, whether it was from Ducati or my baby.

Chapter 9

Giánni

I was so damn nervous. Getting dressed in this formal gown to meet Ford's family had my insides in knots. Although I was a grown-ass, 28-year-old woman, I liked to make good impressions. His family would play a huge role in our lives, so there couldn't be any tension between us. Of course, that would put him right in the middle, and that was the last thing I wanted to happen.

I had about thirty minutes before Ford would get here, so I needed to get a move on. After throwing my robe over my dress, I went to the bathroom to put the finishing touches on my makeup and put on one of my wigs. I didn't have time to get to the salon . . . not without missing my class or having to take off work. This meeting had to be seamless.

When Ford told me that his brother was the mayor of San Antonio and was a hopeful candidate for the governor's office, my anxiety kicked in big time. I knew that his parents weren't as down to earth as he was, so I had to be on my shit. I usually didn't care what people thought of me, especially people I didn't know, but this was his family. So I cared significantly about what Ford thought of me.

These past two weeks have been amazing. Ford was a gentleman in every sense of the word, but I couldn't wait to see that inner nigga come out of him. I skirted on the edge a couple of times and got so excited I nearly orgasmed in my panties. Whenever he grabbed me by my neck, I got glimpses of that side of him. The frown that would grace his face had my body shivering in anticipation. I was hoping he would soon see how fully committed I was. This relationship had to work because I was so all about him I could barely focus on anything else.

The entire time I was in my pole-dancing class, I imagined he was the only one there watching me. That shit had me working even harder, and my instructor was teasing me about it. I'd been celibate for over two years, but it was easy to maintain when I didn't have any prospects. However, with Ford being in my life, this ferocious feline was ready to attack his ass regardless of whether he was ready.

As I finished my makeup and fluffed my wig, the doorbell rang. I quickly took off my robe, gave myself a quick once-over in the mirror, and smiled. This dress hugged every curve my body possessed, but it was still classy. The peek at my cleavage and the split on the side were minor enough to be classy but sufficient to exude the sex appeal I wanted to throw his way.

Making my way to the door, I opened it to find Ford with a bouquet of magnolias dressed impeccably well. His navy three-piece suit was giving everything it was supposed to give. The orange and blue bow tie-hankie set only added to his look. *Jesus*. This man was so damn fine. There was no way I would allow him to go home tonight. "Hey, baby. You look so handsome. Come on in."

He stood there with his mouth partly open, like he was in shock. "Damn, woman." His eyes slowly scanned every inch of me as he licked his lips and stepped inside. "Giánni, you look so damn beautiful. This orange is your fucking color. Shit."

My cheeks heated up under his gaze. He handed me the white magnolias, gently kissing my forehead, cheek, and neck. This was journeying to dangerous territory. If he didn't stop, we'd be missing this dinner altogether. A soft moan escaped me as he slid his arm around my waist, pulling me closer to him. "Ford . . ."

His name had slipped out as a moan, and that only propelled him forward. I quickly backed away from him when his tongue glided up my neck to my ear. "Do you want to go to the dinner or not? I have no problem staying here and giving you everything you're insinuating you want."

"Had my brother not been expecting us, you wouldn't have had time to ask me that question."

He stared at me like he hadn't eaten in days, and I was a five-course meal. The intensity of it caused a shiver to crawl up my spine. My eyes fluttered closed as I thought about his words. He was as ready as I was. Taking a deep breath, I opened my eyes, then went to the kitchen to put my flowers in water. Just the friction below from me walking had my center juicing more than it should be at this moment.

Turning to the sexy man leaning against the cabinet waiting for me, I slowly shook my head. I didn't know how I would control myself tonight. However, I vowed that I would until we were alone again. I couldn't make any promises then.

Once I had the flowers in a vase and grabbed my clutch, we made our way out the door and to his car to head to Cotton Creek Winery.

As we traveled, Ford held my hand, and the closer we got to the restaurant, I could feel his hand tremble. I wasn't sure what he was so nervous about, but he made *me* nervous. Then as if sensing my questions, he turned to me. "I'm not fond of being in front of cameras, and

I believe some news crews will be there. My brother is announcing his plans to run for governor, and I already know that will put the spotlight on us . . . his family. *That's* what has me nervous."

I nodded and smiled. I was somewhat used to being in front of cameras. I'd done a couple of commercials for the bank and had been interviewed by news crews on several occasions. So that didn't bother me. I rubbed his hand between mine. "It's gonna be cool. It's not that bad being in the limelight from time to time. I probably wouldn't be able to handle it all the time, but every now and again is fine."

He lifted my hand to his lips and kissed it. However, what I said didn't seem to ease his nerves, so I could only hope he would calm down once he got around his family. I honestly wasn't a fan of his parents, just from what he told me about them regarding his career, but I would do my best to pretend I had no knowledge of that when I greeted them.

After parking in the lot of the restaurant, I could already see a news van there. Ford took a deep breath, then glanced at me. "Let's get this over with."

I smiled at him, doing my best to ease his nerves. When he helped me out, I fixed my dress and made sure I looked okay, then looped my arm through his. As we proceeded to the entrance, I saw an older woman smiling at us, so I naturally assumed that was his mother. Glancing up at him, I saw a smile on his face as well. When we reached her, she immediately went to Ford and kissed his cheek. He hugged her, then turned to me and said, "Mom, this is my lady, Giánni Judice. Baby, this is my mother, Sherry Noel."

I smiled at her, and we shook hands. "It's so nice to meet you, Ms. Noel."

"Likewise, Ms. Judice," she said as she nodded.

I noticed Ford had gone to speak to an older man, so I knew that had to be his father. I grabbed his hand and stood next to him when he reached out to me. "Dad, this is my lady, Giánni Judice. Giánni, this is my father, Horace Noel."

His dad's eyebrows had risen, and I didn't know how to take that shit. Finally, he smiled and said, "Nice to meet you, ma'am."

"Likewise, Mr. Noel."

No one else said a word as the doors to the restaurant opened, and the hostess allowed us inside. I quickly realized that this was a private dinner. Only those invited to be there could attend. The hostess was checking invites. Ford pulled his out of his pocket and showed the hostess. Then we were led to a table where another gentleman and his date were seated. He stood with a huge smile on his face. Ford went right to him and shook his hand, then hugged him. After he introduced me to his brother, Roman Noel, then to his brother's wife, Kelsey, we were seated.

Several others had arrived, and our state representative and his wife were seated at the table with the six of us. Still, Ford didn't seem any more relaxed than earlier. I leaned over to him and asked, "You okay, baby?"

He nodded, then kissed my forehead. I couldn't help but notice the slight frown on his father's face as he stared at us. Maybe that was what had Ford nervous. Surely his father wouldn't embarrass him in front of all these people. Turning my attention to Roman as he talked, I realized that he was definitely putting on. This wasn't the real him. Hopefully, I would get to meet the real him later. His demeanor seemed forced to me, maybe because I prided myself on being a decent judge of character.

When he turned to us, Ford said, "I really wish you would have returned my call Wednesday."

"I'm sorry. I got so busy, and it slipped by me. We can talk once dinner is over."

Ford nodded, then mumbled, "We may not have to."

I wasn't sure what was happening, but Ford seemed really bothered. I wished he would have clued me in about what was going on. I didn't like being blindsided, but at least I was on guard for the bullshit.

After the server brought our drinks and had taken our orders, conversations commenced, and the representative started engaging with the family. "Mr. Noel, how do you feel about having two successful sons? Roman tells me that Ford owns a successful trucking business."

"I have one successful son. I wouldn't say that trucking is a noteworthy career."

The breath was sucked out of me. I slid my hand to Ford's, and he gripped it tightly. But he didn't say a word, and neither did anyone else. The representative seemed to be caught off guard, so he remained quiet as well. Things quickly became really awkward at the table. To ease the tension, Roman asked, "So, Giánni, what do you do?"

"I'm a commercial lender for Community Bank. It's how I met your extremely successful brother."

I couldn't help myself. I had to speak up for him. Ford cleared his throat and looked away. His brother's face reddened.

"Absolutely. I admire his drive. I believe it's a lot stronger than mine."

"That's where I've seen you," the representative chimed in. "I serve on the board there."

"Yes, sir. I've been employed there for a while now."

As I began conversing with Roman's wife, Kelsey, talking about insignificant things, Mr. Noel blurted,

"When are you making the announcement? I thought this would be a private dinner amongst family."

Roman frowned slightly. "Dad, I told you last night. Kelsey had insisted that I tell you beforehand."

Mr. Noel frowned. "I don't like being caught off guard. This publicity stunt makes it seem like we are the perfect family for your career. Of course, we would be if it weren't for Ford and this woman he probably hired to be his date."

My mouth fell open, and just as I was about to stand, Ford gripped my hand tighter, forcing me to remain seated. "Dad, this isn't necessary. You won't disrespect Giánni."

"I'm sure she's used to the disrespect as big as she is."

My eyebrows lifted as I stared at the old man. Surely he didn't say what I thought he did. Now, Ford stood and pulled me up with him.

"Alzheimer's disease or not, I won't subject my woman to your behavior. She doesn't owe you a thing and has done nothing to warrant your hurtful words toward her. So, Roman, enjoy dinner, and good luck with your run for governor. I'm sorry, but I won't tolerate this shit any longer."

Roman stood as Ford pulled me away from the table and out the door. I had no words for what had just happened. His dad had Alzheimer's. I wish he had told me beforehand. However, I probably still wouldn't have been prepared for the disrespect he spewed my way. We'd never met, so I was stunned. As Ford practically dragged me to his vehicle, I could hear someone running behind us. "Ford! Hold on, man."

I turned to see his brother running to catch up with us. Ford turned as well. His face was so red it made me nervous. When Roman caught up with us, Ford said, "Ducati, if I don't leave, I'm gon' knock out that old man. I can handle the disrespect toward me. I've been handling it for years, but I won't subject my woman to it. Period. She doesn't deserve that."

"Neither do you, bruh. It's about time you stand up to him. I'm sorry you can't stay, but I totally understand. Is that what you wanted to tell me? That he has Alzheimer's?"

"Yeah. I didn't want you to say anything to set off his ass, but it seemed as if my presence alone did that shit."

"I'm sorry, bruh. I love you, and I'll try to get by to see you before we leave town tomorrow. The kids would never forgive me if they didn't get to see Uncle Ford. Giánni, I'm sorry for our father's behavior," he said as he turned to me.

I nodded as he shook my hand, then approached Ford and hugged him tightly. Once he left, Ford helped me inside. We remained quiet for a while and just sat there in the parking lot. Finally, we turned toward each other at the same time. He brought his hand to my face and gently stroked my cheek with his thumb.

"I'm so sorry, Giánni. I never expected him to attack you verbally. I had a feeling he would attack me, but I'm used to that shit. I know you were stunned, and maybe I should have warned you. I'm so, so sorry, baby."

"It's okay, Ford. As your father said, unfortunately, I *am* used to negative comments, but I don't dwell on them. I know who I am and that I'm beautiful. While it shocked me that he said that in this setting and to my face, what he said didn't surprise me. Don't worry about me. I'm cool. I just need you to be cool too."

He nodded. "Do you want something to eat? We didn't get a chance even to enjoy our damn meal."

"No, baby. I'm okay. I have some snacks at home. Maybe we can Netflix and chill. What do you think?"

"Okay. Let's do it."

He pulled out of the parking spot and headed to my house.

Chapter 10

Ford

I'd never been so angry in my entire life. Horace Noel had gone way too far. It was one thing to endure his behavior in private, but that shit was harder to take publicly. When he verbally attacked Giánni, that was my limit. After that, I couldn't stomach anything else. I refuse to subject her to his behavior any longer. I wished I had warned her ahead of time, but as she said, I would have never expected him to attack her.

Before his diagnosis, my father was never a mean and hurtful individual . . . at least not to anyone else. He was only that way toward me. Even with me, his words were never really laced with that much venom. I was just in total shock. Even still, as I sat on Giánni's couch in my suit, I was in disbelief that tonight had gone as it did. Regardless of whether Ducati had called me back, it wouldn't have stopped what happened tonight.

Giánni joined me on the couch, still in her gown, with a glass of liquor. I wasn't sure what kind it was, but it was sorely needed. I gulped it, then set the glass on her coffee table. I glanced at her to see she'd angled her body toward me. She was sitting there watching me like Sylvia in the movie *Life,* duping Claude out of his last two dollars. She took her drink to the head just as I had done as I stared at her neck and cleavage.

She looked so beautiful tonight. I could tell she'd taken her time getting ready, wanting to make a great first impression . . . only to end up facing my father's ridicule and disrespect. After she stood and set her glass on the coffee table next to mine, I pulled her between my legs. Sliding my hands up her gorgeous legs, I couldn't help but moan. My hands continued higher underneath her dress, lifting it in the process. I leaned in closer to her and kissed the outer part of her thigh as she shivered.

When I leaned back into the sofa, Giánni slowly pulled her dress up to her waist, then straddled me on the couch. My hands immediately went to her ass and my lips to her cleavage. Feeling her heat in my crotch assured me of her need to feel me inside her. The way she was ready to stand up to my father in my defense only heightened my feelings for her. I looked up at her as she moaned. Finally, she lowered her head, and her eyes met mine. We stared at each other for a moment, and my dick stiffened even more.

She slid her hand over my cheek and through my beard, then said, "Follow me, baby."

I nodded as she stood from my lap. She pulled her dress down over her hips, and I was disappointed that my view of her fine ass was again obstructed. However, I followed her without complaint. She turned to me when we reached a door that I assumed was her bedroom. "There are rules before you enter."

I frowned slightly, and it caused her to giggle. Giánni rubbed her hands down my chest as I invaded her space, pushing her back against the door. "Once we enter, you can't touch me unless I initiate contact. You must follow my lead, or the show ends."

Her last statement made me aware of what was about to go down. I was so fucking excited my dick nearly burst through my zipper. "Well, can I get a kiss now?"

She smiled, then slid her hand to the back of my neck and pulled me to her. My tongue ravished her mouth because I wanted her to feel how much I wanted her. Maybe she wouldn't tease me for too long if I got her just as riled up as I was. After a few seconds, she opened the door and pulled away from me. "Have a seat, baby."

I walked inside her bedroom to see the pole and a chair not far from it. I gave her a one-cheeked smile as I made my way to my seat. She started some music that I quickly recognized as Alex Isley. We listened to her quite a bit.

"I'm going to change. I'll be right back."

"Don't take too long."

Giánni smiled at me as she headed to her bathroom. I stared at that pole, imagining her spinning around it, and I had to grab my dick to calm him down. I was beyond certain that she would turn me out the moment she touched that damn pole. I sat back and relaxed as my thoughts returned to the disaster at the restaurant. I hated that it could have ruined Ducati's night, but I refused to sit there and allow my father to disrespect Giánni that way. Hopefully, once we left, the night improved, and Ducati could impress those in attendance, waiting to hear what he had to say.

As I thought about how the night could have gone and how I couldn't wait to see my niece and nephews, my baby emerged from the bathroom. My eyes widened as she walked in front of me wearing a long, see-through overlay. I could see the lingerie beneath it, and it felt like I was drooling as I thought about everything I would do to this beautiful body before me. I sat up in my chair as I watched her hips sway to the music. Finally, she turned her back to me, and I damn near came on myself.

I could see her ass cheeks through the material since she was wearing a thong, and watching her make them lift one at a time to the beat of the music wasn't helping matters. I wanted to smack her ass so badly. She looked back at me over her shoulder and smiled, then bit her bottom lip, showing me those sexy-ass dimples. She'd even added a nose ring that hung between her nostrils, a septum piercing. I didn't know whether it was real or fake, but I didn't care. It was sexy as fuck on her.

Giánni allowed the sheer robe to fall off her shoulders and held it in the crooks of her arms as she squatted to the floor and twerked her ass. I grabbed my dick roughly. If I had any doubts about diving into her abyss, they were all gone now. There was no way in hell she was escaping me tonight. "Shiiiit!"

I had little to no restraint left as I watched her stand and allow the overlay to slide off her arms to the floor. She made her way to the pole and slowly walked around it. When she was facing me, she leaned against the pole, her hands gripping it above her head, and slid down it, spreading her legs. Her pussy was eating that damn thong, and I couldn't wait to get some of the action that thong was getting. She stuck her tongue out like she was Megan Thee Stallion, then stood and swung her body around that pole like it was second nature.

Giánni swung again and hopped up on it, twirling around that thing smooth as fuck. She pulled herself higher as Eric Bellinger sang about how much he loved her legs. I couldn't agree with him more. However, I was impressed when she released the pole and leaned over, holding on to it with her legs. She could be a fucking professional. I'd *pay* to see this show. Standing to my feet, I pulled my wallet out, grabbed some bills, and began throwing them at her.

She laughed, but it didn't stop her show. After twirling a couple more times, she quickly fell into a split, never taking her eyes off me. Knowing that she was that flexible would make tonight even more exciting. She was gonna be bent all kinds of ways. I leaked precum when she turned over to her stomach, went up on her knees, and started twerking her ass. She was facedown, ass up. There was only so much more I would be able to take before I snatched her up and sat her on all this dick.

She stood to her feet and pulled the straps of her top off her shoulders. I licked my lips as I scooted forward in my seat. She sexily unclasped the hooks in front, and it fell open, revealing her titties. Walking closer to me, she grabbed my hand and laid it on her chest, permitting me to touch her. But I got carried away, yanked her to me with my other hand, and licked her nipple. Then she grabbed me by my neck and held me away from her.

Giánni had to know that I was allowing her to do that. There was no way she could hold me back if I didn't want her to. As hard as her nipple had gotten, I knew she wouldn't be able to resist me for much longer. She started rolling her hips as she continued holding my neck, then turned around and bent over in my face. I had the perfect view of her wet pussy. After she looked at me around the side of her leg, I popped her ass, then slid two of my fingers along her thong. Just from the bit of pressure I applied, I could see the juices leaking from her pussy.

She moaned as I pulled at her thong. I was desperate as shit now. I began pulling off my clothes while she allowed her top to drop to the floor. Now she was standing in front of me wearing only a thong and heels, so I was definitely overdressed. She was twirling around the pole when I came out of my pants. However, when she stopped, she stared at me in all my naked glory, my dick in my hand.

She licked her lips, then began pulling her thong off. "Ford . . ."

"Yeah, baby?" I said in a low voice.

"I want you to have me . . . inhabit me . . . consume me . . . devour me. Don't waste a drop."

My dick was ready to spit more precum. It was oozing from the head. Just as I was about to wipe it away, she went to her knees and licked it, causing me to shiver. When her mouth covered the head of my dick, I wanted to scream like a bitch. But feeling her soft lips around me made every day of celibacy worth it. Although my celibacy wasn't intentional, I'd accepted it for what it was. Since I wasn't willing to sleep with just anybody, I had no choice but to embrace the life.

I slowly slid more of my dick into her mouth as she stared at me. Then when her hand toyed with my balls, a shiver bolted through me. "Shit," I said as I watched the saliva fall from her lips.

Putting her hands on my ass, she pushed me deeper into her mouth. When the suction noises came from her mouth, and her slight gagging caused her throat to close in around the head of my dick, I lost it. "I'm about to nut. Fuck."

She removed me from her mouth and allowed my cum to shoot on her chest when I released her. "Ahh, fuck," I verbalized.

That was a huge load, so it was probably good that she didn't try to swallow it. I helped her to her feet, then lifted her. She held on to me for dear life like she was scared I was gonna drop her.

"Gi, I gotcha, baby. Yo' man is very capable of handling all of you. Let me show you."

When I laid her on the bed, she rubbed my nut on her skin and lifted one of her breasts to lick the residue from her nipple. I lifted her legs, spread them wide, and then lowered my face to her glistening pussy. It was slick with her juices . . . ripe and ready to be devoured. I went all in, indulging all at once. I didn't do any taste testing. I already knew that her flavor would be intoxicating.

Just as I expected, I enjoyed her taste. I slurped her juices as I gently sucked the inner parts of her lips, then made my way to her clit. Teasing her with my tongue as she moaned, I swirled it around her clit like she was twirling around that pole, occasionally stopping to suck it into my mouth. Then after sliding two of my fingers inside her, I began eating her pussy like it was a sweet kiwi, going after all that juice that was leaking for me, doing my best to suck her dry.

As I rubbed circles on her G-spot with my fingers, I firmly sucked her clit as her legs began quivering. "Ford . . . pleeeaaase. Oh my God . . ."

Within seconds of her calling on the Lord, she released her orgasm. Her creamy goodness slid down my throat and chin as I continued to feast on her soft flesh. I would never get enough of her. No way, no how. When I pulled away from her, I slowly wiped my hand down my chin, then slid on top of her. "Damn, I love your flavor."

"Let me taste it then."

I lowered my lips to hers and slid my tongue into her mouth, giving her all she could handle. The way she sucked my lips, I thought that she loved her flavor too. When I pulled away from her, she reached over to the nightstand. I lifted off her some so she could get what she was searching for. She came back with a shiny gold packet and handed it to me. I didn't waste any time strapping up. Staring into her eyes, I knew this woman was for me. We would be together for the long haul. When my family didn't have my back, having Giánni made everything worth it.

When I entered her paradise, I shuttered as her heat encompassed me. I could barely keep my composure as I stroked her hot box. Her moans and light nail scratches on my back only propelled me forward. "Ford . . . yeeeesss. You feel so good inside of me. Shiiiit."

"Mmm. Yeah, baby. This my shit now."

I stroked her deeper and with more force as she wrapped her legs around my waist. The solo her pussy was singing was one of the best songs I'd ever heard, and it had my dick ready to give it a standing ovation. I knew her pussy would take me down, but I was determined not to go out so soon or without a fight. I pulled out of her and lay next to her. Before I could say a word, she climbed on top of me and slowly slid down my dick.

Watching her rock on my shit was harder to handle than me plunging inside her. But the way she sat on me with her legs spread wide, providing me with a front-row seat to the show she was putting on, was Oscar-worthy. Seeing me disappear within her depths and watching her sex faces was some fantastic shit, especially when I could see her juices coating me. My nut was hanging on to the last thread of dignity that he had . . . until she started bouncing on my shit and playing with her clit at the same time.

Within five bounces, I was nutting in that latex and shivering like a fiend finally getting that high he was searching for. I was seeing fucking stars, and I didn't know how I would face her after nutting so fast. Finally, staring at her as she continued to roll her hips on me, I said, "I can't believe you snatched my nut from me like that. Let me make this shit up to you."

She fell to the bed with a giggle as I pulled off the condom and went to her drawer to get another one. Thankfully, my erection hadn't lost any steam, so I was ready to wear that pussy out now. Strapping up again, I rolled Gi to her stomach, straddled her legs, and entered her. She screamed, causing me to hold my position for a moment. "Fuck! Keep going!"

After that, I commenced to fucking the shit out of her. When her pussy spit at me, I knew I was doing my fucking job. Her juices were leaking to my balls and down my legs. I smacked her ass and continued pounding her, going balls deep inside her until she reached back and scratched my legs. But I simply grabbed her hands and brought them over her head. Then leaning over her, I held them together with one hand and lifted her hips slightly with the other one.

I could feel my dick gut-checking that cervix, and as much as she was trembling, I knew she was about to give up the ghost again. "Fooorrd! Fuck!" she screamed as she excreted her juices all over me again.

But I wasn't done with her. Bringing my legs between hers, I yanked her hips up, stared at the deadly arch she'd perfected, and eased back inside her. "This pussy is magical. It gives me a high I don't wanna come down from, baby."

I watched my dick slide in and out of her as her walls gripped me in a tight embrace. I could tell she hadn't been having sex with her as tight as she was. The cream she released on my dick only made me go harder. I slapped her ass and stroked her hard and deep. Then turning her to her side, I straddled her bottom leg, lifted the other, and pushed inside her once again. This would be something that I wouldn't be able to go a day without. Now that I'd had it, I would never let it go.

My nut was rising, and as I stared at her titties bouncing, she pulled one to her mouth and began flicking her tongue over her nipple as I had done to her clit. That was when my moment of reckoning gripped my dick and squeezed every drop of cum out of it as Giánni detonated all over me again. I nearly collapsed on top of her. For a moment, neither of us spoke. Only our pants could be heard throughout the room.

Falling to the bed beside her, I relaxed as she lay on my chest. Then finally, she said, "Yo' ass gon' have me crazy as hell. You didn't tell me you had Satan in your pants."

I chuckled as I stroked her back. "About like you didn't tell me you had priceless treasures hidden in your depths. So I guess we gon' be crazy as hell together."

She giggled as we lay there together, sweaty and sticky but overwhelmingly satisfied. I slowly stroked her back as I listened to her breathe. It wouldn't take me long to fall for her. Now that I had experienced every part of her, I wouldn't want to do without any of her. At this point, I was ready to move her in with me and keep her all to myself. I kissed her forehead, then rested my cheek against the top of her head.

"Ford, I hope you aren't tired."

"I'm good, gorgeous. I'm just thinking about how I'm gon' go to work Monday when I have a new obsession. So I hope you don't get tired because I plan to be deep in yo' shit until I have to go home."

"Mm. Sounds like fun. Your dick seems at home already. He found his way around quickly and cleaned all the cobwebs out of the corners. I want him to be a permanent fixture, so it's a good thing we're compatible."

"I like yo' nasty ass, but I'm gon' test your limits in a li'l bit. Get ready because I have no limits when it comes to pleasing my woman. Get me another wet suit so that I can go scuba diving."

Chapter 11

Giánni

I was so fucking tired I could barely keep my eyes open. Once Ford had penetrated my folds, we couldn't get enough of each other. He stayed the night, and instead of going to church, we worshipped each other's bodies until we tapped out. We nearly fell asleep on top of the island in the kitchen. Every room in my house had gotten a taste of our action, and the outdoor patio had also seen our backsides.

Sitting at my desk, thinking about how my family clowned me when I got there Sunday evening, I couldn't stop myself from chuckling. I was late for family dinner, and from one look at me, my sister, Jevonna, knew exactly why. She and my mom were all excited, trying to figure out who the new man in my life was. I didn't bring Ford along because I figured meeting one set of parents this weekend was more than enough.

My dad and brother refused to join in on the conversation until I told them about Jermaine's ass harassing me. Of course, that wasn't even supposed to come out, but when my brother brought him up in conversation, making sure he wasn't the one that had me 'glowing and shit,' I spewed how he was on my last nerve with his piss-poor efforts at trying to ease his way back into my life.

Then CoCo was all in my shit when I got to work, asking how dinner went. When I told her about Ford's father, she was just as pissed as I had been. I didn't want to show Ford just how angry his father's words had made me because I didn't want to make the situation worse. However, I was steaming. The pole dance wasn't just for him. It was for me too. Pole dancing always calmed my spirit . . . that along with singing. I wanted to calm him down as well. Had he known how angry I was, he probably would have said more to his father. We'd already made a little scene, and I didn't want it to get out of hand.

After we discussed that, CoCo did just as my family had done Sunday and got all in my shit about why I was so tired looking but happy at the same time. That was a rare combination. While I didn't go into specifics, I told her how Ford had pleased my body *all* weekend. She didn't need details. My man's business was my business and no one else's. All that dick Ford was slanging didn't need to be on nobody's mind but mine. I'd stab a bitch over that man.

It was almost lunchtime, and I didn't know what I would eat today. I didn't prep any meals at home last night because I'd gone straight to my bedroom when I got home from my parents' house. Then I had the audacity to talk to Ford for an hour on the phone about how much I enjoyed him. My body crashed after that. Seeing it was twelve thirty already, I stood from my desk as my legs screamed in agony and grabbed my purse from the file cabinet.

When I turned back to the door, Ford was leaning against my door frame. Damn, he looked so sexy. He only wore blue jeans, a T-shirt, and a baseball cap, but his swag shined through no matter what he wore. I smiled big as I made my way to him. "Hey, baby. What are you doing here?"

"I'm here to take you to lunch. Work is going to pick up in a little bit, so I want to cater to you while I can. So, where do you want to go?"

"Aww, that's so sweet," I said, then pecked his lips.

He grabbed my hand and led me out of the bank as I thought about where we could eat. After opening the door for me to get inside his truck, he walked around and joined me inside. Once he started the engine, he turned to me, awaiting instruction. "Longhorn? Do you like them?"

"Longhorn it is. I'm not picky when it comes to food, baby. As long as it's good, it's a winner."

I smiled as we headed that way. It was only about ten minutes from my job, with the lunch traffic. Usually, it took less time than that since it was only about three miles away. However, there were six traffic lights between here and there, which slowed traffic. As I sang along with Ella Mai, I could see Ford staring at me in my peripheral. I stopped singing. "Sir, I need you to focus on the road."

I turned to him and sang a little. When the cars started blowing their horns, he took off from the light. I had stolen all his attention. "Damn, Giánni, I had no idea that your singing voice was *that* beautiful. You gon' be singing to me all the time now."

I chuckled as he grabbed my hand and kissed it. "It's not *that* great. Quit swelling my head, Ford. I can hold a tune. I'm decent."

"You must not hear yourself. Don't worry. I'm gon' make you realize just how great you are. Friday night, you're mine, so don't make plans."

"I planned to be with you. Weekends are totally for you. Maybe you can meet my parents Sunday. They won't let me rest until I take you to meet them now."

He chuckled. "No problem. I'd love to meet them. From how you speak of them, especially your dad, I know it will be a pleasure to make their acquaintance."

I smiled at him as he turned into the parking lot and parked. Then before he could open my door, I hopped out of his truck. That fried okra and medium-well steak were on my mind heavy. When he joined me, he said sexily, "Next time you just hop out of a vehicle like that when I'm with you, I'm gon' fuck up your pretty ass."

"Mm. You promise?"

He chuckled as he wrapped his arms around my waist. "You so nasty. You oughta be tired."

"Shit, I am. But if you wanna feel my insides, I'm gonna let you."

He kissed my puckered lips, then led me inside. "That's good to know, baby."

I smiled at him as he opened the door, but my smile soon turned to an eye roll. There was Jermaine, waiting to be seated. I turned to Ford, and he noticed him as well. "Ford, we can go somewhere else."

"Why? Don't give him that kind of power. Let him see just how happy you are. That's his loss."

I stared into his eyes and took a deep breath. "You're right. Fuck him."

He gave me a gentle smile, but then his facial expression hardened. I knew that was his protective stance. When I turned back around, Jermaine was gone. *Thank God.* Going to the hostess, Ford requested seats for two, and we were immediately led to a table . . . right across from Jermaine and his lunch date. I held my head high, knowing that I was in a much better situation than I had been with him. The woman he was with was probably the one footing the bill.

"Charli?" Ford called out.

"Hi, Mr. Noel. How are you?"

"I'm good. I can't wait for you to start."

"Me either. Monday next week can't come fast enough."

I frowned slightly as he turned back to me. "She's going to be one of my drivers."

I nodded as I glanced at her. She was a beautiful woman. I just hoped she wasn't falling for Jermaine's bullshit. I stared into Ford's eyes as we sat waiting for our waiter. He smiled, then stretched his hands across the table to hold mine. "I told you that he was going to move on. I do not intend to mess things up with you for him to even be worried about getting back with you. He's not crazy enough to approach you with me sitting here. But if he is, he will be handled accordingly."

Ford winked his eye at me, then greeted our waiter. Once we gave him our drink orders, he walked away, and my gaze landed on my man again. He was so perfect for me in every way. While I knew he was still feeling a way about his father, he still showed me love. *Love.* It was much too soon to be talking about love, but there was no other way to describe what I felt from him.

Once our waiter returned with our drinks and had taken our orders for our meals, he left us alone, and we talked the entire time. I'd forgotten Jermaine was even sitting directly across from us. Ford was just that engaging and intoxicating. Taking my attention away from him to give Jermaine even a glance would have been wrong as hell. Like Ford had already said, Jermaine didn't deserve the steam I gave him. He'd fucked up years ago. I was seated in this amazing restaurant with a man I knew would be my forever.

As we ate our meals and I was preparing to ask for a box, Jermaine's ass had the nerve . . . the *audacity* . . . to approach our table. I didn't miss the danger I saw in Ford's eyes. I hoped he wasn't standing here on no bullshit. "I just wanted to speak, Gi. I hope all is well with you. Good to see you again."

He nodded at Ford and walked toward the door before I could utter a word. *Hmm.* That was different. I could only hope that this wasn't the quiet before the storm. I frowned as I turned back to Ford. He had a look of amusement on his face . . . a slight smirk, and his eyebrows were slightly lifted. "Maybe he's done like he said he would be, baby."

"I hope so," I said as I got a not-so-good feeling in the pit of my stomach.

"Can you step into my office for a moment, Ms. Judice?"

"Yes, sir. Be right there."

I returned from lunch about an hour ago, and my supervisor called me into his office. While I wanted to be nervous, I knew I hadn't done anything wrong. So I practiced my breathing techniques as I walked to his office. Once there, I knocked on his door, and he yelled for me to come in. When he smiled at me, it eased my nerves even more about why he had summoned me to his office. "Have a seat, Giánni."

I did as he requested, then crossed my hands on my lap. I noticed he was playing around. Instead of getting right to it like he usually did, he was shuffling shit around on his desk and writing shit on his calendar. I wanted to choke the hell out of him, then tell him to spit it out. As I frowned slightly, he looked up at me and chuckled. I twisted my mouth sideways. I was glad he found my impatience funny. "I just wanted you to know that your name was thrown into the hat to be a VP. Of course, I did the throwing."

Multiple people could hold that title. It was one of prestige and guaranteed a nice raise. My eyebrows shot up as my eyes widened. "Are you serious?" I asked.

"Yep. You deserve the title. You know how much money you've profited this bank? In my opinion, you deserved it long before now. I was waiting on one of the higher-ups to throw your name in the hat last year, especially after you got that huge loan for that church. But this year, I decided not to wait."

"Wow. Thank you. I appreciate this so much, Mr. Hammon. I really do," I said as I held my hand to my chest.

Today was shaping out to be a great day. I couldn't believe this.

"That was all I wanted to tell you. Congratulations on a job well done, and good luck."

"Thank you again."

I stood from my seat and exited his office, wanting to skip all the way to mine. That was just how happy I was. After my vocal session today, I would have to pop up on Ford so we could celebrate. I didn't care how sore my legs were. The best way to celebrate would be all over his dick. Plus, I knew he would want to celebrate with me. We could celebrate with my family when the weekend rolled around. However, I still had to call my daddy with the good news.

"Hello?"

"Hey, Daddy. How's your day going?"

"It's going well, baby girl. How about yours?"

"Well . . . I was just informed that my name was thrown in the hat for the next promotion to vice president."

"Wow! That's great news, baby. Congratulations. When will you find out if you got the title?"

"You know, I was so excited about it, I didn't even ask," I responded and chuckled.

He laughed too. I could hear the excitement in his voice when he congratulated me. "So, what are we going to do to celebrate?"

"Well, I was hoping we could all celebrate on Sunday with everybody."

"That sounds like a plan. Is your new boyfriend still coming? I need to put my eyes on him."

"Yes, sir. He's pretty excited about meeting you. He said he can see my excitement and love when I speak about my family, especially you."

"Hmm. I'm gonna still be on guard . . . just in case. I can't have you enduring no shit like you did with that bum-ass nigga you used to be with."

I slightly rolled my eyes. "Slow down, killa. Ford and Jermaine are in totally different categories. Ford is about his business, and he cares for me a lot. I can tell. He's definitely not ashamed to take me in public, and I've met his family. He's great, Daddy."

I refused to mention how his father disrespected me. That wasn't a battle my dad needed to be involved in. That would only make the situation worse and cause tension between him and Ford and, ultimately, Ford and me. I was sure that Ford would confront his dad about what happened in due time, although I wasn't sure it would even matter since I knew he had Alzheimer's. He probably wouldn't even remember what happened that night.

"Okay. But I still need to see for myself. I love you too much to allow that bullshit again, and I hope you love yourself too much for that shit as well."

"Way too much, Daddy. I've been single for two years by choice. Men have approached me, but they weren't what I wanted for my life. I made a conscious decision to be with Ford. I was by no means desperate. I was content with being alone."

While I had begun to feel lonely, I was far from desperate for a man's attention. I'd matured significantly, but I knew my family would always be on guard for bullshit because of my past with Jermaine. I didn't get offended by it because I knew it was because they loved me so much and were in protective mode.

"Okay, baby. Is it okay if I tell your mom the good news?"

"Of course. I don't mind the family knowing. You were just the first person I called. I need to get back to work. So spread the word that we turning up Sunday afternoon."

He laughed, and that did my soul good. His laughter always made me feel extremely happy. "I gotcha, baby girl. Hopefully, we'll see you before then, right?"

"Yes, sir. Most likely, I'll come by tomorrow after my class."

"Okay. Enjoy the rest of your day, Giánni."

"Thanks, Daddy. You too."

I ended the call feeling happy as hell. While I wanted to call Ford and tell him the good news, I would wait until I surprised him tonight.

Chapter 12

Ford

My doorbell rang as I dumped a load of clothes on the couch. I never had pop-up visitors, not even my parents. I set the basket on the floor and then went to the door. I'd only been home an hour or so, time enough to shower, throw my clothes in the dryer, and eat something. I only had on some basketball shorts, free balling. Checking the peephole, I was pleasantly surprised to see Giánni. My dick woke up the moment I saw her standing there.

Quickly opening the door, I said, "Hey, baby. What'chu doing here? Come on in."

She smiled at me, then walked inside. Going to her tippy toes, she puckered her lips for a kiss that I readily gave her. After closing and locking the door, I checked the time to see it was eight o'clock. She usually went to bed by ten on the weekdays, so I supposed she had a little time to kill. I followed her to my couch and hurriedly put my clothes back into the basket.

"I have good news, and I want to celebrate with you. I'm up for a promotion to vice president. I don't know if I'll get it, but just knowing that my name is on the list of people being considered is a high like no other. So I wanted to share that high with you," she said as she unbuttoned her shirt.

"Mmm. Well, congratulations. We gon' speak into existence that the promotion is yours." My eyes dipped to her breasts as she exposed them. After fully unbuttoning her shirt, she took it off, then stood and took off her pants. "Damn. This how we celebrating?"

"Yeah. You have any objections, Ford?"

"Hell naw. Come ride this Ford Power Stroke. He already ready for you," I said as I pulled off my basketball shorts.

I stroked him several times as I watched Giánni pull off her underwear. She made her way to me, then straddled me. My dick was resting against her ass, mad as hell that she didn't immediately greet him. She laid her lips on mine and brought her hands to both sides of my face as I caressed her ass. However, my dick wouldn't allow me to be patient, so I lifted her and filled her to capacity.

"Ooohh, fuck," she yelled.

I loved her dirty mouth. That shit always made my dick twitch in excitement. I closed my eyes as she began rolling her hips on me. That shit felt amazing. Opening my eyes, I went to her breasts and began teasing her nipples with my tongue and fingertips, alternating between the two. Scooting to the edge of the sofa, I leaned back, taking Giánni with me, and wrapped my arms around her waist.

When I began thrusting into her, she gushed all over me. "Oh, fuck! *That's* how you feeling, baby?"

"Mmm-hmm," she moaned.

I quickened my pace, enjoying every stroke into her wetness, and realized I didn't have a condom on. It was too late for that shit because there was no way I was leaving this paradise now. I gripped her ass as I continued to assail her and listen to her screams. "Ahh, got damn, Gi. This pussy always this good?"

"Only for you, it will be. Only for you, baby."

I released my hold slightly as she lifted her head to stare into my eyes. We held each other's gazes for a moment as I slowly drove into her. "Sing to me, baby."

"Right now?" she said through her pants.

"Hell yeah. Right now. Let me hear that beautiful voice."

She lowered her head, and I immediately lifted it. "While you look at me. Sing while you stare into my eyes, Gi."

"*You make me feel like I can love again,*" she sang softly.

I recognized the song as Alex Isley's "Love Again." We'd just listened to the song this weekend. She sang the same line again, and I felt her soul in it. She was really singing that to me. She meant those words. I felt the same way. My stroke got stronger as she panted.

"Keep going, baby," I said softly as I stared at her.

"*Ain't know redemption tasted oh, so sweet,*" she sang, then moaned, threatening to close her eyes.

She rolled her hips on me as she sat up slightly. "*Paper faith and I landed on my feet.*" She barely got that line out. Her voice had gotten louder as her climax neared. "*Up in the air but so easy to breathe. Doubled my hopes and gave them back to meeeeee. Shiiit!*"

She was coming like a river. I could feel her juices all over my balls as I plunged inside her, chasing my own orgasm. Then just as I was about to nut, she lifted from me, went to her knees, and sucked that shit right out of me. "Oh fuuuck, Gi."

She had my damn toes curling so tight I was destined to get a cramp. I dropped my head to the back of the sofa as she stood to her feet and straddled me again. Finally, she lay her head on my chest as she whispered, "I want to fall in love with you, Ford."

I kissed her head as my heart swelled with emotion. I would have never guessed that she would move as quickly as I wanted to move, but I suppose when you know, you just know. "I want to fall in love with you too, Yanni."

She lifted her head and smiled at me. "I like that nickname better than you calling me Gi like everybody else."

"Good. I'm glad we're feeling the same way. There's only one thing I didn't say."

"What's that?"

"I'm already falling. I haven't made a full descent yet, but I'm falling in love with you, baby. You're everything I want and need in my life. I know we have a lot to talk about and disclose, but there is nothing you can say to stop what's happening."

The tears fell freely from her eyes as she stared at me. I hoped she saw the sincerity in my eyes because everything I said was factual. I was falling in love with Giánni Lecrae Judice after only a couple of weeks of dating but months of watching and admiring her. I suppose that was what made it easier for me to fall. I had all these preconceived notions of what I thought she would be like, and she exceeded those expectations by a mile.

"That makes me feel amazing," she said as I gently wiped the tears from her cheeks. "I've always wanted a love that would fully consume me . . . one that would be able to stand against anything and conquer it. I feel like I can have that with you, and it's beyond refreshing that you feel the same way . . . that you've even surpassed me in how I feel. Your feelings are so deep, which only reduces the doubt and hesitancy I can feel at times. Damn, Ford."

I bit my bottom lip as my dick sought out her opening again. Her words were beyond beautiful, and I couldn't help but try my best to make love to her. Slowly lowering her to the couch, I slid on top of her and reentered what had to be heaven. I closed my eyes, and my groans mingled with her moans, taking us to ecstasy even faster than before. Her legs were already quivering, and my dick felt like it was about to fire off sooner than right now.

Lord knows I didn't want to pull out of this furnace, but I knew I had to. So, just as her orgasm slipped from her restraint and her walls gripped me, I had to withdraw and litter her mound and abdomen with my seed. She was going to be my wife sooner than she knew.

"Ford! Hey, baby. I, umm . . . I didn't think you would come today, so I didn't cook a big meal."

"It's okay. You doing all right, Mom?"

"Yeah."

She walked away from me and began taking breakfast food out to cook for me. "Mom, you don't have to do that. I'll be fine. The main reason for me coming is to check on y'all. I designated Wednesdays because it was your idea to have family dinners. It's okay. I'll go spend time with Giánni when I leave."

She nodded, then put the eggs back in the fridge. Once she did, I hugged her and went to see my father. I tried to put what happened the other night out of my mind because I knew that he probably wouldn't even remember. However, I refused to bring my Yanni around him ever again. When I walked into the family room where he was sitting watching TV, I said, "Hey, Dad. How are you today?"

He looked up at me and smiled. "Hey, son. I'm doing okay. How are you?"

"I'm okay."

He doesn't remember a thing. So I sat on the couch across from him to see he was watching a western. He always liked those, so I purposely chose not to because he liked them. I never wanted to be like him. As a kid, I didn't even understand why, but the minute I wanted to do my own thing, I figured it out plain as day. He was controlling. My mother never really voiced her opinion on things. She just went along with whatever he said.

He watched TV for a while, then turned to me. "I guess your mom wasn't feeling good today. She didn't cook a big meal. But maybe there's enough for you."

"It's okay. I'm gonna meet my girlfriend when I leave," I said, testing his memory.

"You have a girlfriend? What's her name? What does she do?"

He didn't remember shit about what happened the other night. I wondered if he even remembered Ducati and the kids coming to town. He'd brought the kids by to see me Sunday evening after Giánni left. "Her name is Giánni, and she works for Community Bank as a commercial lending specialist."

"That's great, son. Hopefully, she's the one so you can give us some grandkids before my time is up."

He chuckled, so I joined him. "You'll be around for a while, but I think she's the one. I'm falling for her more and more every day. She supports me in my business, and she gets me."

He fiddled with his fingers for a minute and then turned back to me. "I'm dying, son. I don't think I have much time. I'm sorry for all the trouble I have given you concerning your career. I didn't see it becoming what you've turned it into. But maybe it wasn't for me to see. The vision wasn't given to me. I'm proud of you, Ford. I wanted to tell you that before I couldn't. My days are running together. I barely remember anything anymore. I'm scared, son. What if I forget all of you? Your mother?"

He started crying, and that shit almost took me down with him. I'd never seen my dad cry or even be this sensitive. I grabbed his hand. "It's gon' be okay. We're all here with you."

Hearing him say he was proud of me made my soul light. His apology helped me release the lingering anger in my heart toward him. I knew he would probably do or say something else to piss me off in this process, but today, the slate was now clean. As I held his hand, he turned his attention back to his western. For the first time in my life, I consciously tried to sit here and watch it with him.

When I looked toward the kitchen, my mom was standing there with tears streaming down her face. "I'll be right back, Dad."

He never responded to me. I didn't think he even saw me leave because he was so engrossed in his show. When I reached Mom, I gently pulled her into the kitchen out of Dad's view and into my arms. The soft sobs that left her broke my heart. This was going to be an uphill battle, but knowing I would be here to help them through it gave me a sense of peace.

When she pulled away from me, she wiped her face, then sat at the table. I sat with her, and she grabbed my hand. "I heard the conversation. He already forgets me, Ford. He didn't know who I was yesterday. He thought I was a nurse. I mean . . . I am a retired nurse, but the fact that he didn't know me was a hard pill to swallow."

"I'm sorry, Mom. I'll do my best to check on you more and give you breaks so you can have time to yourself. Instead of going to meet Giánni, I'll just hang out here. We'll be fine if you need to get away for a little while." I lowered my head, then looked back up at her. "I came here prepared to go to war with him about my girlfriend if I had to, and he doesn't even remember."

I slowly shook my head as my mom caressed my hand. "She's a beautiful woman, Ford. She really cares for you. When your dad insulted you, I could tell it took a lot for her not to jump to your defense. When she finally said something about you being extremely successful, I could only thank God that you met a woman with a backbone. I feel like I sacrificed who I was to be everything your father wanted me to be. Unfortunately, I feel like Kelsey is doing the same for Ducati."

"Mom, you loved your husband, and that was what was required of you. Sometimes, I wish you would have stood up for me, but I get it. I love you, and now you can get the time you need, okay?"

I didn't want to make her feel worse than she already did. She refused to go against my father even when he was wrong. I hated that shit about her . . . mainly when it came to me. I could tell she thought differently when he was getting on to me, but she wouldn't say a word. At least she never said a word to him in front of me. However, just like he had a clean slate starting today, so did she.

She smiled at me. "I'm going to take a little time to myself. Do you want me to pick up something for you to eat?"

"Please. You know what I like, so it doesn't matter what you bring back."

I took a twenty-dollar bill from my wallet, handed it to her, and kissed her cheek. Making my way back to the den with my dad before laying eyes on him, I knew he was asleep. His snoring filled the room. I slowly shook my head, sat back on the couch, and texted Ducati. Hey, bruh. Dad doesn't remember this weekend, and he believes he's dying. He apologized for all the shit he gave me about my career and said he was proud of me. Can you believe that shit?

I smirked as I sent the message. While I knew tomorrow Dad could be back to bashing my career, I accepted today as a win and chose to regard the words he spoke today as his true feelings. As I stared at him, I accepted the thoughts swirling through my mind. My father did his best to raise us and only wanted what was best for us. Unfortunately, I didn't know a thing about his upbringing and what he was taught to believe. Both his parents were deceased before I was born. The only grandparents I had the pleasure of knowing were my mom's parents.

I didn't know his life journey to becoming the successful attorney he once was. He wasn't that forthcoming with his past, just that his parents expected his best, and that was what he gave them. However, I knew he attended Baylor Law School and ranked at the top of his class. Maybe he would be more forthcoming with information before he forgot everything. So, I chose to forgive him because I didn't know about any of the struggles he had to overcome or the situations he endured.

Ducati responded to my text quicker than I expected him to. What's up, bruh? Ain't that some shit? I'm happy for you. I know you've been waiting to hear that from him for years.

How did the rest of the dinner go?

I had been meaning to ask him about it, but shit, my eyes were laser-focused on Giánni over the weekend. When he brought the kids by, it never came up. He probably didn't want to talk about it in front of them anyway since they were still relatively young, all under the age of ten. He responded right away, once again.

It went well despite the outbursts by Dad. He yelled at Mom a few times while I was speaking, but he finally got it together. I made a statement about his condition, just so there would be no negative publicity about him. It would piss me off to no end if I saw a news outlet bashing him. We're the only ones that can do that. LOL.

I chuckled silently at his last statement. Well, good luck in your run to the governor's mansion. Lord knows we can use someone like you in the office.

Thanks, bruh. I'll talk to you later. I have a meeting to get to. Love you, man.

Love you too.

I was glad that everything had gone well. As I stared at Dad, I could only nod repeatedly. I was happy that in all my years, I had never disrespected him. Although I still followed my own path, I had no regrets about how I treated my parents. So, if God chose to take him anytime soon, I would be at peace knowing I did right by him.

Chapter 13

Giánni

"You going to pole-dancing class tonight? I haven't been in a week, and I know Melissa will be tripping when I walk through the door."

"No. I went yesterday. I'm spending this evening with my dad. I'm thinking of inviting Ford over to meet him. Something has been nagging me to do so instead of waiting until Sunday."

"Sunday is only three days away."

"I know. We'll see. Let me get my shit together so I can get out of here, CoCo. You working late?"

"Yeah. I have to close the drive-thru. Well, I'll talk to you later. You barely have time for me, slut, but I'm happy for you."

I slowly shook my head as she left my office. I'd had a busy day today and had gotten two loans approved. One was for nearly $2 million. That should look good on my file whenever they evaluate me for the promotion. Before I could leave, I called Ford. I couldn't take lightly the feeling I was having. "Hello?"

"Hi, baby. Are you off work yet?" I inquired.

"I'm just leaving the office. Everything okay?"

"I wanted to see if you would come to meet my parents this evening instead of Sunday. I don't know what the hurry is or why something is tugging at me to allow you to meet them now, but it is."

"Yeah. I'll go home and shower and meet you at your place."

"Okay. I'll stop and get us something to eat. You good with Subway?"

"Yeah. You can get me the steak and cheese on flatbread. Only spinach as a vegetable with sweet onion sauce. Pepper jack cheese."

"Gotchu, baby. See you in a little while."

"A'ight."

I ended the call and grabbed my things to head to Subway. Once I got into my car, I called my dad to tell him that Ford and I would come this evening. I could hear my mama screaming in the background. That only caused me to chuckle. I was excited already, but her shenanigans had me wanting to be as dramatic as her.

After getting home, I took a quick shower and changed into something more comfortable. I was excited to be connecting my worlds. Knowing my mama, she would probably call Jevonna and Jules to come over. Just as I took our sandwiches from the fridge, the doorbell rang. I knew it was my baby. I went to the door to find him in sweats and a T-shirt, looking sexy as hell. "Hey, baby. Come on in."

He smiled, then kissed my lips. "Hey, Yanni. I missed you today."

We'd barely talked all day. Usually, we talked for lunch or even went out together. We also spoke during my break times and whenever I had a quick break at work. "I missed you too. I was so damn busy," I said as I closed the door.

I absolutely loved that he called me Yanni. It was the cutest nickname that somehow felt like love to me. When I turned back to him, he pulled me into his arms and kissed me passionately. My heart rate sped up, and my temperature rose as it always did in his presence. Then as I pulled away, I added, "Damn, you so good to me."

He chuckled, then bit his bottom lip for a moment. "You good to me too, baby."

"Okay, let's eat our sandwiches before we don't leave."

He chuckled as he followed me to my table. He was somewhat quiet, or rather, quieter than usual. Most times, I led the conversation, and he usually had things to say. Once we sat and dug into our sandwiches, I asked, "Everything okay? You're kind of quiet. Oh! How did dinner go last night?"

He smiled as he stared at his sandwich. I stopped eating and waited for his reply. "It went well. He didn't remember anything about what happened this weekend, and he apologized to me for the hard time he'd been giving me about my career. He told me he was proud of me for the first time. He feels like he's dying, and when he voiced it, it softened me. He was excited that I had a girlfriend and can't wait to meet our babies."

He stared into my eyes after his last statement, and I knew I had to be red. My face heated up tremendously at the thought of having Ford's children. Of course, I wanted kids eventually, but I wanted to be sure that this was real first. Only time will tell. Once the excitement of being a new couple wore off and we fell into our routine, that would be the deciding factor. But I hoped that the real excitement never wore off.

"Well, one day, I would love to have your babies, Ford. I'm happy that you had a good evening with your parents," I said softly as I thought about our possibilities.

"I won't bring you around them anymore because I never know what type of day he's having. Hearing him talk to you that way angered me so much. I could never subject you to that again."

"What if I want to go?" I asked.

I didn't like how it felt not to be included. Although I knew Ford meant well, not being able to be around him when he was with his family didn't sit right with me. He stared at me for a moment, then said, "I don't know, baby. Let's just play it by ear, okay?"

I nodded and ate the rest of my sandwich so we could head out. He kept staring at me, I suppose trying to gauge how I was feeling, but he didn't say a word. Finally, once we were done and were about to leave my house, I insisted that he follow me there. I didn't want him to stay longer than he wanted to, and I didn't want to cut my time with my parents short, either. He reluctantly agreed and got in his truck to trail me.

When we arrived, I grabbed my purse from the seat, and Ford appeared at my driver's door to open it for me. After I got out, he gently pinned me against my car and stared into my eyes.

"I'm sorry, Yanni, if I made you feel a way. You're always welcome to be anywhere that I am. I was only thinking of myself and not how you would feel. I just don't want to have to pop my old man in the mouth." He slid his fingertips down the side of my face, heating my entire body. "You forgive me, baby?"

I wrapped my arms around his waist, thankful that he got me without me even having to say anything. He was so attentive to me. I couldn't ask for more. "I forgive you. I understand where you're coming from. Whenever I want to go visit, I'll try to let you gauge the situation first to make sure he's having a good day."

Ford leaned over and kissed my lips. I smiled big as he backed away and grabbed my hand. Just that quickly, I was feeling overly excited again. There were no other cars in the driveway, so I knew we would be the only ones here with my parents. I led Ford to the back door, and before I could knock, my mama opened the door with a huge smile. "Hey, y'all, come on in."

I smiled at her theatrics as Ford brought his hand to the small of my back and followed me inside. "Hey,

Mama. This is my boyfriend, Ford Noel. Ford, this is my mother, Morgan Judice."

He grabbed her hand and kissed it. "It's very nice to make your acquaintance."

My mama was blushing and shit. I narrowed my eyes at her as she said, "The pleasure is all mine. Y'all come on in. Lloyd is in front of the TV waiting on you."

I walked past my mother and lightly shoulder-bumped her as she giggled. I was going to get on her ass later about flirting with my man. I slowly shook my head at the thought. She was a mess. When we entered the den, my dad stood from his seat and hugged me. "Hey, baby girl."

"Hey, Daddy," I responded and kissed his cheek.

I immediately turned to Ford and introduced the two of them. They shook hands, and then we had a seat. My dad didn't waste any time diving in. "So, Ford, what do you do for a living?"

I knew I had told him all of that already, but I suppose he wanted to hear it from Ford. "I own a trucking company, F.A.N. Transport Service. I just expanded by adding two rigs and a dump truck. Your beautiful daughter assisted with getting the loan."

My dad glanced at me, and I knew what he was thinking. So I added, "I only talked to my boss, offering my input to help him get the loan. He looked great on paper."

My dad nodded, and somehow, Ford realized how my dad had taken what he had to say. "I'm sorry, Mr. Judice, if I wasn't clear. I'm self-sufficient, and I'm very capable of taking care of Giánni's heart. I don't want to sound stalkerish or nothing, but I went inside the bank to conduct business for months before I gathered the nerve to talk to her. I just wanted to see her."

Ford turned to me and smiled, then kissed the side of my head as my dad responded. "That's my baby girl, and

I'm very protective of her. She's my heart. I don't know if you can tell, Ford, but she's a daddy's girl, and we don't play about our relationship."

"I can tell, sir. Whenever she talks about family, even if she's talking about someone else, she always brings your name into the conversation."

My daddy nodded, and they began making small talk about the weather and sports. Then Daddy asked about his family and their closeness. I was hoping Ford didn't go into too much detail about that and what happened this past weekend, and he didn't. "We're close, and I can feel us getting even closer now as we learn more about my dad's illness. He has Alzheimer's. While he's known for a while, they are just making my brother and me aware of how serious it is."

"I'm sorry to hear that. My grandfather had Alzheimer's, and there was little to no research on it back then. So I know where you're coming from with that. If you need help with anything, let me know. I'm retired and have plenty of free time on my hands."

I smiled at my father's generosity. He could already see in Ford just what I saw in him . . . his sincerity. "Thank you, Mr. Judice. Now what are you watching on this TV? I know good and well that ain't those sorry Celtics."

My dad laughed and said, "Hell yeah, it is, but that's the only game on right now. I love basketball, so I'll even watch the teams I don't really like."

That started an entire conversation, so I removed myself from it and went to the other room, searching for my mother. When I didn't find her, I followed my nose to the kitchen. She was pulling a damn peach cobbler from the oven. "I know you didn't make a peach cobbler."

She looked up at me and smiled. "Giiirrrlll, that man is fine. Jermaine could never. You hear me?"

I slowly shook my head as I laughed at her. "I know. I was mesmerized but tried to play it cool at first."

"Yeah. I know that shit didn't last long."

"Not at all. He told me what his intentions were on our first date. Told me I was gon' be his. Scared the hell out of me. I ghosted him for a few days until his ass sent me a bouquet of purple magnolias. That shit broke me all the way down. Mama . . . he's the one. I feel it. If we don't let outside distractions force us apart, he will be mine forever. I feel that in my soul."

She gave me the "aww, that's so sweet" look. Her eyebrows were raised and slightly scrunched together, and she had a slight smile on her face. "Baby, I've wanted that for you, especially after dealing with that dog nigga. God blessed you, baby. I'm so happy for you."

Ford and Daddy yelled at the TV, causing us both to jump. I laughed afterward because I was so happy that they were getting along. However, I never felt like they wouldn't. Ford could practically get along with anyone. After fixing them bowls of peach cobbler and vanilla ice cream, we brought them to the men. Ford sat up in his seat, his eyes wide. "Oh man, Mrs. Judice, you done messed up, na. I'm gon' be expecting this all the time."

He chuckled, and my mama blushed again.

"Ma, really? Come on here in this kitchen, woman."

She laughed and responded to Ford. "Anytime, son."

He winked at her and said, "Thank you so much." Then turning his attention to me, he gave me a playful smile. "Thank you, Yanni."

I smiled as I pulled my mama into the kitchen. "Yanni?" my mom questioned. "Okay, boo. I love it."

"Uh-huh. You gon' quit flirting with my man before I lock you in your room."

She laughed as we fixed our dessert and joined the men. We were having a fantastic time as Ford got to know them. It felt like they'd known one another forever by the time we were about to leave. We'd been here for two hours, and I knew Ford had to be beyond tired. He'd gone to work at three this morning, and here it was nearly eight o'clock in the evening. After saying our goodbyes and making promises to see them Sunday, he walked me to my car.

When we got to my driver's door, I turned to him and gave him a soft kiss on the lips. "Thank you for coming tonight. I don't know why my spirit wanted to be here now, but I'm glad we came."

"You don't have to thank me. Your parents are cool. Although I think yo' mama tryna snatch me up as her side nigga with that peach cobbler."

I laughed so damn loud, then hit his arm. "Both of you are a mess. But I do appreciate you coming this evening."

"Show me how much you appreciate that, and come stay with me tonight."

"Only if you promise to let me sleep."

"Sleep . . . mmm," he said as he nuzzled his nose against my ear. "I'll let you sleep, Yanni, but only after you put *me* to sleep."

I giggled as he playfully bit my neck. "Fine. Let me go home and get clothes, and I'll be there."

He backed away from me, then opened my door. Once I was in, he said, "Be careful. See you in a li'l bit."

"Okay."

I quickly made my way home and packed clothes for work tomorrow and my toiletries. There was no need for pajamas. As I headed out, I got a call from my daddy. I smiled as I answered because I knew he wanted to give me his feedback on how great of a person Ford was. "Hey, Daddy," I answered.

"I'm sorry, ma'am, but I found this phone at the scene of an accident. If this is your father's, you need to get here as soon as possible. The ambulance is on its way."

"Oh my God! Where is he?"

"He's on Highway 69 North, near the Dowlen Road exit."

"Shit, I'm on my way!"

I ended the call and phoned my mama. "Hey."

"Mama, I'm on my way to get you. Daddy was in an accident. Someone called me from his phone. Where was he going?"

"Oh my God. He was going to Walmart to get some gloves to be ready whenever Ford solicited his help. Oh my God. I'm going to the porch to wait for you."

I sped down Delaware to get to my parents' house. I was only about five minutes away, and their house wasn't far from the direction I had to go to get to the scene. I ran the traffic light to cross Eleventh Street, then hooked a left on Minglewood Drive. After getting to South Willowood Lane, I saw my mama running down the driveway. I turned in and unlocked my doors for her. But before she could fully get in, I was already backing out.

As I got back to Eleventh Street, my phone was ringing. I glanced at the radio to see who was calling. When I saw Ford's picture, I quickly answered. "Daddy was in an accident! I'm heading to the scene. I'll call you as soon as I know more."

I ended the call before he could even respond. There wasn't time because we were almost at the scene. When we crossed the Lucas Drive overpass, I saw the lights of emergency vehicles. I got as close as possible. Then my mom and I hopped out of my car and ran toward the ambulance. A cop stopped us to identify who we were. Once verification was done, he led us safely to the scene. There was debris everywhere. As we approached my dad's wrecked car, I screamed. His car alone looked like the accident could have been fatal.

They pulled my dad from the car, and he was conscious. My mama got inside the ambulance with him as they headed to Victory Medical Center right up the road. He looked to be in a great deal of pain and was holding his side. I could only pray that he would be okay.

I ran back to my car to drive to Victory when I saw someone conducting a sobriety test. As I stared for a moment, I realized Jermaine was taking the test. His drunk ass had hit my dad. As badly as I wanted to get out of the car and attack him, I stayed focused on the man that mattered and took off for Victory.

Chapter 14

Ford

I wasn't sure what was going on or how Mr. Judice had gotten into an accident when he was just at home. As I paced, waiting for Giánni to call back, I arranged for one of my drivers to cover my load for tomorrow. I was still short one driver I needed to hire, but I wasn't overwhelming us with work just yet. Not until everyone had fallen into a routine and gotten comfortable.

I grabbed my keys from the countertop and went to my truck. That way, whenever Giánni called, I could take off immediately and meet her. No sooner had I'd gotten in than she called. "Hey, baby," I said.

"Hey. We're at Victory Medical Center on Dowlen. I had to give blood just in case he needed it. He's O positive. They're always running low because it's so common. Plus, with this being a small hospital, their supply is even more scarce. He has some internal bleeding from a small laceration in his liver that they know of so far. He broke a rib during impact, and it slightly punctured it. A drunk driver hit him. Motherfucking Jermaine Brown," I rambled.

"Your ex?"

"Yes. I saw him sitting on the side of the road, taking a breathalyzer test. I wanted to wild out on him, but I needed to get here for my daddy. He's in surgery to reset some bones, mainly his forearm, but they will also check everything else out as well. His car was slammed into the median and rolled over a couple of times."

"Damn. Okay. I'm on my way. I can hear the panic in your voice. Is everyone there already?"

"I picked up my mom on my way to the accident, and my brother just walked in the door. My sister is on her way. They'll probably take him to give blood also."

"Okay. I should be there in ten minutes. I'm on my way now."

"All right."

She ended the call as I rushed to get there to be there for her. I couldn't imagine how she was feeling right now. I was feeling slightly nervous for her. Not knowing was a crazy beast to deal with in any situation. When I got there, I parked and quickly went inside to find Giánni having a whole-ass meltdown. I immediately thought the worst. *Her dad has died.* I got to her and scooped her up as I saw her mother's tears. A man I assumed to be her brother was pacing.

"I gotcha, baby."

She was fighting against me as she said, "No. Put me down."

I did as she requested, and she ran back to the doctor standing near her mother. "Tell me again because I couldn't have heard you correctly. Repeat it," Giánni said.

Her voice sounded eerily calm, so I made sure I was close to her just in case she erupted again.

"I'm sorry, ma'am, but your blood type is AB and isn't a match. We're testing your brother's for compatibility now. Blood type doesn't dictate paternity. That's a misconception. However, you should have a DNA test done to be sure."

"That's what I thought you said." Giánni turned to her mother as I stood there stunned. "What's your blood type, Ma?"

Her mom fidgeted some. *What in the entire fuck is going on?* She looked away as tears streamed down her cheeks. She turned back to Yanni and almost looked to be pleading with her eyes. "A," she finally said softly.

"That doctor said my blood type was AB. Ain't no way type O and type A can create an AB. So you fucked around on my daddy? I don't give a shit what that blood says. That's *my* daddy in there. Does *he* know?"

Her mom shook her head. "He knows about the affair. We were having a really tough time. I'd been staying with my parents for nearly a month. It wasn't as cold as you think it was."

"But you had to know there was a possibility. How could you not express that to him? I'm so disgusted with you right now. That blood needed to be on hand for him. What if this is a matter of life and death, and they don't have enough in their reserve? Then his blood will be on *your* hands if it is!"

Giánni stormed away from her, and I followed her along with her brother. He got to her first and hugged her tightly. He said some things in her ear as I stood aside and watched. When she pulled away from him, tears were streaming down her face. She grabbed his hand and led him to me. She introduced us, then fell into me as I shook Jules's hand. I kissed her head as I embraced her.

That was the last thing I expected to hear. I just knew that he'd died, but I suppose this was just as bad for Yanni. The man she'd known as her father for her entire life could possibly *not* be her father.

While I knew this paternity situation could turn out differently, I would be here to support her. Her mother could be wrong about her blood type. Maybe she was indeed AB. Just from high school biology, I knew if her father was an O, he could only produce O alleles. Genetics was the most interesting part of the science class for me. We'd even learned what our blood types were. So for her mother to be type A, she could be AA or AO, passing down an A or O to her children, but I didn't think there would be a possibility of her producing any B alleles. As the doctor said, Yanni needed to get a DNA test done to be totally sure.

I felt for her in this situation. But she was stronger than me. After that revelation, I would be right in my mom's face asking all sorts of questions. Maybe she wanted to cool down, and I could understand that too. She lifted her head and said, "This is why I had a strong urge to see him tonight."

I gently rubbed her back, then led her to a seat. I wanted to sit close to her mother but didn't want to set Yanni off again. She was the spitting image of her mother. They could almost pass for twins. Her mother obviously looked a little older, but not by much. *Black don't crack.* I put my arm around her as she bounced her leg nervously.

Her mom was constantly glancing at her. She wanted to explain and maybe apologize. I could sense it from where I was seated. She was a nice woman, and I could only imagine the stress she was under when she found out she was pregnant with Giánni. I wondered if she even tried to tell her husband about her uncertainty at the time.

As I consoled Yanni, the doctor came out once again to confirm that Jules's donation was a match. "Lucky you," Giánni mumbled.

She stood and walked closer to engage with the doctor on how her dad was doing and how soon they would be able to see him. While she talked, I moved closer to them and sat next to her mother. She glanced over at me with tears in her eyes. While I wanted to comfort her, I didn't want to set Giánni off. She was angry, and she had every right to be.

As the doctor explained how they had to watch his blood loss from the laceration and how they'd repaired his broken forearm and stitched a few minor cuts, Yanni turned to me, her eyes filled with relief that her father would be okay. After the doctor assured them that they would be able to see him within a couple of hours, she sat on the other side of me. However, she kept glancing at her mother. Finally, she leaned over and said, "Tell me what happened."

Standing from my seat, I had her switch chairs, and I sat in hers. Her mother turned toward her and grabbed her hand. "When Jevonna was born, your dad and I had only been married a year. I'd gotten pregnant almost immediately. I feel like we really didn't have time to learn to cohabitate with each other truly. When I had her, everything he did worked my last nerve. We argued more than a little bit. Although doctors weren't diagnosing it at the time, I think I went through post-partum depression. Since I didn't work outside the home, your dad figured all he had to do was go to work. Everything else literally fell on my shoulders . . . cleaning the house, taking care of Jevonna, cooking, serving him, paying the bills . . . everything."

I grabbed Yanni's hand and gently rubbed it as she continued to listen to her mother explain. I almost felt like I shouldn't have been privy to the things her mother was saying, but they didn't seem to mind talking in front of me.

"I caught him cheating on me when Jevonna was six months old. I was devastated. Despite how miserable and depressed I felt, I loved your dad and had been loyal to him, but when I heard him talking to that woman and followed him to her house, I was broken. I stayed with my parents for about three weeks, but they made me go back home to Lloyd. Nothing had changed other than his apology. He still saw that skank, so I decided to get even."

Yanni squeezed my hand as she quietly listened to her mother pour her heart out. I could tell where this story was headed, and I was sure Yanni could too. However, she didn't interrupt. "It was an old boyfriend from high school. We used a condom, so I assumed Lloyd was the father when I got pregnant. I'd had sex with him, although we were still arguing and fighting about his whorish ways."

"Did Dad know I could be from this other man?"

She shook her head. "*I* didn't think it was a possibility. I told him about the affair because I felt so guilty afterward. However, I also wanted him to know that whatever he could do, I could do too. He was crushed. From that day forward, he promised to stop messing around and agreed to help more with Jevonna. We made up, and we've been doing well ever since. However, this will crush him, just like it crushed you. I'm so sorry, Gi."

Her mother cried audibly, and Yanni just stared at her for a moment. I rubbed her hand as she loosened her grip. She pulled away from me and put her arms around her mother. "Believe me, Gi, I'm just as devastated as you are."

When Giánni released her, she asked, "Who is he? Does he have other kids?"

Mrs. Judice lowered her head and fidgeted slightly. "Leonard Spivey. He died three years ago. He has a son that's the same age as Jules."

Giánni stood from her seat. I sympathized with her completely. To find out that the man you've known your entire life as your father possibly wasn't your father was a heavy blow. However, itis even worse to learn that the other man involved in this situation,who could possibly *be* your biological father, is already deceased. She walked toward the exit, so I followed her outside. She was no longer crying, but I could tell she was deeply bothered.

I didn't offer her any words of comfort. I just wanted to be there for her. Honestly, I had no clue what to say. My nerves would be rattled if it were me, but I could also sympathize with her mother. She had the story of so many women her age. Not necessarily her having an affair but being left to do everything while their husband got off easy. I learned from Steve Harvey that if the man wasn't providing, protecting, and professing his love through words and deeds, then what was he doing? While Mr. Judice was providing financially, he wasn't doing anything else.

His wife felt forgotten by a man who she gave her all to. That had to be hard for any woman. It was a hard pill to swallow to feel like they were navigating through life alone, especially when they had a nigga living with them that should have been making things easier. Instead, his fucking around only made things worse. I stood behind Giánni and wrapped my arms around her, doing my best to provide the solace she desperately needed.

She leaned back and rested her head against me. I noticed her eyes were closed, and she was taking deep breaths. I couldn't help but take deep breaths with her. This shit was stressful, and I suppose since I was trying to bear it for her, it was stressing me the hell out like it was my parents. Shit, I had enough going on with my family already, but maybe I was supposed to be here to hear all of this so I could help Yanni digest it.

She slowly spun around in my arms, and I gently caressed her back as I stared out at the night sky. She finally stared at me and said, "This is hard, Ford."

"I can imagine it is, baby."

"What do I do now? Do I seek out this brother? Do I try to get to know his family . . . my family?"

"I think you should get a DNA test, as the doctor suggested, to be sure. If he's not your biological father, then you should do whatever brings you peace. Seeking them out may bring a little more chaos to your life right now. If I were you and the DNA test established a different paternity, I would find peace with the situation and talk to your dad about it. Once your family has gotten over this blow, if you still want to connect with them, go for it."

She nodded, then rested against my chest, resuming the breathing techniques she was doing. She quickly threw that by the wayside when she started verbalizing her thoughts again. "I was angry at my mom initially, but now, I feel sorry for her. This has to be a hell of a situation to be in. It's like she has to relive something that happened over twenty-eight years ago. But my dad . . . How's he going to feel knowing that he could have possibly raised another man's child?"

"*You're* his child—no matter what blood says. Just like you said earlier, you're his baby girl. I don't believe blood will change that for him. He may be hurt to know there's a chance that someone else could be your bio father, just as you and your mom were, but after the initial blow of it, I think he'll come around."

She stared up at me and puckered her lips. I lowered my head and kissed her. As we continued to stand there, her brother appeared next to us. "Gi, I'm so sorry how this turned out."

"Sorry about what? Is Daddy okay?" a woman asked.

When Giánni turned to her, she said, "Hey, Jevonna. Dad is going to be fine. He has a couple of broken bones and a small liver laceration that will heal within a few weeks. Jules donated blood for him because of internal bleeding. So we should be able to see him soon."

"So what are you sorry for, Jules?" She immediately turned to me and smiled slightly. "Hi. You must be Ford. I'm Jevonna, the oldest Judice child."

I smiled and then shook her outstretched hand. "Nice to meet you."

She turned back to her siblings and raised her eyebrows questioningly.

"Biologically, I may not be a Judice. It's possible that Dad isn't my biological father, and I found out because our blood wasn't a match."

Jevonna's hand flew to her mouth as her eyes seemed to be pleading with Giánni to tell her it was a joke or something. "Wait. Don't you get blood from Mom *and* Dad? It's possible for your blood not to match, Gi."

"Dad is O positive. Mom is A. I'm AB. That combination isn't possible from those two blood types, Von."

"I don't know, Gi. I heard O positive can maybe produce AB as well."

"It doesn't matter, since Mama confessed."

"Mama had an affair?"

"Yeah. When you were only a year old. Supposedly in retaliation to Daddy fucking around. Honestly, it's a fucked-up situation, but I don't blame her. I'm not angry now that I know the story of what happened. She didn't know it could be possible, and Daddy still doesn't know."

"When are y'all going to tell him?" she asked.

"I don't know, but I don't think tonight is a good time. Maybe tomorrow after he's gotten some rest. We need to get a DNA test to be sure."

"Okay. I'm going to head inside," Jevonna said.

Their brother followed her, leaving us outside alone once again. Yanni found her way back to my arms, and I was grateful that I was the one she turned to for consolation. I kissed the top of her head and held on to her for as long as she held on to me.

Chapter 15

Giánni

As I stared at my daddy, tears flowed down my cheeks. He was awake, but he was in a lot of pain. The nurse had just given him something for it through his IV and had exited the room. "Gi, I'm okay, baby. Stop crying."

I nodded and wiped my cheeks, trying to get my emotions under control. I focused on Jermaine's ass so I could hang on to my anger. "The person that hit you was drunk. Guess who the nigga was?"

He frowned slightly as he and everyone in the room waited for me to reveal what I knew. "Jermaine's punk ass. Had I not been trying to get to you, I would have run up on him while he was sitting on the ground and kicked him right in the mouth."

Everyone's mouths fell open in disbelief. "When did he become a drunk?" my dad asked.

"I don't know. He was always a drinker, but I'd never known him to drive drunk. I suppose people change."

No one else said a word. It seemed everyone was thinking about our situation and trying not to let on that something was wrong, but my dad was an intelligent man. He caught on to our silence. "What's going on? Am I worse off than what they're telling me? Y'all looked like you swallowed the canary. Spit it out."

We all turned to my mother, waiting for her to say something. Rightfully, she should have been the one to reveal what was going on. She cleared her throat when she realized we were all staring at her. "Lloyd, there's something I need to tell you."

Everyone sort of turned away, I suppose not wanting to witness our dad's reaction to what she had to say.

"Go ahead, Morgan. What is it?"

"You needed blood when we got here. Giánni was the only one here at the time, so she donated. But unfortunately, they returned and told us she wasn't a match. The doctor said that it's possible that Gi could have a different blood type, but because of the history between us, I knew I needed to tell you."

There was complete silence, so I turned to look at my dad. He was staring at my mother, and I could see the moment the recollection of what happened twenty-eight years ago surfaced. His eyes widened somewhat and held a sadness I'd never seen before. But suddenly, that sadness turned to anger. Many people believed the misconception that if the child didn't have the father's blood type, the child wasn't his. Although my mama explained what the doctor said, I could see that it didn't matter. I hated that we even had to tell him. I could have snuck a hair follicle or something for a DNA test.

"Get out."

"Lloyd, I didn't know either. I would never deceive you that way."

"What do you mean you *didn't know*, Morgan? Having unprotected sex without being on birth control can cause pregnancy. You should have made me aware of that when you came back."

"We *did* use protection, Lloyd. *That's* what I'm telling you. When I discovered I was pregnant, I knew she was yours because you are the only man I've ever had unprotected sex with."

"Please, just leave. All of you. I need time to myself."

I stared at my dad, pleading for him to say something to me. Instead, he refused to even look at me. That tore me to pieces. I walked over to his bedside, the tears falling down my face. "You're still my dad. You're the only father I know. Please don't shut us out. Don't shut me out, Daddy. We still don't know for sure. We need to take a DNA test."

"Giánni, I need time. Give me that."

The cries of desperation left my body as I left the room. I was in despair, and I didn't know what to feel. When I entered the lobby area, Ford stood and made his way to me. "Can you take me home? Please?"

He frowned slightly as he watched everyone else enter the waiting area. Finally, my mom sat in a chair and said, "I can't leave as long as he's here. So y'all go home and get some rest. Jevonna, go tend to your family, baby. Gi, I'm so sorry. My heart hurts for you, baby girl. But I feel like he'll come around. He just needs time to process things, okay?"

I nodded, then walked out, feeling like a zombie. Jules sat next to my mom. I suppose he was going to stay with her. Jevonna stopped me and wrapped her arms around me. "I love you, sis. If you need to talk, please call me."

"I love you too," I mumbled as she released me from her embrace.

"Take care of her, Ford."

He nodded at Jevonna and said, "It will be my pleasure."

When we got to his truck, he opened my door and helped me inside, nearly picking me up and placing me on the seat. Unfortunately, my car would have to stay here for the night. He buckled my seat belt and kissed my cheek. I had no words for how I felt. My mom's revelation had knocked the wind out of me, but my dad's reaction felt like a stab wound to the heart. Just the fact that he couldn't even look at me hurt more than anything. According to Jevonna, I could still possibly be his daughter. I'd go through every horrible decision I'd made in life all over again just not to have to deal with this pain.

Once Ford had gotten inside and cranked the engine, he grabbed my hand to get my attention. I turned to him as he said, "I'm gonna go to my house and get some clothes, okay?"

I only nodded. While I didn't want to talk, I was beyond grateful that he would be with me through this. It wouldn't have been good if I had to deal with this all alone. I wanted to shut out the world and wallow in my despair. But at least I knew Ford wouldn't allow me to do that. Just him being here for me would help me stay afloat. My dad was my best friend, and I didn't know what I would do if I didn't have him anymore.

After we'd gone to Ford's house and he'd come out with a duffle bag, we made our way to my house. He rubbed my hand and said, "I suppose y'all weren't able to wait until tomorrow to tell him, huh?"

"No," I responded softly. "He wouldn't look at me afterward. He asked all of us to leave."

"He'll come around, baby. Once the shock of the news wears off, he'll be right back in your life."

"But what if the shock lingers and the DNA test proves that he's not my biological father? Am I supposed to move on without him? I talk to my dad every day. How am I going to function without him?"

"Let's not think like that, okay? Let's just bank on you seeing him tomorrow and talking through things. Did he talk to your mom?"

"He asked her how she could do that to him. She explained that she didn't know either and why she was so sure I was his. She even told him what the doctor said and how I could still be his daughter. That was when he told all of us to leave."

"It's hard for him to fathom. I don't believe he'll be able to go too long without you, regardless of paternity. I've witnessed your connection, and I admire it. The love the two of you have for each other is something I wish I had had with my dad. Watching your interaction earlier tonight brightened my soul. He won't be able to throw that by the wayside. Try not to worry your pretty head about it."

"Thank you, Ford, for being here for me."

He turned into my driveway, then turned to me. "I'm your man. I'm supposed to be here." He touched my cheek and gently caressed it with his thumb. "I'm just happy that you're *allowing* me to be here for you."

He pulled away, got out of the truck, and walked around to help me. Following me to the door, he gently rested his hand on the small of my back. That simple gesture from him always made me feel protected. I loved the feeling. After unlocking the door and going inside, I dropped my keys on the countertop. Ford lifted me from my feet and into his arms as I dropped my purse.

I wrapped my arms around his neck as he cradled me like I was the most precious gift he'd ever gotten. When we got to my bedroom, he lowered me to the bed and took off my shoes. "Do you want to take a shower?"

"I took one before we went to my parents' house. I'll take one in the morning."

"Okay."

He pulled my shirt over my head, unfastened my bra, and pulled off my pants. I watched him as he folded my clothes and laid them across the chair. He smiled slightly as he glanced at the pole, causing me to offer a small smile as well. Then Ford took off his shirt and pants and joined me in bed. It was late, but I knew I probably wouldn't be able to sleep. Thoughts of my dad disowning me had me nervous.

Pulling my body close to his, he kissed my cheek, then my lips. We lay there staring at each other like we were trying to memorize the smallest details about the other's face. I didn't know what got into me, but I whispered, "I love you, Ford."

He didn't seem to be surprised by my admission. Instead, his hands slowly descended and made their way to my ass. After gently squeezing it, he lowered his lips to mine and kissed me like he would never get the chance again. Once he separated our lips, he rested his forehead against mine. "I love you too, Yanni."

I took a deep breath, then exhaled as I got comfortable in his embrace, silently praying that everything would be okay tomorrow.

I woke up to Ford's tongue between my legs, bringing pleasure that was damn near unfathomable. Even in my sleep, my body was extremely sensitive to him. I hoped that never changed. I rubbed my hand over his head as I moaned. "Mmm . . . yes, Ford."

He lifted his head and stared at me for a moment while my juices navigated through his beard. "Good morning, beautiful."

"Good morning," I whispered.

He returned to what he was doing, and my breath caught in my throat. My head was spinning as he brought me closer to orgasmic pleasure. The gentleness that he gave me was overwhelming, and I was about to be overwhelmed all over his face. He was sucking my clit with so much passion that I couldn't help but be fully engrossed in the moment. When I felt a warm feeling between my legs, like someone had poured a cup of warm water down there, I immediately sat straight up.

Ford put his hand on my stomach and gently pushed me back down. "You squirted, baby. So fucking sexy. Now, cream on my tongue."

He dove back in and once again took my breath away. Bringing my hands to his head, I let out a guttural moan that surprised even me. The pleasure his tongue was bringing me was something I never wanted to let go of. I lifted my hips slightly and began rolling them against his face. He fell in rhythm with me, and before long, my orgasm rained down on him just as he commanded it to.

When he lifted his head, and I saw the creamy goodness in his beard, it turned me on even more so. He wasted no time sliding into my pussy. It was like there was a fire he needed to put out. We both moaned the moment he entered me. I wrapped my legs around his waist as he expertly fed me the dick. "Yanni . . . shit . . ."

I opened my eyes to stare at him, and he stared right back at me. I noticed that he rarely closed his eyes. I didn't know how he could control his nut that way. Whenever I stared at him, it made the moment even more intense. We stared into each other's eyes, and after a few deep-ass strokes, he said, "I love you so much already. You've become my everything in such a short amount of time."

"I love you too, Ford. God . . . You're so good to me . . . and for me. Ooohh, shit."

My legs began trembling as Ford pushed them to my head and watched the action below. He had dick for days, and it seemed it was crafted just for me. He filled me perfectly, and sometimes, it felt like I wasn't deep enough for him, but the feeling of him gently caressing my cervix was just as powerful as my orgasms. He wasn't on no beat-the-pussy-up shit when he was that deep, and I appreciated him for that.

However, I loved when he went to war with my shit too. Those quick, powerful strokes brought me to orgasm just as quickly as his slow, deep ones. The fact that I'd squirted showed how gone I was in his love. "I'm about to nut, baby," he said, breaking me out of my daze.

Just as he tried to pull out, I put my hands on his ass and pushed him deep inside me. His eyes widened somewhat as he released. His gaze never left mine. I may have been stupid for taking that risk, but I needed to feel him finish inside me. Lowering his head, he kissed me softly and rested his head on mine, allowing his dick to marinate in my juices without saying a word.

When I walked into my dad's hospital room holding a DNA kit I'd gotten from Walgreens, no one else was there. I didn't care that he hadn't called for us to come back. My mom had gone home to shower and get something to eat. He was asleep when I walked in, but his eyes landed on mine as soon as I closed the door. He didn't look away. Instead, a few tears left him. I went to his bedside and grabbed his hand as tears graced my cheeks.

"I'm sorry, baby girl. Last night was so hard to stomach. With our bond, it seemed unreal that you might belong to someone else. I was angry, hurt, and consumed with grief. I felt betrayed at first. But during my time alone, I realized that it was my fault. I'd pushed your mama away. I was sleeping around, and I just wasn't a good husband to her or father to Jevonna. I was horrible, actually. It wasn't until I realized that she had other options, too, that I decided to honor my vows. I couldn't take the same shit I was dishing out to her."

The tears continued to fall from his eyes as he took a slow, deep breath. I knew it hurt because of his broken rib. He winced in pain as he exhaled. "Had I been the husband I vowed to be, your mother wouldn't have done what she did. She's not that kind of woman. Gi, you'll always be mine, baby girl. I'm sorry for the way I made you feel last night."

I nodded, unable to speak at that moment. He continued. "I could never disown you. You my road dog, my dominoes buddy, and my partner in crime. Blood means nothing. It won't change our relationship. I love you so much and hate that I made you feel unwanted."

I leaned over and kissed his head, thankful he'd come around like everyone said he would. "I bought this DNA test kit from Walgreens. I just need to swab your cheek and mine. Then I can send it off for testing."

"Okay. How long does it take to get results?"

"Once the lab gets it, two to five days. I assume that window is for if they receive it later in the week, close to the weekend."

"Okay. Let's do it, baby girl."

I tore the box open and took out both sample packets. After reading the instructions, swabbing my cheek, and storing it correctly, I did the same to him. I closed my eyes, took a deep breath, silently praying for favorable results, and sealed the shipping envelope. I gave him a soft smile as he stared at me. "I suppose I can tell Ford he can come in now."

My dad gave me a slight smile as well. "He's a good man. I'm glad you've finally found happiness. He's the one, baby girl. He's going to be your husband."

I smiled, leaned over, and kissed him again. I was beyond happy that my dad was still in my life. Then leaving his side, I walked to the lobby to get Ford. When he looked at me, questioning me with his eyes, I smiled and waved him over. He smiled back and stood to his feet, rushing over to me. "Everything is good now, baby. Just like you said it would be."

He kissed my forehead and followed me back to my dad's room . . . with his hand at the small of my back.

This had to be what love was supposed to feel like. The realization of how I felt caught me off guard, and I couldn't stop myself from verbalizing it to the man I knew felt the same way I did. He was right about what he said on our first date. I would be his, and he prepared to take care of me for the rest of my life.

Chapter 16

Ford

It had been a couple of weeks since Yanni's father's accident. He was home and doing well. He had to return to the doctor in a week so that they could check the small laceration in his liver. His rib would take another couple of months to heal, along with his arm. When he'd gone home, the tension was still a little thick between him and his wife, especially since the DNA test results had confirmed that he wasn't Giánni's biological father. It wasn't an angry type of tension but one of pain and sadness. It was heartbreaking, but I believed they would get through it together.

Yanni had taken the results better than I thought she would. I suppose she was already convinced that he wasn't her father. While blood types and whether they were compatible could be tricky, in her case, it wasn't tricky at all. The two of them didn't produce her. Instead, another man was involved in creating such a beautiful display of love. We talked about it the day the results came in, and she took time to be with her dad. After that, she was done with it altogether.

I was able to speak to Charli about her date with Jermaine. What Yanni and I had assumed was the total opposite. Jermaine was her cousin, and she had been trying to talk some sense into him. I was surprised

Giánni had never met her. She apologized profusely when I'd told her about it being Yanni's father that he'd hit. I had to remind her that it wasn't her that needed to apologize. She said he'd been binge drinking through the depression he felt about losing Giánni, and I felt sorry for him—for a split second. Only a split second, though. His fuckup was how I was blessed with such an amazing woman. It was just crazy that the depression he felt about losing her caused him to hurt her further by running into her dad.

My company was finally fully staffed, and I couldn't be happier. The time I gained from having a full staff gave me more free time to spend with my parents and Yanni. For an hour a day, I gave my mom her free time away from the house. I wasn't sure what she was doing during that time, but I almost didn't care. She earned that time to herself, plus some. Of course, some days with my dad were worse than others, but we were managing.

It was Wednesday, and my mom was cooking a Mexican feast in the kitchen. As I sat watching westerns with my dad, my phone rang.

"Hello?"

"Hey, baby. I know you're probably at your parents' house, but I wanted to see if today was a good day. I would love to spend that time with y'all. I'm not going to my pole-dancing class."

"Absolutely. I would love to spend time with you and have you get to know them."

After giving her the address, she told me she was on her way. It seemed I'd fallen more in love with her the past two weeks, and all I could think about was how I nutted inside her. We hadn't talked about it, but I'd been wearing a condom since then. I believed she felt sensitive about her dad at the time and just wanted to feel me completely, no matter the consequence. While I knew I wanted to be with her for the rest of my life, I wasn't in a hurry to raise kids. I wanted to enjoy our time together without children at first. But if she was pregnant, I would adjust and be the best father in the world.

I stood from my seat to go to the kitchen to inform my mother that she was coming. "Mom, Giánni is coming for dinner. She's on her way."

She smiled brightly. "I'm so glad we will get a do-over, and she isn't taking our first meeting to heart."

"She's an amazing woman I've had the pleasure of falling in love with. She's it for me. She'll be the woman I marry and create a family with. There's no doubt in my mind. I feel that strongly about her."

"I'm happy for you, baby. What God has for you is for you. I'm sorry for allowing your dad to belittle you and pressure you into doing what he wanted you to do. I must admit that I wasn't completely on board when you turned down that scholarship. I was upset with you, thinking you were throwing away an opportunity that few people got. You were smart and an amazing basketball player. However, you proved us wrong. Now, you are a successful business owner, and you've made my heart proud. Even with the lack of support, you walked to the beat of your own drum. Your decision in your career led you to the woman of your dreams."

She gently stroked my cheek with her hand as she smiled at me. I was happy I didn't let the pressure get to me, either. Although Yanni and I had only been together for a month or so, I couldn't imagine life without her now. We saw each other almost daily, and when we didn't, we whined on the phone about how much we missed each other. "Thank you, Mom. I'm glad God gave me the strength to keep going. Ducati was extremely supportive. He even fronted me a few dollars in the beginning."

"That makes me happy, son. I'm glad that despite your dad's constant comparisons, the two of you remained close." She huffed and slowly shook her head. "We could have destroyed you. Thank God . . . He kept you."

I smiled slightly at her, kissed her cheek, and then returned to my dad. A commercial was on, so he turned to me and said, "I didn't see you leave."

I chuckled. "That's because you were all up in *The Rifleman*."

He laughed and said, "You don't know what you're missing."

"If you say so. My girlfriend is joining us for dinner."

His eyes brightened as he stared at me. "That's great! I'm glad I get to meet her finally."

I smiled at him, but I silently prayed that he remained in his mood. While I knew that his condition could have him saying any and everything, that wouldn't stop me from getting angry. Once his show came back on, he focused on the TV, and I was able to check in with my dispatcher to see how the day had gone. I'd been here for most of the day. I'd met Yanni for lunch at noon, and I'd gone to a meeting at Dow Chemical to try to get a contract there to haul hazardous materials.

After that was done, I'd come right back here and had been watching westerns all day, from *Bonanza* to *John Wayne* to *Gunsmoke* and now *The Rifleman*. After my dispatcher confirmed that all was well, the doorbell rang. My dad looked up at me as I stood and smiled. He was a totally different man. It was days like today that gave me the strength to endure the rough days.

Once I got to the front door, I welcomed Yanni inside, then kissed her lips. I was nervous as hell. "Hey, baby. How did the rest of your day go?"

"It went well. I've made it to the final three being considered for VP."

"That's good, baby. I'm proud of you."

"How did your meeting go?"

"It went great. I got the contract."

"Great news. I'm happy for you."

I grabbed her hand and led her to the den, where my dad was still seated. My mother had joined him. They both stood when we entered, and I introduced Giánni like they'd never met. My mom hugged and welcomed her to the family like we were already married. My dad was just staring at her, and my wall immediately went up, preparing to defend Yanni at all costs. "I can't believe she's your girlfriend," he said as he shook his head slowly.

I frowned. Instead of ignoring him, I probed. "Why do you say that?"

"Because she's way too pretty for you." He burst into laughter, and I exhaled. He hugged her and said, "It's so nice to meet you, Giánni."

She smiled big. "It's nice to meet you also. You know Ford is quite the catch himself. It looks like he may have gotten that from you."

My dad had the nerve to blush and smile. "He *is* a chip off the old block."

I slightly rolled my eyes. She was buttering him up. That was an excellent strategy to keep him in a good mood for the rest of her visit. When she sat next to me, I noticed his eyes had stayed on her. I swore this man had me on edge. "Giánni, what do you do for a living?"

"I'm a commercial lender at Community Bank."

"That's nice. Did you have to go to school for that?"

"I didn't have to, but I have an accounting degree. It helps a little bit. Had I known that I would have been doing this, I would have gone for finance."

"That's good. Sometimes life takes us in a different direction. I thought my entire childhood that I would be a doctor. I quickly changed my mind when I got to college and took a few science classes. I wasn't a fan of science, but I loved political science and debating. That propelled me to pursue a law degree."

"That's amazing, Mr. Noel."

He smiled and said, "Call me Horace, daughter-in-law. Or, I mean, if you feel comfortable, you can call me Dad."

I almost swallowed my damn tongue. He frowned at me. "What's wrong with you, Ford? You jealous at how me and uhh . . ." He lowered his head for a moment, then turned to Giánni. "What's your name again, baby doll?"

She blushed and said, "Giánni."

Turning back to me, he continued. "You jealous at how me and Yanni have hit it off?"

My eyebrows shot up. "Hol'on, old man. *I'm* the only one that calls her Yanni. She's *Giánni* to you."

He chuckled some more, and I was grateful that he was having such a good day. "Well . . . looks like we'll both be calling her Yanni."

"Nope. You can call her Gi. That's what everyone else calls her."

He shrugged his shoulders as my mama stole Giánni from us and brought her to the kitchen. When they were gone, he turned to me and said not so quietly, "She's beautiful, son. I think she's going to be your wife."

Everyone was seeing just what I saw in her. For once, my vision was shared with others. They accepted it and believed in it. "I *know* that she's going to be my wife. No doubt about it."

"That was how I felt the first time I saw your mother. She was like a ray of sunshine in my life. Although my father gave her a hard time, she still loved me and wanted to be with me."

I frowned slightly. I had never heard this before. "What did he do?"

"He told her she was too independent for me. That I needed a woman who would allow me to provide and be the man of the house. She was too opinionated and didn't know how to submit. Sherry changed who she was to be accepted by them, and I allowed it. Don't ever allow anyone to disrespect your wife. Don't allow her to change to please anyone. You fell in love with her just the way she is. Encourage her always to stay true to who she is. She's so beautiful. When did y'all get married? Was I there?"

I lowered my head slightly. "We aren't married just yet, Dad. But I promise that you'll be in attendance when we tie the knot."

He nodded as my baby returned from the kitchen and sat beside me. "Dinner is almost ready. The enchiladas need a couple more minutes in the oven."

"Okay."

"Daughter-in-law, do you want to have babies?"

Yanni smiled big as she turned to me. "Only with Ford. I'll have as many as he wants."

"Be careful with that, baby. I may want a basketball team."

She rolled her eyes, and I tickled her, causing her to burst into laughter. She quickly covered her mouth and slapped my arm. "Remember I told you not to cover that beautiful smile or stifle that laughter? That still holds true. A wise man told me always to encourage my wife to stay true to who she is. So, I'm telling you, wife, that I fell in love with you just the way you are. Don't change."

She blushed. I knew it was because I referred to her as my wife. My dad nodded in agreement and said, "Very wise man."

I chuckled because I wasn't sure if he was talking about himself or if he'd already forgotten and was just agreeing with me. I grabbed Yanni's hand and kissed it as she smiled at me. "Have you checked on your dad? How's he doing?"

"I called him before I got here, letting him know that I would go by there tomorrow. He's doing okay. He and my mom have been talking about everything and trying to get over the shock of it all."

"That's good."

"Yeah. I'm still struggling with whether I want to know my other family or not."

"It's only been a week since you've known. You have time to think about it. When will they reach a decision at the bank?"

"By next week, but it could be sooner. The sooner, the better. My nerves are going crazy being in limbo like this."

"I can imagine."

"Food is ready, everyone," my mom yelled from the kitchen.

Yanni was the first one up to go and help while I helped Dad from his chair. He'd fallen asleep just that fast. The medication, Donepezil, made him tired and drowsy, he'd told me. Thankfully, he didn't have many other side effects, like nausea and muscle cramps.

Once we got to the kitchen, my mom and Yanni placed our food plates on the table. I smiled at her. "Thank you, baby."

"You're welcome."

"Did I tell you that your wife was so pretty?" my dad asked me.

"Yes. You told me. She's gorgeous."

"Hopefully, your kids all look like her."

He chuckled as I twisted my lips to the side. I liked this playful side of him. Once he sat, I pulled Yanni to me by her waist and kissed her near her ear. "I hope *all* of our babies look like you too."

Epilogue

Giánni

Nine months later . . .

"Had I known y'all would get married this fast, I would have visited more often to get to know you," Ducati said.

"It's okay. We have plenty of time to get to know each other."

He smiled, then kissed my cheek and Naima's hand. Ford and I married three months ago while I was big and pregnant. That day before seeing my father in the hospital was definitely the conception date. It was the only time we'd gone all the way, letting him nut inside me, before finding out I was pregnant. My dad refused to let us go to the courthouse to get married. Instead, he and my mom planned an intimate but beautiful wedding in their backyard. Besides Daddy Horace repeatedly asking why we were getting married again, everything went beautifully.

When Ford and I found out I was pregnant, he'd held his hands to my stomach and promised to be the best father he could be. He then asked for my hand in marriage. Said we were only prolonging the inevitable. He was right about that. He put his house up for sale and moved in with me since my house was bigger. We thought about getting married in Jamaica since he accompanied me on my vacation there, but it would have been much too difficult for our parents at the time.

Naima was born a month ago, and she was doted on like a princess. No one could get enough of her ample cheeks and thick, black hair. She looked just like me, and Daddy Horace had thanked the good Lord for that. Of course, we all laughed when he said it. He'd been doing well, and his Alzheimer's seemed to be at a standstill. We could only thank God that it hadn't gotten any worse.

"Can I hold my niece?"

I looked up to see my brother, Leonard Junior. I finally reached out to my other family about six months ago. They were shocked, but they accepted me when I told them who my mother was. They knew Morgan wouldn't lie about such a thing, and they loved her for their brother and son. I wished I could have gotten to meet Leonard before he died. They talked about how much he loved my mama, and I was in awe of how great they made him sound. From the pictures I'd seen, my brother was a replica of him.

Leonard Junior and I had still gotten a DNA test done to confirm things, proving that he was indeed my brother. We talked almost daily, as much as I spoke with Jules and Jevonna. I was grateful to connect with not just him but my grandparents, aunts, and uncles. "Of course," I said to Leonard.

Once he sat with her, I stood to find my honey. His business had grown significantly. So much so that he had to purchase another rig. His loan was almost entirely paid off. I was so proud of him. When I caught up with him in the backyard, I smiled at the sight. He was barbecuing with my dad standing next to him, applying the sauce. Still, by far, my two favorite guys.

My dad was doing great and had healed amazingly well. Thankfully, Jermaine had been arrested and was still doing time for a DWI and vehicular assault. He was set to get out in a couple of years unless he became eligible for parole. The judge had sentenced him to three years in prison. He'd sent my dad a letter apologizing for the accident and hoping that all of us would forgive him. The jury was still out on that. Daddy and Mama had grown closer through all the turmoil and seemed more in love than before.

"Hey, VP. Whatchu need? We got it out here," my dad said when he saw me.

Ever since they'd awarded me the promotion nearly nine months ago, my daddy had been calling me "VP," like he'd forgotten my real name. I slightly rolled my eyes as I always did when he called me that.

"I was looking for my husband. But since you wanna put your two cents in, we can get these bones poppin' expeditiously. I owe you an ass whooping."

I kissed Ford's cheek as he chuckled at our shenanigans. It was the same shit every time we were together. "See, Ford, she tryna make me embarrass her in front of your family." He turned his attention back to me and said, "But that's okay. I don't mind them watching how I'm gon' school the hell outta yo' ass. Let me get this set up. You good, Ford?"

"Yes, sir. I got it," he responded with a slight chuckle.

I wrapped my arms around my husband. "Now that he has something to do, I need to feel your lips, husband."

He lowered the lid on the barbeque pit and turned to me. "As I said in our vows, whatever you need from me, you got that shit. Even though it was fast, love wouldn't let me wait." He lifted me, bringing us face-to-face, and said, "Take what you want, Yanni."

I laid my lips on his and promised with my soul that I would never let our flame dim. Instead, we would work hard and constantly communicate to make sure it would always shine bright.

The End

Plus One

a novella by

Treasure Hernandez

Chapter 1

Pretty Brown Eyes

"Trick, what the fuck do you have on?" Gizelle asked as she stood in her best friend's doorway. Immediately upon Bae opening the door, Gizelle's face twisted like a pretzel on a New York street cart. "You look like Piggy Smalls, or better yet, a pregnant prostitute about to go into labor."

Bae took a step back into her luxury penthouse on the top floor of an apartment building near South Point Hotel and Casino on Las Vegas Boulevard. It was the one she'd dreamed of living in when she first landed in Sin City, a.k.a. Las Vegas, twelve years ago.

"For one," Bae started, with the white-tipped acrylic nail of her index finger moving up and down, scanning the entire length of Gizelle's body, "A *trick*? Never. Not when *I'm* the one doing all the magic, which means *I* control the tricks. So, call me the Magician."

"And what's two?" Gizelle asked, throwing her hands on her twenty-five-inch waist. "And three, four, five, and six, too. 'Cause I'm here for all the excuses about why you think I don't love you enough to let you go out looking like the fat Elvis in drag."

Bae put the full weight of her five-foot-six-inch, 227-pound frame on her left leg and then continued. "For two, your skinny, coke-whore-looking self just mad because the fellas can't pull up to the bumper and hit curves like they do with *alllll* this." Bae ran her hands down the length of her beautiful body, her hands hitting the perfectly placed curves throughout the journey. "With you," she again pointed her finger at Gizelle, "it's just flat terrain, which makes for such a boring ride." Bae winked and shifted her weight to her right leg. Her firm, solid, well-toned calf had no trouble sustaining her delicious mound of flesh as she balanced effortlessly in her clear pumps sprinkled with Swarovski crystals. "And for three, since you want me to count down like I'm Beyoncé, don't come up in here greeting me with all that cussing. You know better than that. Bitch, I'm saved." Bae rolled her eyes as she sashayed away from the front door, heading to her bedroom.

Gizelle laughed as she shooed her hand at Bae, letting her have the last word, as usual. "Where you going?" Gizelle asked as she entered Bae's penthouse, closing the door behind her.

"Where you think?" Bae asked, not even looking back over her shoulder at Gizelle as she strutted on with confidence. "To get out of this little-ass dress that makes me look like the glitter dust that pops out of the top hat after the magician says, 'Abracadabra. Tah-da! Poof!'" Bae opened her balled fist into the air to symbolize her throwing up glitter dust.

Both women burst out laughing.

"Oh, so you *do* know you look crazy in that blingy-ass tube dress that barely covers Miss Kitty." Gizelle headed straight to the bar that rested in the corner of Bae's living room. She admired her reflection in the ceiling-to-floor window that enabled a view of the best of both worlds when it came to the Valley: the mountains and the Strip.

"Kitty? Girl, you mean Miss *Lioness*." Bae stopped in her bedroom doorway, turned around, and feigned clawing the air.

"I can't with you." Gizelle smiled and shook her head as she scanned the selection of cocktails. "Leos, y'all so damn dramatic."

"I know, right?" Bae proceeded into her owner's suite, decorated with just a few choice pieces of furniture.

There was her California king bed with a gray velvet head and footboard trimmed and decorated in rhinestones, her chest, dresser, and a nightstand. No pictures, paintings, or any type of artwork on the walls. No rugs. No vases, plants, or the like. And it was just enough for Bae. When it came to life, Bae wanted the world. But when it came to her domicile, she was a minimalist, preferring to spend her fortune on a few nice quality things than a bunch of inexpensive items. But whether expensive or inexpensive, Bae didn't like a lot of stuff in her surroundings. She didn't want anything taking the attention away from her.

"But, girl, yeah," Bae said, raising her voice the farther she walked into her walk-in closet and away from Gizelle.

Now, when it came to her closet, *that's* where one would beg to differ that Bae was a minimalist, as Bae had garments and shoes stacked wall-to-wall and corner-to-corner. Finally, she ran out of room in her closet and resorted to using the guest bedroom closet, chest, and dresser to store her overflow of clothing and accessories.

"I was about to change out of this dress when you buzzed." Bae slid a few hangers back and forth and then shook her head, not finding what she was looking for.

"Fix me a drink while you're at it," Bae said, exiting her bedroom and heading to the guest bedroom closet.

"I got you." Gizelle was in heaven at her favorite part of the penthouse. Although she loved her some cocktails, she didn't keep any at her own house. She was what one refers to as a social drinker, only drinking when she was out with friends, at an event, et cetera.

Once upon a time, her cupboards and fridge stayed on fleek with everything from top-shelf liquor to Two Buck Chuck wine from Trader Joe's. But when her mother came to visit her from their hometown of Detroit, Michigan, and decided to stay in Vegas, living with Gizelle until she could get a job and her own place, Gizelle stopped stocking anything that had alcohol in it, including cough syrup. Her mother had been clean and sober for six months when she joined Gizelle in Vegas, and Gizelle didn't want to tempt her.

The first few months of her mother being in Vegas were good. Gizelle's mom found a recruiting job and was doing so well that she received a promotion, raise, and a bonus within five months. But everything went downhill when her mother's boss celebrated the promotion, raise, and bonus during a happy hour. Then, just one drink was the snowball that turned avalanche.

Gizelle's mother ended up back in Detroit in a rehab facility. But even with her mother no longer in her residence, Gizelle still doesn't keep alcohol in her home for fear that the saying was true . . . that alcoholism is a hereditary disease. However, Gizelle's grandmother begged to differ. "Yo' momma's just a stone-cold drunk," her grandmother would say. "That disease mess is something white folk made up when their precious white woman, Betty Ford, stayed full and tipsy out of her mind. So they had to put a cute little label on it at that point because they didn't want to hold her accountable or make her take accountability for being exactly what she was, which was a stone-cold drunk just like yo' momma."

True or not, Gizelle didn't want to take any chances by making access to it so convenient—it being alcohol and the disease.

She squinted her eyes as she looked among what she referred to as the drinks' "seasonings," a.k.a. the mixers. "Where's the Monin Orange Spritz Syrup?" she frowned.

"You used the last of it the last time you were over," Bae reminded her as she shouted from the guest room while sliding hung outfits along the closet bar.

"And you didn't get any more?" Gizelle's tone was one of offense. "You *know* I can't drink liquor without the right seasonings. That's like trying to eat collard greens with no Lawry's Seasoning Salt." Gizelle stomped her foot like a two-year-old refused candy in the checkout line. "And I was all set to drink this peach Cîroc with my splash of Monin. Damn, Bae."

"Damn you for showing up empty-handed," Bae said. "You drink up my stuff on a regular and don't ever come through with a replacement. Just because you don't buy alcohol and seasonings for your own house don't mean you can't buy them for mine. Especially when you know the first thing you'll do is run over to that bar." As Bae fussed, she took the exact same dress she was wearing—only in a larger size—off the hanger and held it up against her body. "Besides, you be totally disrespecting the Cîroc with all that sweet syrup, juices, fruit, and stuff you be putting in it. Syrup, orange juice, pineapple juice, soda water, cherries, and orange slices. Puffy would be pissed if he saw what you were doing to his drink." Bae shook her head.

"Nah, he'd call it the P Diddy remix and keep it moving." So Gizelle did Sean Puffy Comb's signature dance as she continued to make her drink, minus her favorite seasoning.

A few minutes later, Bae reappeared in the living room. "How's this?" She spun around in the silver, blinged-out tube dress to which she'd added a thick black belt.

"A hundred times better now that it fits," Gizelle said with her usual backhanded compliment/shade. "What did you do, go throw up last night's meal until you could fit in that dress? Or did you buy it in three different sizes like you do with an outfit you absolutely love?" She took a sip of her drink, not totally pleased with it, but it would have to do for now.

"Girl, you know I stopped making myself throw up in college." She stopped in her tracks and gave Gizelle the once-over. "Unlike yo' ass, who looks like if you swallowed an olive, you'd have a baby bump." She pranced over to the bar. Once there, she paused. "Where's my drink?" She looked from one end of the bar to the other.

"I drank it and threw it up, bitch." Gizelle sucked her teeth and took another sip of her drink.

Bae huffed as she proceeded to make her own drink.

The back-and-forth banter between the two could very well be seen as offensive on the outside looking in, but not to Gizelle and Bae. The two had been friends since middle school, and even back then, they would play The Dozens to see who could trade the best insults about each other. It was the baker's dozen for them, because Bae was always one-up on Gizelle.

Bae was so slick, smooth, and creative with her words. She always was sure to get the last one in. That's why it was no surprise to her classmates that Bae chose to be a writer and author as her career. She had always been great at manipulating and mastering words, which she used to her advantage and greatly benefited from. Not only is Bae a *New York Times* bestselling author with an option for each of the five books she's written and published—the first adapted to film and released just two weeks ago—but she's also the most sought-after celebrity ghostwriter for A-list African American celebrities.

Ever since their first shopping trip together in high school, passersby mistook Bae and Gizelle as enemies. They even had security called on them a time or two. But when seen sharing fries, shakes, and pizza in the food court moments after their back-and-forth displays, there was no mistaking that these two were best friends—and would remain as such for life.

And there is no mistaking this among the other three women in their tight-knit circle who were already fifteen minutes late meeting. Playing The Dozens was Bae's and Gizelle's own love language. As expected, they loved it. And although seventy-five percent of their conversation was slinging insults, they loved each other too.

As a matter of fact, out of the Fab Five, the nickname for their circle of friends, Gizelle and Bae had the most special relationship of them all. For the most part, outside of Bae and Gizelle, none of the other girls hooked up with one another and did anything outside their full circle. The ladies even did group FaceTime chats and calls together. However, during the 2020 pandemic, Zoom became the circle's primary platform for connecting.

"I ain't got time to be pouring the tea four times," Tyra, one of the Fab Five, decided years ago. "Plus, whenever I tell Bae something, by the time she spills the tea I poured into her cup, she done added sugar, fake sugar substitutes, honey, and all kinds of stuff to try to sweeten it up."

All the women agreed, including Bae herself.

"I'm a storyteller," Bae said in her defense. "I can't help but embellish."

"No, you're a Leo," Tyra shot back. "Y'all always gotta add yeast to something to make it rise, to make everything larger than life."

"Yeah, that too," Bae said before all agreed. From then on, as many women as possible would be on the call or present to sip tea. And with Zoom allowing them to record their conversations if, for some reason, one of the women wasn't present during a Zoom tea party, as they referred to their group chats, then all she had to do was click the link to watch or listen to the replay on demand. But she only had a week to do so. After that, all recordings were deleted for life, and the download feature was disabled. So, whatever went on in the Fab Five tea parties stayed at the tea parties, the conversation ultimately dissolving like sugar in a cup of tea.

But Bae and Gizelle were the exceptions, having been friends the longest. They always met up before meeting the rest of the girls, called each other first, or signed on to Zoom a few minutes before the other girls to get some one-on-one. What one member of the clique knew about another member, the other members knew as well. But that wasn't the case with Gizelle and Bae. Some things were just between the two of them, and it would stay that way forever . . . maybe.

The circle members were one another's best friends, but Bae and Gizelle were besties. And besties are the best of the best.

"You about ret' to go?" Bae asked as she finished up her drink.

Gizelle swallowed her last drop. "Aaah," she said. "I guess so. I mean, I would have made me a second drink, but a bitch don't have no Monin. And drinking without my favorite seasoning is like getting ate out by a dude with no tongue."

Bae's mouth dropped open in shock. And rarely was she shocked by anything that came out of Gizelle's mouth. In the same way Bae allowed her big presence and personality to make her stand out in the crowd, Gizelle used her big mouth.

"I can't with you." Bae gave Gizelle a serious side-eye. "But I can use that line in my next book." She slammed her empty glass on the bar. "Let's go."

Gizelle stood up, flattening out her sheer, long-sleeved, color-blocked maxi dress that hugged her size four slender frame. "Then make sure you run me my money. I want two percent royalties on every book sold with that line in it."

Bae pulled her head back and smiled. "Oooh, look at you knowing about book business and shit. You wanna be my agent? You can be the Samantha to my Carrie."

Gizelle's eyes lit up. "Oh yeah. *Sex in Sin City.*" Suddenly, she paused and frowned. "Or is it *Sex and Sin City?*" Gizelle headed to the door mumbling under her breath, "*Sex in the City* or *Sex and the City.* Damn, I can never get it right."

"Don't hurt your brain like that. Google it later. Right now, we need to hit them streets. The girls are probably already there waiting on us."

And as usual, Tyra, Jackie, and Angelina were already seated at their regular section at Blue Martin in Town Square when Bae and Gizelle arrived. Town Square was a few miles from the middle of the Las Vegas Strip. It was right off Las Vegas Boulevard. But one could still see the Strip from Town Square, day or night. That's the thing about the Vegas Strip. All the tall, lit-up, and decorated casinos were larger than life. Like 4-D larger-than-life. So much so that everything seemed closer than it actually was.

Tourists would swear up and down that one hotel wasn't too far from its neighboring hotel because on the Strip, even though a hotel might have been right next door and appeared as if you could reach out and touch it, that was never the case. Once a person gets to walking, they soon realize that their closest neighbor could be up to a mile away. A single hotel could have several towers stretching five city blocks, making it its own island on the Vegas Strip. Couple that with the desert heat, and you didn't know if the hotel you thought you could reach out and touch was a mirage or if it was really there. And let's not even add the fact that most folks walking the Strip have a yard of alcohol they are sipping on along the way. Heat, alcohol, and age have landed many tourists flat on their behinds. How so many forget that the beautiful and fabulous Las Vegas, Nevada, is a desert . . .

For the most part, the girls didn't meet up on the Strip. Anywhere but the Strip. Despite popular belief, Las Vegas residents didn't regularly frequent the Strip hotels and casinos. If someone asked locals how often they visited the Strip, most would say only when family or friends were in town or if there was some type of networking event or business function at one of the hotels.

It's hard to convince tourists that there is more to Las Vegas than the Strip. Some people visit every year— sometimes twice—and never leave the Strip. And if they do, it's only to visit Fremont Steet, which is like a French Quarter version of the Strip experience. This is why hotels offer free parking to locals, discounts on excursions, spas, and restaurants to lure them into the heart of Sin City.

"About time y'all showed up," Tyra said, flipping her long, blond wig. It complemented her caramel complexion.

"Ditto," Jackie said, tapping her watch.

"For real, Jackie?" Gizelle said. "You *really* want to add your two cents? Even when you are late, you're on time. So, I'll *always* be late in your book."

Bae laughed as she squeezed into the booth next to Jackie.

"Oh, wait, let me guess," Jackie said mockingly, "you're on CP time, as y'all call it. Right? Did I get it right?" Jackie looked from each of her four friends to the next, proud that she just might have nailed some of the Black slang she often heard them use over the last five years of knowing them. A white girl raised in Summerlin, an affluent suburb in the Valley, she never tried to be Black, talk Black, or act Black, for whatever *that* meant to society. Jackie genuinely and honestly wanted to knock down any language barriers to communication.

Gizelle stopped midway from sitting on the opposite side of the booth where Bae sat. "As a matter of fact, I was on VT. *Vegas Traffic* time." Her face was etched in offense.

Jackie swallowed so hard it could be heard over the live band playing. "I'm-I'm so sorry," she apologized. "I didn't mean anything by it. I just thought . . . I mean, I've heard you guys say—"

"You guys." Bae put her hand on her hip and shot Jackie the look of death. "As in *you people?*"

"Or are you referring to this table full of beautiful women as guys as in *men?*" Gizelle asked. "I know I'm rocking my natural low 'fro." She patted each side of her hair, twisting her head, "but my pronouns are *she, her,* and *hers.*"

Jackie swallowed hard again. She looked at Tyra and Angelina for help.

Tyra sucked her teeth and then addressed Gizelle and Bae. "Lucy and Ethel, if the two of you don't stop messing with Jackie, I swear—"

Gizelle, Bae, Tyra, and Angelina burst out laughing as Gizelle finally took her seat.

"Jackie knows I'm just messing with her." Gizelle blew Jackie a kiss and turned her attention to Tyra. "I like getting her all flustered because I just love that shade of red on her cheeks." She turned back to Jackie. "It never gets old." She laughed and used her cell phone to scan the QR code on the table to pull up the drink menu.

Jackie exhaled as her hot red face turned carnation pink and then back to its normal fair complexion. "You got me . . . again." She rolled her eyes and took a sip of her drink.

"And you keep letting us get you," Tyra said. "After being around us all this time, when are you going to realize we ain't got no sense, and we ain't got no filter either?"

And that was the truth. Although Gizelle and Bae were notorious for throwing shade, all the girls could hold their own. And that's what made the bond between them so strong. None of them walked in offense and therefore wasn't always getting offended by something the other did or said. This resulted in very few arguments and one member being mad at another, forcing others to take sides. As a result, this circle was drama-free, the kind of drama that bore negativity, anyway. But there was the good kind of drama that kept there from ever being a dull moment amongst them.

"Don't have any sense," Jackie corrected Tyra.

Tyra snapped her neck back. "Huh?"

"You said 'ain't got no sense.' Proper English is 'don't have any sense.' And it's not 'huh,' it's 'excuse me,'" Jackie continued. "*That's* how they taught us proper English in the school I went to, but I know *your people* didn't always get the same quality of education as some of *us,* so I'm just here to help," Jackie said in a bubbly tone, bouncing her shoulders up and down. "You're never too old to learn how to speak proper English." Jackie smiled at Tyra, shrugged her shoulders, and took another sip of her drink.

All four sets of eyes surrounding Jackie at the table were glued to her. Not like regular Elmer's Glue, but that Gorilla Glue chicks used on their hair to slick down their edges.

Jackie looked over the rim of her glass that rested at her lips. "Gotcha, bitches." She burst out laughing as did the other ladies . . . after they exhaled, of course.

Jackie did a little victory wiggle in her seat. She rarely participated in the ladies' shenanigans. Instead, she typically sat back, watched the show, and enjoyed it. So, it was easier for her to catch her friends off guard because they didn't expect to see anything fly coming from her.

"Jackie, girl, there is a five-second rule," Angelina told her. "You have *five seconds* to say, 'psyche your mind' before you get jumped."

A couple of the ladies chuckled.

"You gotta be quicker with the punch line," Angelina said, stirring her drink with the straw that sat in it . . . "much quicker."

"Yeah, too long of a pause between the joke and the drink. Too long," Bae said. "Speaking of drink . . ." She looked around. "Where is our barmaid, bartender, or whoever?"

Tyra, Jackie, and Angelina looked around for the waitress who served them their drinks.

"There she is." Tyra pointed and waved her hand to get their server's attention.

After making eye contact, their server nodded at Tyra, acknowledging her, and then raised her index finger to signal her to wait a minute. All of this was done with a pleasant, gleaming smile.

Bae didn't witness any of it because she was too busy scanning the drink menu on her cell phone.

Less than a minute later, their server arrived at their table. "I see the rest of your party has joined you," said their waitress, who looked to be Black and Latino, as she smiled and looked from Bae to Gizelle. "Can I get you two lovely ladies something to wet your whistle?" She spoke with an accent.

Gizelle looked over at Jackie. "See, our waitress can see we aren't guys." Gizelle stuck her tongue out at Jackie.

Although the waitress wasn't privy to the joke, she still laughed along.

Gizelle placed her order. "Peach Cîroc with . . ." She ordered her usual and then looked up from the menu at the waitress. "Do y'all have orange syrup?"

"Indeed, we do, dear," the waitress replied.

"And a splash of that to top off my drink." Gizelle placed her phone in her purse.

"Hmmm." Bae continued to go over the drink menu, undecided. "I'll have a margarita on ice."

"Salt, sugar, or topless?" their waitress asked.

"Salt *and* sugar," Bae said, a smile spread across her lips, signifying her satisfaction with her choice of drink. She shut down the menu on her phone and then looked up at the waitress. Her smile instantaneously evaporated as she looked the waitress up and down.

"Sugar and salt," the waitress said with her thick, glossed lips. She showed Bae reciprocity by looking her up and down for as much as she could see of Bae since Bae was sitting down. "I've been waitressing for some years now. And I can tell a lot about a person by the drink they order." She licked her lips and placed the pen that she was writing their orders down with to her chin. "Let me guess. You're like one of those gummy thingies the kids here in the States love. Sweet and sour, depending on which side of the bed you wake up in the morning, right?" The waitress stood smiling, waiting to see if she'd nailed Bae's personality.

Bae sat stoically in the face, not at all interested in playing games.

There was a cold silence. It was as if even the band had stopped playing. And the look Bae gave the waitress was just as cold.

Realizing that Bae was not amused, nor would she entertain the waitress's comment, the waitress breathed in and out. "Oh well, your drink sounds quite delightful, nonetheless." She maintained her genuine, polite, and bubbly warm energy.

"It is," Jackie jumped in, hoping to diffuse the awkwardness of the moment. "I forgot to ask for the same when I ordered my margarita." Jackie raised her near-empty glass. "Oh well," she shrugged.

"Oh, no worries, my dear," the waitress said. "I'll bring you one on the house. How's that?"

"That's bomb," Jackie said with a smile. "You rock, Flower."

"Thank you, love," Flower replied. "I'll be right back with the three drinks." She looked at Angelina and Tyra. "You ladies still good? Can I bring you anything else?"

Both Angelina and Tyra assured her they were good for now.

"Okeydoke, then off I go," Flower said. "Be back in a jiff." She twirled around and walked away.

As Flower left, Bae stared at her for a few seconds before rolling her eyes and turning her attention back to the ladies. "She must be new." The girls frequented Blue Martini at least three times a month. Bae would have remembered seeing Flower there before.

"She is," Tyra said. "She just moved here from London."

Bae let out a harrumph. "Explains that accent and the way she puts her sentences together. Sound like a character right out of the *Bridgerton*."

"Don't you just love it?" Jackie said. "She's so cute and friendly. And I absolutely love the way she talks. She sat with us on her break while we waited on the two of you to show up." Jackie looked from Bae to Gizelle. "I could have listened to her talk with that accent for hours."

"She just had a baby. Her little girl is only three months," Tyra added.

"Well, I can't tell," Gizelle said.

"Right. That's what I told her," Angelina said. "I complimented her on how good she looked in her dress. She said she wasn't going to wear it at first because she's a little self-conscious about her weight. But I told her, 'Mami, you look good as hell.' Not for a woman her size and not for a woman who just gave birth to a baby. But she looks good for a woman. Period."

"I know *that's* right." Tyra gave Angelina a high five.

Bae watched the women carry on about their waitress. "What's her blood type?" Bae asked.

"What?" the four women asked simultaneously.

"I mean, y'all know everything else about the ho," Bae said. "I figured she told y'all of her blood type as well." Bae tried her best to imitate Flower's accent with her last statement.

"Why she gotta be a ho?" Gizelle asked. "And, bitch, why you sound like you speaking Dutch or some shit?"

The other women laughed.

"But really, she seems like a nice girl," Gizelle added.

"She is," Tyra agreed. "She chopped it up with us like we've known her for years. I could see her rolling with us. She would fit right in."

Jackie and Angelina nodded in agreement.

"Squares don't fit in circles," Bae said quickly. "Besides, look at her." She nodded to the bar where Flower stood, speaking to the bartender and placing the ladies' drink orders. "Size eighteen–twenty. Two hundred thirty pounds, give or take. Thick. Not flabby thick. Solid, toned, thick."

"Just like you, Bae," Tyra said.

"Exactly." Bae hit the table with her fist. "And y'all bitches know the deal. I *have* to be the biggest person in the room . . . literally. There's only room for one delicious big Bae in this clique. Plus, adding one more to our circle would make things even. There'd be no tiebreaker when we're voting on stuff." A lightbulb went off in Bae's eyes. "Speaking of which, we need to vote on where we're going for our girls' trip."

"Oooh, she's right," Tyra agreed. "We're less than four months out, and y'all know ticket prices will be a mutha the closer we get."

"What do we care about the cost of the tickets?" Gizelle asked. "Our girl got this." She started snapping her fingers to the beat of the band.

Bae proudly raised the roof by pumping her open palms toward the ceiling. "Yass, queens. Money isn't an object when it comes to my girls. Like I told y'all, ya girl got y'all for this trip. It's my way of celebrating my six-figure book deal and thanking my aces for all the love and support y'all have shown me over the years. When everybody else thought this book thing was just a hobby, each of you had my back. Buying multiple copies of my first self-published manuscript that was jacked up because I couldn't afford to hire a professional editor."

The ladies laughed.

"Yeah, you owe us big time for figuring out which version of the words 'their,' 'there,' and 'they're,' and 'two,' 'to,' and 'too' you meant to use," Jackie said.

"Don't be shading me. I didn't know my grammar program wasn't going to catch that kind of stuff," Bae laughed.

Just then, Flower returned with the ladies' drinks. "This is for you." She handed Gizelle her drink. "And you. On the house, of course." She placed Jackie's drink in front of her. "Last but not least, this one's for you, dear." She put Bae's drink in front of her. "By the way, what's your name?" She stood staring at Bae.

"Bae. Her name is Bae," Jackie said, then lightly elbowed Bae and mimed the word, "Rude."

"The Bae," Flower said. "That's what I'll call this drink from here on out. The Bae." She winked at Bae and then looked at the other women at the table. "I'll be back to check on you ladies shortly. Enjoy, all right?" She nodded and walked away.

"I thought y'all said she just had a baby," Gizelle said.

"That's what she told us," Tyra said.

"Like she was pregnant carrying the baby? Not adopted a baby?" Gizelle wanted clarification.

"Uh, yeah," Tyra said.

"Could have fooled me." Gizelle let out a knowingly harrumph and then sipped her drink.

The other ladies looked at one another, confused. What did Gizelle know that they didn't?

"Why you say that?" Tyra spoke up and asked.

"Y'all don't see the way she's looking at Bae and the way she's talking to her?" Gizelle let out a tsk.

Tyra, Jackie, and Angelina said in unison, "No."

"Blind as the wife and the sidechick." She shook her head and took another sip of her drink.

Bae didn't even bother to respond or entertain Gizelle's query.

"Never mind." Gizelle shooed her hand at the ladies. "So, back to our girls' trip at the end of July. Where we going?"

The girls discussed several options and the pros and cons of the various destinations before deciding on Saint Martin.

"To Saint Martin." Bae raised her glass.

"To Saint Martin," the girls sang as everyone clinked their glasses and drank their drinks down to their last couple of swallows.

"One more round," Jackie said. She signaled Flower to come to the table. "And since Bae's paying for our trip, I'll at least pay for this round of drinks."

"Okay, with your white-privilege ass," Gizelle joked.

"Then what the hell . . . to white privilege." Jackie held her glass out that rested solo in the air. She turned and looked at Angelina when none of the other girls engaged. "Too much?" she asked Angelina.

"Too much," Angelina said.

"Hello, again, my favorite ladies in the place tonight," Flower said, approaching the table. "Can I get you all another round of drinks, yeah?"

"Yes, and put them on my bill, please, and thank you," Jackie said.

"Got it." Flower smiled as she started to walk away.

"Uh, Flower." Gizelle stopped her.

"Yes, dear," Flower said.

"I hear congratulation are in order. So you had a baby not too long ago?" Gizelle fished.

A proud smile spread across Flower's face. "Yes, I'm a new mum." Flower lit up like the Vegas sky on the Fourth of July.

"Got any pics?" Gizelle asked.

The look on Flower's face showed delight that someone had asked to see her pride and joy. She started whipping out her cell phone before Gizelle could even get the complete sentence out. She searched her photos and then placed her phone in front of Gizelle's face.

Gizelle took the phone out of her hand. "Aww, what a cutie-pie." She looked from the phone to Flower, then back to the phone. "She has your pretty brown eyes. I bet she has your lovely smile as well. Do you have one of her smiling?"

Flower eagerly began swiping through pictures.

"Oh wait. She's pretty . . . who's she? The baby's other mum?" Gizelle asked, her head down but her eyes looking up at the girls.

Flower pulled back in shock. "As a matter of fact, it is."

Gizelle looked at each of the girls, her eyes finally landing on Bae. She looked back down at the phone. "Anyway, I know you need to get back to work. I wouldn't want you to lose your job. I don't have any myself, but I hear little ones can be quite expensive." She held the phone out. "Thank you so much for sharing pics."

"My absolute pleasure." Flower took her phone back from Gizelle. "What mum, especially a new mum, doesn't love the opportunity to boast about her child?" She put the phone in her pocket. "I'll be back with your round of drinks." She smiled and walked away.

Tyra could hardly wait for Flower to get out of earshot. "Oh my God, Gizelle, how did you know?"

"Right," Angelina said. "I just assumed she had a baby daddy."

"Well, it's a new day in America. You can no longer assume anything about anyone," Gizelle said.

"Still doesn't answer how you knew she was into chicks, not dick," Tyra said to Gizelle.

"Yeah, Gizelle, so how did *you* know?" Bae asked, raising an eyebrow.

Gizelle took a sip of her drink and then leaned forward with her arms folded on the table. "Perhaps it's a gift or something." She shrugged her shoulders. "But I just knew."

Bae stared into Gizelle's eyes momentarily. "Well, here's to Gizelle's gift of knowing." She raised her glass, and the other women followed suit.

"To Gizelle knowing!" the ladies said, none the wiser of just how much Gizelle actually knew.

Chapter 2

Goodbye, Dolly

Although the Fab Five had done a couple of Zooms since their meetup at Blue Martini two months ago, tonight would be their first in-person gathering since that time. The ladies had been crazy busy at work, making sure they stayed caught up on work so that no one would have to do any work on their trip, which was a little over a month away. Tonight's get-together was to celebrate the series based on Bae's book having been released on Netflix several months ago, where it instantly hit number one in streams and has been in the Top Ten ever since.

It was an impromptu celebration/book signing. Her publisher put it together last minute in hopes of bringing even more awareness to her debut title that sat in the Top Ten in the *New York Times* for two fifteen weeks straight upon its release a few years ago. More attention meant more book sales, a way for her and her publisher to make new money from an old book. Bae was all for the celebration since she didn't have to flip the tab or wrack her brain putting it together on such short notice, not that an event couldn't be thrown together on short notice in Vegas.

Her publisher barely even had to come out of pocket. The venue, The Draper, had been glad to host the event at no charge, knowing it would bring awareness not only to Bae's book and film but also to their new luxury coworking and event space in downtown Las Vegas near the Fremont Experience. A local Black-owned business supplied the wine at no charge. Of course, they were listed as a sponsor on all the marketing material, as was the catering company that provided the appetizers. Instead of having Barnes & Noble be the official bookseller, or even Writers Block, a well-known bookstore near the downtown Vegas area, a Black business owner named Roderick, who sold books in a kiosk in Meadows Mall, served as the official bookseller of the event.

The event brought out a full house to support and celebrate Bae, including a few members of the media and press.

"I'm so glad you could make it." Bae hugged a local author who also came out to support and celebrate her achievements.

"I wouldn't have missed it for the world," the author replied. "Congratulations and continued success, my scribe sister."

Bae met and greeted as many guests as she could for the first hour of the event until she was summoned to the mic by her editor, introduced, and asked to share a little bit about her literary journey, read an excerpt from her book, and then sign copies of her book and take photo ops with guests.

By that time, all the members of the Fab Five had arrived except for Gizelle. Bae even watched the door several times while speaking and signing books, looking for Gizelle to walk through it. Gizelle promised Bae she would be there. She hadn't been able to meet with her beforehand because it was Thursday early evening, and Gizelle had a meeting with her team at work.

Bae figured the meeting must have run late because her bestie assured her she'd be there. But even with it being a work night and Gizelle having to attend a meeting, when flying solo, Gizelle was rarely on time. Not that she was ever on time when she was the wind beneath Bae's wings. But she had never been two hours late to any event. Not since Bae had known her, anyway. Which had been forever.

After signing her last book before completely selling out, Bae got up from the folding table and walked over to where Tyra, Jackie, and Angelina were standing. "Have y'all heard from Gizelle?"

Tyra opened her mouth to respond but suddenly paused. "Speak of the devil."

All eyes followed to where Tyra was staring . . . the entryway.

"And the devil appears," Bae said, staring intently. Not at Gizelle, but at the person standing next to Gizelle who entered the room with her. "I know she didn't," Bae whispered under her breath. "No, she didn't bring somebody to my event without asking." But before she got all riled up, she paused and thought for a minute.

There was a chance that Gizelle wasn't with this person at all. It could have been that Gizelle and this person just happened to show up at the same time. They could very well be complete strangers.

Bae watched as Gizelle whispered something in the ear of the woman standing next to her as the woman scanned the room. At first thought, this was proof to Bae that Gizelle was, in fact, with this woman. But on second thought, perhaps they ran into each other outside. And the woman wasn't from Vegas. She didn't know if she was in the right place. She was supposed to be meeting someone at the event. And Gizelle was being a Good Samaritan and helping her out.

Yeah, that's probably all it is, Bae thought, letting out a less-than-confident chuckle.

When Gizelle's eyes finally landed on her group of friends, she raised her arm and waved with excitement. She quickly grabbed the woman next to her by the arm and pulled her along in their direction.

So much for the woman being a stray. Looks like Gizelle was the Seeing-Eye dog.

"Ladies, ladies, ladies, sorry I'm late," Gizelle said as she hugged each of her friends.

"This is my new coworker I told y'all about," Gizelle introduced, "the one I said just moved here from L.A."

"Oh yeah," the women said. Except for Bae, who stood there as clueless as Alicia Silverstone.

Gizelle noticed the expression on Bae's face. "What?"

"I thought we had a rule, *that's* what," Bae snapped, never one to bite her tongue. Not even in front of company. That was one trait about Bae that all the ladies loved and respected: they never had to wonder if she ever said something about them behind their backs because Mike Tyson couldn't hold her back from telling the truth. "How come everybody knows about your new coworker but me? I thought we only spill the tea when everyone is at the tea party."

"Didn't you get the Zoom link from Tuesday's tea party?" Tyra asked Bae, the comment turning Bae's look of victory for catching the girls breaking a rule into a look of embarrassment. "Mm-hmm, you didn't watch the Zoom link yet."

"I've been busy preparing for tonight," Bae reminded them.

"Well, that's on you," Tyra said. She then turned her attention to Gizelle's coworker. "I'm Tyra. Nice to meet you." She shook the woman's hand.

"Anyway," Gizelle continued, "like I was saying, this is my coworker." She looked at the woman. "Honey, this is—"

"The rest of the 'Famous Fab Five'," Honey finished.

"It's not famous Fab Five," Bae said. "Just Fab Five. Five as in one, two, three, four, five." She pointed to each official member of the Fab Five as she counted.

"I meant famous, as in the Fab Five is famous," Honey said in a nonconfrontational tone.

"Oh," Bae said, feeling even more embarrassed now.

"I see our reputation precedes us." Jackie smiled and stuck out her hand. "Hi, Honey, I'm Jackie. Nice to meet you."

Angelina introduced herself to Honey next. Then everyone looked at Bae since she was the last one up to bat.

Bae looked at everyone right back as an awkward silence accompanied the very awkward moment. Finally, Honey cleared her throat and looked at Bae, an apparent sign that she was free to introduce herself. But still, Bae remained silent.

"And this chatterbox right here is Bae," Gizelle said sarcastically.

"Hi, Bae." Honey stuck her hand out. "Congratulations on your—"

"It looks like my editor is getting ready to leave," Bae said abruptly, totally ignoring Honey's hand. "I better go tell her goodbye." Bae exited stage left, walking over to her editor, who was midconversation with a drink in one hand and a shrimp cocktail in the other. Leaving the event appeared to be the least of her intentions.

Bae stood and talked to her editor until Tyra finally walked over to her.

"Excuse me." Tyra smiled at Bae's editor and the gentleman Bae's editor had been hounding all night, giving him looks as if he was going to be her nightcap before she had to get up the following day and fly back to New York. "Can I borrow the guest of honor for a moment, please?" Tyra pulled Bae away by the arm without waiting on permission. Once the two were in a space out of earshot from the other guests, Tyra tore into Bae. "What's your problem?" she asked through gritted teeth, all up in Bae's face.

"What do you mean?" Bae feigned ignorance. She swiped her hand across her nose, swatting Tyra's alcohol-smelling breath out of her face.

"The way you just treated Gizelle's coworker and then ghosted us like that. What's going on?"

"Nothing . . . I just . . ." Bae decided against trying to mince her words. She'd never bitten her tongue before and saw no need to start now. "Who the hell does she think she is bringing a plus one to *my* event without even letting *me* know? And showing up hours late with her so that she knows darn well when they enter, all eyes will be on them instead of me." Bae was darn near out of breath by the time she finished speaking. So, she took another deep breath, like during yoga, and started up again. "It's just plain rude to bring a plus one to an event that someone else is having without telling them. That's just one more mouth to feed. You know what I'm saying?"

Tyra looked around the room, totally confused. "No, I don't," she said. "Bitch, you ain't out of pocket one red cent. Why do you care who shows up and drinks the juice and eats the cookies? You said yourself that your publisher hooked all this up. So, no, I *don't* know what you're saying. I have no idea why you're not only mad, but you're also *super* mad. Like, where the fuck is your cape right now? 'Cause your superpower is straight up being mad as hell."

Bae put her arms straight to her side and balled her fists in frustration. "You *do* know what I mean." She stomped her foot that was donned in a clear strappy sandal decorated in rhinestones with the straps trailing up to her calves.

"I said no, I don't. So, why I gotta lie?" Tyra asked, getting more and more frustrated by Bae's behavior. "You went from acting like Big Bae, the queen bee up in here, to a Big Baby. *That's* why I came over there and snatched you up from your editor, who ain't thinking about leaving, not until she gets her some, anyway. I need to know what the hell is going on with you so I can stop you from looking crazy right now."

Bae threw her hands on her hips. "What do you care if I'm looking crazy or not?" she asked. "Let me wear my cape by myself. Ain't nobody asking you to be Robin to my Batman."

"I care because, for one, it's just plain unprofessional. You never know who is watching you. Readers don't want to buy books from and support no crab. And for two, you are representing the Fab Five. People assume a pack is cut from the same cloth, and I don't want anybody to think I act ugly like this or that I hang around people who act ugly. And that, my friend, is *why* I care." Now it was Tyra who was out of breath.

Both women stood there trying to catch their breath so they could be the first to speak again to continue making their point. Unfortunately, neither really wanted to listen—just talk. And be right.

"I don't know why you're tripping so hard lately, like someone is trying to replace you. Or if the fact that you'll be turning forty soon has you developing insecurities or what, but you've been acting really crabby around anybody you think has a remote chance of stealing Bae's thunder." She turned her attention over to the girls and looked back at Bae. "First, it was Flower back at Blue Martini, someone we may never see again. And now, it's Honey. Same. Someone we will more than likely never see again."

Bae looked over at the ladies and glared at how chummy they were with Honey. She rolled her eyes and let out a tsk.

"I get it," Tyra said, snapping her fingers as if she'd figured out the answer to her question on her own. "It's not just people you think will steal your shine you hate." She pointed an accusing finger at Bae but still had excitement in her voice. "You hate *fat* girls!" Her arms flailed as she talked.

The four glasses of wine Tyra drank that night were showing themselves in the form of her speaking way louder than she needed to and slurring a word here and there.

"Shhhh." Bae roughly pushed Tyra's arms back down to her side. "Will you stop talking so loudly?" She looked around to see if their animated interaction had garnered any attention, which it hadn't. Kudos to the music playing over the speaker for drowning them out.

"It's true." With a huge smile on her face, Tyra began pacing. "You use Gizelle to deflect your true hatred. Because the only skinny person you shoot darts at is her. And that's just because, well, she's Gizelle. That's what y'all do. But when it comes to girls like Flower and now Honey . . ." Tyra's words trailed off with a cliffhanging slur. She thumped herself on the forehead. "How am I just noticing this after ten years of knowing you?" She paused. "Wait, I would have noticed. So, again, like I said, this new deep-seeded insecurity finally starting to sprout."

Bae exhaled in disgust. "Ugh, that's the wine talking. But even if you were right, the word is deep-seated, fool." She rolled her eyes.

"Deep-seated, deep-seeded. To-may-toe, Tah-ma-toe," Tyra said and then started cackling.

"Po-tay-toe, po-tah-to. You're wrong either way," Bae growled. "Look at all the thick and lovely women I've been here cackling with, hugging on, taking photo ops with, and everything else all night." She flung her arm horizontally across the room.

Tyra looked around, stumbling slightly. She noticed all the thick, full-figured, voluptuous women Bae had been rubbing elbows with all night, attitude-free. "Oh, yeah." Her energy deflated.

Bae was right. The room was full of curvy, plus-size, full-figured divas working the room. Several could have given Bae a run for her money by dominating the attention in the room if Bae hadn't been the guest of honor.

Women were women in Bae's book. She never tripped on size or felt that her own size was an asset or deficit. Her body was just her body. And the same went for other women. So until now, and only to prove a point to Tyra, Bae never had a reason to specifically scan a room to count how many plus-size ladies were present, how many skinny girls, medium build, or what have you. And it frustrated Bae that Tyra didn't know that about her. But how could she?

On the flip side, Tyra was partially right about Bae. No, she didn't want any other girl stealing the spotlight from her, regardless of size. And, no—hell to the no—she didn't want another girl stealing her spot in their circle. They were five amazingly diverse women who still had more things in common than differences. Their differences, though, are what made them so unique and stand out. And no more than they needed another brunette to steal Jackie's thunder, or another redhead with freckles like Tyra, did they need another queen-size diva like Bae.

Period.

"Well, maybe I am wrong," Tyra said, throwing her arms up and allowing them to flop down to her side. "I just can't think of any other reason you're tripping. But I guess it's for you to know and for me to find out. All I know is that I just want you to chill. You are killing the book game. You are living your best life. So just choose happy, okay?" Tyra grabbed Bae by her cheeks and stared into her eyes. "Okay?"

Exhausted from the conversation, Bae gave in. "Okay, Tyra. Okay. Just get your hands off my face." She swatted away Tyra's hands.

"But you know, it's okay if really somewhere deep inside," she poked Bae's chest, "you do hate fat girls, it's okay. Because you know what?"

Bae stood there hoping Tyra would hurry up already and just say what she needed to say. Apparently, it wasn't a rhetorical question, though, because Tyra waited for her to respond.

"What, Tyra?" She closed her eyes, shook her head, and sighed.

Tyra leaned into Bae's ear and did a hard whisper, her hot breath practically melting Bae's ear. "I hate them, too." She pulled back and put her hand over her mouth. "I hate fat girls."

Bae buried her face in her hands, totally exasperated at this point.

"No, no, no, seriously," Tyra said, removing Bae's hands from her face. "But I hate them in a good way, though, you know?"

Bae shook her head. "No, Tyra, I don't know, but I'm sure you will tell me."

"At the pools and beaches, *that's* when I hate fat girls." Tyra scrunched up her face. "And you know why I hate 'em? Because they look way better than me in two-piece swimsuits and bikinis." Tyra nodded. "It's true. Yeah, I'm a size six, but after giving birth to three kids, I have all this extra tummy skin." Tyra grabbed her tummy skin through the thin, sheer top she was wearing.

It took everything in Bae not to laugh in this girl's face. Even though the truth serum, a.k.a. wine, had Tyra pouring her little heart out, it was funny as heck to Bae. All Bae could picture was that scene in the movie *White Chicks* when the girl in the dressing room was trying on clothes that made her feel fat.

"Look at this." Tyra tugged on her tummy. "This is just far too much skin to be trying to tuck into swimwear bottoms. It pokes out of my dresses if I don't wear Spanx. It flops whenever I'm in a dog position during yoga. Because of this tummy fat, I now refuse to have sex doggie style with my husband. Between the sound of my tummy flapping and these deflated tits that I've fed three children with until they were three years old, slinging and flapping back and forth, it sounds like little girls on the playground playing the Tweedle-Lee-Dee Rockin' Robin hand-clapping game."

Up to this point, Tyra and Bae hadn't drawn any attention to their conversation, but Bae roaring out in laughter changed all that. She immediately threw her hand over her mouth when she realized she'd let out such a squealing yelp. She couldn't help it. Tyra had her on the floor. So much so that she forgot all about being pissed off at Gizelle.

"Look, Tyra," Bae said, getting her laughter under control. "You don't hate fat girls. You're just a little jealous of them." Bae said those words to comfort Tyra, but her efforts backfired.

"Oh no," Tyra exclaimed. "I've gone from wrath to envy. I'm going to hell, Bae. I'm going to hell."

"Now, now, Little Grasshopper," Bae said, hugging Tyra, "just make sure you pray real good tonight and ask God for forgiveness, and you'll be just fine. Okay?"

Tyra nodded. "Okay." She pulled out of Bae's hug and straightened up. "What was I over here talking to you about again?" Tyra thought for a minute. "Oh yeah, your stank mode you've been in."

"We got past that already, Tyra," Bae said, crossing her fingers that Tyra would just let it go because, at this point, that's certainly what Bae was ready to do.

"So, you're not mad anymore that Gizelle strolled in here late as fuck with an uninvited guest who got everybody's attention and who the clique seems to simply adore?" Tyra pointed to Honey, laughing it up and getting along just fine with the other ladies in their clique.

Bae took a deep breath and kept her composure, reminding herself to blame it on the wine and not the friend. "No, Tyra, I'm not mad at all." And that was the truth. She was no longer mad. She was tired.

"Good, because that's on Gizelle, not Honey, so no need to act funny toward her. I mean, I get it now that you like to be the center of attention, and you usually are."

Bae took a step back with one hand on her hip.

Tyra corrected herself. "You always are. So, if you're worried about Honey getting a little bit of your shine for the evening, okay, I get it, but it's one night. After that, we'll never see her again." Tyra poked out her lips and feigned sadness. "And you can handle a little healthy competition for a few more minutes, can't you?"

"Competition, girl? Bye." Bae was offended, and it showed in her tone. "She's cute." Bae looked over at Honey and eyeballed her up and down, "but not as fine as me," she said, mocking an interlude from Jill Scott's first CD.

Tyra looked over at Honey, who wore a long, honey-colored flowing dress with cream flowers. She was about the same size as Bae, but several inches taller, even without the nude stilettos she wore. "Agreed," Tyra said, giving Bae a high five. She grabbed Bae by the arm. "So, come on and play nice."

Tyra reminded Bae of when she was little and her mother forced her to let her cousins play with her favorite doll. "Just let them play with it, Bae," her mom would say. "They'll only have it for a little while. You will have it forever."

Since it worked when she was a little girl, she said a little prayer that it would still work now that she was in her big girl panties versus her Underoos. Bae took a deep breath. "You're right, Tyra. No need for me to take anything out on Sugar, insecurities, attitude, quirks, or otherwise."

Tyra sucked her teeth. "Honey. The girl's name is Honey."

"Whatever." Bae shooed her hand. "It's Gizelle I'm going to get with. But that can wait until tomorrow. I don't want anything to ruin this wonderful evening. Life's too short."

"Amen. You got this." Tyra encouraged as they walked toward the ladies. "As I said, thirty more minutes tops to play nice."

"Yeah, just thirty more minutes," Bae chanted, encouraging herself as they approached the ladies. "And then I can have my dolly back."

"Huh?" Tyra asked, puzzled.

"Nothing," Bae responded. "Let's just do this."

"You good?" Tyra confirmed as they were just a few steps from reaching the women.

"I'm better than good. I'm great," Bae replied as if everything was everything. "My editor just told me that the film adaption of my book is now streaming number one on Netflix and is probably sure to make it number one on the *Times* again. I just sold out of books at this last-minute shindig that turned out to be a full house." Bae looked around the room at the event that was taking place in her honor. "I'm Gucci, yo. And this time next month, I'll be out of the country living my best life in the Caribbean with the Fab Five, about to turn Fab Forty. Yass."

Bae had pumped herself and Tyra up.

"Yass," Tyra cheered.

Neither Bae nor Tyra could ignore the awkward silence that greeted them when they approached the group. It was even more uncomfortable than it had been before Bae stormed off. Surely, they weren't picking up where they left off a few minutes ago. So, what had occurred between the group that neither Bae nor Tyra were privy to?

"Did we miss something?" Tyra asked.

Jackie, Angelina, and Gizelle looked at one another to see who was going to be brave enough to drop the bomb that was sure to blow the night away.

Since Bae was already pissed at Gizelle, it only made sense that she be the one to pull the pin out of the grenade. She'd be the one to go through the fire while Jackie, Angelina, and Tyra simply stood back and smelled the smoke. "Well, uh, actually, we were just talking about our amazing upcoming girls' trip when Honey said she's never been on a girl's trip anywhere, let alone out of the country."

"You've never been out of the country?" Tyra exclaimed. "Chile, Bae and I were just saying how life is too short." She elbowed Bae. "Weren't we, Bae?" She continued without allowing Bae to respond. "Way too short not to experience the world. I told my husband I didn't care if we had to take our children out of the country one at a time. They have to experience that there is so much more than the United States of America, as beautiful as it may be."

"Funny you should say that, Tyra," Gizelle said precariously. "Because that's exactly what we told Honey. Didn't we, girls?" she said to Jackie and Angelina.

Angelina tightened her lips and shot proverbial darts at Gizelle. How *dare* she attempt to pull them into the fire. But neither Jackie nor Angelina was falling for it. They said nothing.

"Yeah, well, my ex, who was my high school sweetheart, hated traveling. A two-hour car ride was the furthest he was willing to go," Honey said. "If we had to hop on a plane to get to our destination, it was out of the question."

"Well, your ex is an ex for a reason," Tyra said. "And now that he's no longer in the picture, take a selfie. A selfie of you out of the country." Tyra sucked in a heap of air as a thought entered her mind. "I have a brilliant idea. Why don't you come with us on our girls' trip, Honey?"

Gizelle, Jackie, and Angelina exhaled so hard it put out the entire fire.

Praise be to drunken Tyra, who wasn't in her right mind, because she had to be out of her mind to invite the plus-one Bae didn't even want to spend the next thirty minutes with on their five-night girls' trip.

Bae looked at Tyra in disbelief. She didn't care how many glasses of wine Tyra drank. There is no way she forgot that quickly the conversation the two of them just had. At this point, Bae forgot all about being pissed at Gizelle. It was Tyra's neck she wanted to wring.

"Actually," Honey started, "that's exactly what—" before Angelina cut her off.

"Going on a girls' trip is always a great idea," Angelina said. "That's why we plan a trip out of the country every year, but that's in addition to the other little getaways we take throughout the year."

At this point, Bae felt totally removed from the conversation. Totally removed from the clique. In fact, she felt invisible. As if she weren't there. As if she'd never been there. She was on the outside looking in. She wanted out from the outside so that she could get it. As quiet as it was kept, Bae didn't know what she wanted . . . except for Honey *not* going on their girls' trip.

Gizelle hoped to cut through and silence all the loud tension that surfaced through the air. "Well, uh, Honey doesn't have many girlfriends to go on a girls' trip with." She was set on justifying why Honey should go on the trip with them.

"More like any," Honey added. "My ex was pretty possessive. Not controlling, abusive, or anything like that. Just, in his world, it was only him and me. He didn't have any friends either. And until now, hearing about and seeing for myself this beautiful bond the five of you have, I didn't know what I was missing. He always made me feel as if no other woman in the world even existed . . . for him or me." A smile, unsure of whether it belonged on her lips, warmed Honey's face. "And I have to say, I kinda like it." She exhaled, holding back tears. "I was content living in his world, the one he created just for me, it seemed. So, I didn't really miss out on traveling the world. Or having girlfriends." Honey shrugged and looked down sadly.

A sympathetic expression rested on each of the women's faces . . . except for Bae's.

"Humph. Not me. I got crazy stamps on my passport," Bae said, breaking the monotony. "And plan on getting crazy more. Starting next month in Saint Martin with the Fab Five. It's going to be lit."

And just like that, the awkward silence was back as the rest of the girls looked back and forth from one another.

But not for long.

"I hope so." Honey smiled. "Just in case it ends up being my last, I want my first trip out of the country, my first girls' trip, to be as lit as can be." She looked around at the ladies. "Thank you so much for inviting me. It means so much, especially since y'all just met me and don't even know me like that."

Once again, Bae felt like she was on the outside looking in. But what the hell had she missed? The first thing she would do when she got home was watch that Zoom video. Perhaps the answers to all the questions and confusion she had twirling through her head were there.

Who was this Honey chick?
Where did she come from?
Why did Gizelle like her so much?
Why did the girls like her so much?
Why was she infiltrating Bae's circle?
Bae's life?

There was no hiding the expression on Bae's face. She was fit to be tied. Anger was an understatement.

"Well, we have thirty days to get to know you better," Tyra said.

The entire time Gizelle remained silent. Instead, her focus was on Bae's reactions. She was reading her like one of the many books Bae had written.

The other ladies started chatting excitedly about their upcoming trip. They shared with Honey memories, adventures, and experiences. All Bae could do was shake her head in disgust.

"Thirty more minutes, huh?" she snarled into Tyra's ear, who completely ignored her as she chatted with the other ladies.

Bae crossed her arms across her chest in a huff. From the looks of things, she wouldn't get her dolly back for a very long time.

Chapter 3

Honey Changes Everything

Bae showed up at the emergency Zoom meeting for the Fab Five fifteen minutes early like she always did. As suspected, Gizelle wasn't there like she usually would have been. But things were anything but normal.

Gizelle had been avoiding—or at least that's how Bae felt—talking to Bae ever since the book celebration event at The Draper. Yeah, that was just last night, less than twenty-four hours ago, but never had the two of them not hopped on the phone right after an event to talk, usually while driving home from the event. Or to call or text, letting the other know they arrived home safely. Or if all else fails, they would have at least called each other the following day.

But never—absolutely never—since they met in junior high and started meeting up at the public library after school—had a day gone by where Gizelle and Bae hadn't talked two or three times within a twenty-four-hour period.

Bae gave Gizelle a pass for not calling her on the way home last night, considering she had an additional pair of ears since she decided to bring a plus one. But why not call her to let her know she got home okay after dropping Honey off? Or her getting dropped off, depending on who drove? So, why not call Bae the following day?

"Why not get on the fucking Zoom early?" Bae shouted. "Oh, shit," she exclaimed, searching frantically to see if the session was recording. The air from her mouth escaped like a gust of wind pre-tornado. "Thank God," she said when she realized the session wasn't yet recording.

Five minutes later, still no Gizelle. Bae was fuming and almost stroked out until a black square appeared on the screen with Gizelle's name.

"What up, bitch?" Gizelle said once her camera and sound were on.

"Don't even," Bae spat. Knowing they only had a few minutes to chat one-on-one before the other three ladies hopped on, she jumped right in. "What was that shit you pulled last night? Not only inviting some random to my event but also for the girls' trip as well? *Really?*" Bae huffed. "And the fact that you sprang it on me like that proves you knew what you were doing was foul. Otherwise, you would have given me a heads-up."

"Bae, you were the only one caught by surprise," Gizelle said nonchalantly, which surprised Bae that Gizelle wasn't in fight mode. "We talked about this on our last group Zoom, which you would have known about had you watched the replay. So wasn't nobody trying to spring nothing on you, despite your belief that everything is about Bae and must be run by Bae. You may rule the world with your pen, but this is the real world, and the only surprise I have for you is that you don't rule the real world."

Bae was on fire. Livid. Beyond pissed. "Bullshit. Bullshit, and I call even more bullshit."

"You assume if there is a bad odor in the room, it must be a bull's shit because Bae Bee Anthony's shit don't stink. Well, seems like I've got yet another surprise for you," Gizelle said. "It does." *Now* she was in fight mode. But before Bae could throw her next punch, a black square popped up on the screen with a face in it, followed by another, like the intro to the old family sitcom, *The Brady Bunch.*

"Hey, ladies," Tyra chimed in before taking a bite of her apple.

One by one, the remaining ladies of the group signed on.

"What I miss, chichas?" Angelina asked as she appeared on the screen with a red plastic cup in her hand.

"I think the question is, what did *I* miss?" Bae asked, full of attitude. "I miss one Zoom, and y'all bitches done met a new best friend, not only invited her to *my* shit last night but also to *my* bigger shit. Our trip. That *I'm* paying for. How the fuck y'all gon' spend a bitch's money?" Bae ranted on for a good ten minutes straight, not allowing the other girls to get a word in edgewise.

"If you shut the hell up and let somebody else talk, maybe you'll get the answers you need."

Every mouth on the screen dropped open as Jackie's words rang through their ears.

"Who you cussing at?" Bae asked. "I know you ain't cussin' at me because, bitch, I'm saved."

"No, bitch, you jealous," Gizelle said.

"Of what? Of whom?" Bae's head wobbled.

"Shut up!" Jackie yelled again. "Sorry," she said, sincerely regretful. Her cheeks were flushed.

"Oh, shit, Jackie poppin' off." Tyra stuck her tongue out as she laughed. "I see you, Jackie boo."

"It's *always* the quiet ones," Angelina said.

"I'm sorry, Bae. No disrespect," Jackie said, her voice about to break any minute now. "But it's been a long fucking day over here at Kennedy Manor, okay?" Jackie breathed heavily to keep her composure and hold back her tears.

"Oh, Jackie, sweetheart," Angelina said. "What's going on at Kennedy Manor?"

Kennedy Manor was what the girls referred to Jackie's home as, even though her last name wasn't Kennedy. They sometimes called her Jackie O in reference to the former first lady of the United States. Not only was her hair the same color and the same length, but she also carried herself so classy. Always put together like the pretty finished picture of a puzzle. And as a doctor's wife, she was always so regal around his colleagues, especially when she hosted the other doctors' wives at her home. Jackie was nothing like those rachet, *Married to Medicine* doctors' wives portrayed on reality TV. That is when she wasn't hanging out with Fab Five, of course. She referred to her time with the girls as being off camera, even though, ironically, they actually were on camera on Zoom. But when the cameras were rolling, in other words, when the world was watching, she was very mindful of how she carried herself. She was a representation of her husband. Not that when cameras weren't rolling, she was a lunatic. Her genuine characteristic was nonconfrontational, partial, and soft-spoken, which is why the way she just spoke to Bae was surprising.

"I see you done let Jacqué out to play," Bae said to Jackie. "So, I forgive you because I know you only let her out to play when it's rough. Besides, I like Jacqué. She's fun. Not that Jackie isn't fun," Bae said, cleaning up her last statement.

Jacqué was Jackie's alter ego who surfaced whenever Jackie was overwhelmed and felt she would lose control and she would, therefore, let Jacqué take control.

"It must be bad at Kennedy Manor for you to invite Jacqué over," Tyra said. "Why I never imagined Kennedy Manor being anything but perfect," Tyra said, using the most proper English accent she could muster up.

"Me either," Angelina said. "If it's that bad, I don't know if I want to know what's going on. I don't want my image of Kennedy Manor distorted."

The girls loved visiting Jackie's home whenever she and her husband hosted an evening gala or what have you. They said it always felt like they saw a place other than the lights and action of Vegas. There was always some unique and fancy theme Jackie would create in her home. The last time it was set as if they were at an English ball. All the ladies wore big, fancy gowns with bodices and short sleeves, and the men in white ruffled shirts, ties, stockings, and shoes. It took a special kind of man to play along with *that* theme.

Kennedy Manor wasn't the most expensive of all the ladies' dwellings, which would be Bae's penthouse. Neither was it the biggest. That would be Tyra's home in North Las Vegas. But it had a lot of land surrounding it, which wasn't typical for a Vegas residence. Homes with yards, yards with grass especially, were rare in Vegas in the average neighborhood. But Jackie was originally from Arkansas, where green was everywhere. So while most people budget for décor to design their homes, Jackie opted to spend her budget on grass and maintaining it. Of course, not all the two acres surrounding her home were grass. There were various trees, including palm trees, along a creek her husband had made, a gazebo, and a stone trail with a white wooden bench at the end of it. No livestock or crops like a real manor would have, but still, it seemed to suit the nickname given to it by the girls.

"Theodore just told me we must host the quarterly partners' dinner in two days. Bradly's wife, who all but slit the throat of any of the other wives who even suggested they host the dinner, caught COVID and bailed," Jackie complained.

"Uhh, you kind of don't want someone with COVID hosting a dinner at their house," Tyra said.

"Right," Bae said. "The only good thing that came out of COVID for me was that I got more writing done and that the Big Mac was deemed essential, and I still had fries in my bag by the time I got home. Because I wasn't about to be touching my steering wheel, eating fries, and none of that mess." She made a face to reflect her disgust.

"I get that, but like, who hasn't had COVID already?" Jackie said. "Or at least those fifty immunization and booster shots the FDA suggested people get? Besides, everyone there is a doctor or married to one. So they can treat each other or themselves if someone catches it."

"Jackie," Bae shouted, "come on now. COVID is not to be played with. It ain't the damn chickenpox. And even chickenpox can kill a grown-up who catches it." Bae lowered her voice and softened her tone as she continued. "I know I go hard in the paint when I talk shit, but I don't even fuck with COVID. I don't care how old it gets. It killed people and still can. It's just like AIDS. Even though they have it more under control than when it first came out and was an epidemic, it *still* kills. So you still must be mindful of it."

"I know that's right," Gizelle agreed. "These days, we already take a chance going to events, not knowing who has what."

Hearing Gizelle say those words reminded Bae how pissed off she was at her. "Says the girl who brought someone who could not only have COVID to my event last night but also invited her on our girls' trip out of the country."

"It is not that serious, Bae," Gizelle said. "You act like we haven't been on a million trips together and won't go on a million more. This is just one trip."

"But this is supposed to be *our* trip. The Fab Five. This is *our* thing," Bae whined. "Actually, this one was *my* thing. It was to show my appreciation to my ride or dies who have been down with me and supported me through my literary journey, from when I was selling books out of the trunk of my car, to a million rejection letters, to now million-dollar contracts. So this one meant something to me, and I wanted to do this with my girls. *My* girls. Not my girls *plus one.*"

There was silence.

Everyone waited for Gizelle to have some kind of comeback, but what could she say? And what could they say because they had initially supported the idea of inviting Honey along? But now, hearing how much it meant to Bae, they were second-guessing their decision to do so.

"Bae Bear," Tyra said in a pacifying tone, "Us sorry. We didn't really think about it all like that."

"You're right. This isn't just another girls' trip," Angelina said. "This one is special, and we should have thought about it before we invited Honey to join us."

"Y'all didn't invite her," Bae corrected, "Tyra did in her drunken stupor." Bae rolled her eyes.

Tyra looked down and scratched her head, avoiding eye contact with Bae as she took a bite of her apple.

Angelina took a drink from her cup.

All the girls were looking quite suspicious at this point.

"Right, Tyra?" Bae said. "We're blaming it on the alcohol, *right?*"

"Umm, this is so good." Tyra took another bite of her apple.

"Now that I think about it, I've watched you drink a fishbowl of wine like you're Olivia Pope and do the Electric Slide without missing a beat," Bae said. "You weren't drunk, were you?" she snapped, waiting on Tyra to respond.

Now, Tyra took a *huge* gulp bite of her apple. "Wait a minute." She held up her index finger and took another bite. The juice from the apple slid out of the corner of her mouth and down her chin. "Umm . . . Hold on." Her words ran together in a mumble.

"I hope a worm is in that damn apple," Bae said. "Or poison!"

Angelina spat out the mouthful of liquid in her mouth and burst out laughing.

"Y'all played me," Bae said. "Y'all heifers set me up." She zoned in on Tyra. "You came and pulled me away from my editor to butter and warm me up because y'all had already invited her before you even walked over to me." Bae started repeating words Tyra said to her during their conversation at her event. "'*We'll never see her again. Thirty more minutes.*' Shame on you, Tyra. Shame on all of you," Bae spat.

"It just came up during the conversation when we were all standing there talking," Jackie confessed. "You stormed off to go talk to your editor—"

"I didn't storm off," Bae shot back.

"Well, walked away quickly," Jackie said. "We all felt bad for the way you were treating Honey. She's never had girlfriends. And how you were acting was not the impression or the first experience we wanted her to have when it comes to the sisterhood of girlfriends."

"Who cares what she thinks? It's not like she's going to be a part of our sisterhood," Bae said.

"That's not what she's saying, Bae," Gizelle said calmly. "The only world she's been a part of for the past few years is her ex's. So any image she's seen of girl cliques, groups, and circles has been reality TV. And you were about to make that her reality. And it wasn't cool. It wasn't a good look at all."

That stung Bae's spirit to the core. That is absolutely *not* the impression she wants to give any woman. Her girls are her everything. They have nothing but love and respect for one another. They don't play that "we fight, but we love each other" crap. They pride themselves on *not* being that type of circle, which, in their opinion, is more like a cage.

"I hear you, sis," Bae said, nodding. "I heard and hear all of you. And that's my bad. I know I be on some old-school Mýa *It's All About Me* and 'I have to be the center of attention'-ish. And y'all let me get away with it."

"Most of the time. When we think it's cute," Tyra said. "Because that's who you are, and you are cute. And we love you." Tyra kissed the air.

"Muah," Jackie said, kissing the air.

"But when it starts to get ugly, we have to call you on it," Gizelle said. "Because we love you."

Bae nodded her understanding. "And I'm way too damn cute ever to act ugly. Okayyy." Bae used her hands to frame her face as she started striking poses.

The girls chuckled and waited for the answer to the million-dollar question.

"I can't wait to get away and spend some time with my girls," Bae said.

The ladies continued waiting.

Bae looked at each one of them. "And plus one."

The other ladies cheered.

"But I ain't paying for plus one," Bae added with a pout.

"Yay," Tyra said while clapping. She abruptly stopped clapping. "But you're not going to call her Plus One the whole time, are you?"

"Her name is Honey," Gizelle said as if teaching a child the alphabet. "And she's paying her own way, thank you," she added.

"I know, I know," Bae said, flailing her arms. "But seriously, Gizelle, not to start anything again, but what's up with this Honey chick anyway? I mean, you know how territorial I am, so for you to bring her all up in our space—why? What's so special about her? Why her after all these years?" Bae stared at Gizelle intently, waiting for an answer.

Gizelle shrugged, which kind of pissed Bae off all over again. Why was her ace acting like the joker to the queen? Why was she acting so nonchalant about this? How could she not know how Bae would react to this Honey situation? After all, Gizelle knew Bae better than anybody. She knew how petty Bae was and how sensitive and territorial she was about her clique. Probably the same way Honey's ex was about her.

So . . . why?

Bae never had a problem voicing or expressing how she felt about the Fab Five. And it didn't bother the girls a bit. On the contrary, it was almost flattering to them. Bae could befriend and roll with so many people. She was a multimillionaire, for crying out loud. And the girls didn't take it for granted that money hadn't changed her.

But little did they all know . . . Honey would.

Chapter 4

Sixth Wheel Keep on Rollin'

"Thanks again for letting me go on this trip with you lovely ladies," Honey said as they all got situated in the seats of their first leg to Saint Martin. She sat comfortably between Jackie, who had the window seat, and Gizelle, who was sitting in the aisle seat. "And these nice, roomy seats too. People are always talking about how uncomfortable planes are. Small seats. Little leg room." She let out a harrumph. "That's probably why I never argued with my ex about not traveling. I didn't think they made seats for big bodies. Just like they don't really make parking spaces for big-body vehicles."

"That's because Bae splurged for the economy deluxe," Gizelle boasted.

"Yeah, I downgraded from our first-class seats because they only had the five seats for *us* . . . and since now there's *six* of us . . ." Bae said, not at all happy that when they went to add Honey to their itinerary through the travel agency, there were no more first-class seats.

"We can't just put her in the economy while we all fly first-class," Tyra had argued.

"And *why* can't we?" Bae wanted to know.

"Come on, now, Bae. How would you feel if the shoe were on the other foot?" Jackie asked.

"Privileged to be going on the damn trip in the first place," Bae said. "Besides, it won't be economy. It's *deluxe* economy. They have tons of those still available." It was at that moment Bae could have kicked herself. Or "accidentally" ended the Zoom meeting for all.

"Are you ladies thinking what I'm thinking?" Tyra asked with a grin.

"No," Bae shouted.

"No, you're not thinking what I'm thinking, or—"

"No, we are *not* flying economy. Deluxe or otherwise," Bae said. "Besides, deluxe economy is the airlines' way of not charging big people for two seats. They get to sneak charge us for one and a half."

Gizelle started laughing—until Bae shot her a look of death.

"Girl, please," Gizelle said, "you know that was funny. You stay trying to be funny, and you know it, so don't trip when people laugh."

"Speaking of 'trip,' let's get back to discussing our trip," Jackie said, circling back to the issue at hand, in which Bae was outvoted four to one on keeping their five first-class seats and letting Honey fly solo, literally, or cashing in their five first-class seats for six economy-deluxe seats.

As a result, the animosity Bae thought she could keep at bay regarding Honey joining them on the trip in the first place resurfaced like a tidal wave. And she wanted them all to drown in it. But she wanted Honey to pay her back for the cost of her ticket first. It wasn't that Bae needed the money. But in agreeing to allow Honey to join them on the trip, she made a point to mention that no way in hell was she going to pay Honey's way. And she wanted to remain a woman of her word.

"We're glad to have you join us," Jackie said, putting her hand atop Honey's hand and patting it.

Honey flipped her hand, palm up, squeezed Jackie's, and shot her a smile.

"We sure are," Gizelle said, then looked across the aisle at Bae.

When the ladies traveled, Gizelle and Bae, who both loved aisle seats, always sat in the aisle seats across from each other. "Isn't that right, Bae?" Gizelle made a face at Bae to let her know she was intentionally getting under her skin. Nothing new.

Bae painted on a fake smile and tilted her head to the side. "Absolutely. A plus one is always delightful." She overexaggerated her words by rocking her head from side to side with each word she spoke, stretching her smile even wider. Finally, however, she abruptly replaced the smile with a serious look, rolled her eyes at Gizelle, and looked straight ahead.

Gizelle looked over at Honey, who kept a genuine smile on her face, and then shrugged her shoulders.

"Don't pay her any mind. It's just who she is. And she'll never change. She's like, uh, what someone once called a 'sour-patch kid.' Sometimes sweet. Sometimes sour. But just a yummy, squishy person at her core."

"I get it," Honey said with a chuckle. "Sometimes, people aren't necessarily on the outside who they appear to be on the inside."

"I couldn't have put that more perfectly," Gizelle said.

"It can be like this protection mechanism," Jackie chimed in. "Or something like that. My husband's a psychiatrist, and I sometimes hear him talk about that stuff. Only with Bae . . ." Jackie leaned forward and looked over at Bae, who was putting in her earbuds, "I probably wouldn't diagnose her as such. That woman doesn't have to hide behind any type of fake exterior. She's just who she is." Jackie smiled genuinely while staring at Bae. "And we love her." She turned and looked at Honey. "And you will too. Trust me." She patted Honey on the knee and then turned to look out the window.

"I'm sure I'll love *all* you ladies," Honey said.

"Some more than others, I expect," Gizelle said under her breath as she plugged in her own earbuds, leaned her seat back, closed her eyes, and enjoyed the flight.

One layover and eight hours later, the girls arrived at their rented mansion in Saint Martin.

"OMG," Tyra exclaimed when she entered the home they rented for the next few nights. "This is a hundred times bigger than the one we stayed at in Jamaica."

"This place could sit on both acres of Kennedy Manor," Jackie exaggerated as she spun around, her yellow, checkered printed sundress fluttering about. "And this is just the foyer," she added. She walked over and sat down on the double-size queen bench that sat up against the wall on the marble floor. A large live plant crawled up the wall and hung slightly over it, high enough where someone could sit down without it touching their head. "I could sleep out here." She stretched out and the bench almost accommodated the entire length of her body. "Better than that room with those bunk beds I got stuck with in the DR." She referred to the Dominican Republic three years earlier.

"You're the one who missed your flight and arrived late," Gizelle reminded her. "Last one to show up, last one to pick the room."

"Unless you're paying for the room," Bae said, entering the foyer, "or, in this case, paying for the whole damn house." At that moment, Bae made a mental note that Honey needed to pay her back for her flight ticket *and* what her share of the house would have been had they been splitting it evenly among the ladies.

At that moment, their driver entered the house carrying as much luggage as possible in a single trip.

"You can start setting stuff right there." Bae pointed toward the wall-length bookshelf that stood opposite the queen bench in the foyer. "Once the ladies pick their rooms, they'll tell you which suitcase goes where."

The nice Haitian man who drove them from the airport to their rental smiled and nodded as he placed the luggage in his hands where Bae had instructed him to before heading back out to grab more.

"Well, we're all here at the same time this go-round, so how will we do this?" Jackie sat upward on the bench.

"I don't care what you hoes do," Bae started, "but I'm going to go find the upstairs master bedroom with—"

"I thought we didn't call it the master bedroom anymore," Angelina said and then looked at Gizelle. "Didn't you say y'all learned something about that during that DEI training session y'all took on your job?"

"Girl, I'm not trying to talk about no diversity, equity, and inclusion right now," Bae said. "I'm trying to talk about the biggest bedroom in this mother. The one with the full-size balcony and French doors, separate shower from the kidney-shaped jet tub with an Alaskan King bed and fireplace. Okurrr." Bae dipped low and dropped it like it was hot. She bounced a couple of times, butterflied her knees, and then effortlessly brought it back up. Next, she threw her right hand back while looking over her right shoulder and swished up the spiral staircase leading to the four upstairs bedrooms.

"I think there might be a broom in the kitchen if y'all want to draw straws to see who gets the other rooms. There are three others upstairs and two down here. Toodles." Bae let out a wicked laugh as she trotted up the steps to claim her room.

Gizelle sucked her teeth and huffed. When they first talked about going on the trip, Bae said she'd stamp her name on a room. So now, she was leaving her to fend for herself. Apparently, you don't always get more bees with honey, because all Gizelle was getting was the blues for bringing Honey on the trip.

"All I wanted was to do something nice for a girl going through a hard breakup from a jerk she should have left a thousand times," Gizelle had continued to plead her case during their in-person meet-up last night.

The girls always had a "we're going out of town tomorrow" celebration the night before they departed for their vacations, which was why Jackie ended up with the bunk bedroom in the Dominican Republic. Unfortunately, she drank one too many and ended up as sick as a dog the following day. She woke up less than an hour before the gates closed but only lived twenty minutes from the airport. She got ticketed, her luggage checked in with fifteen minutes to spare, and she *almost* managed to get through security. But when TSA asked her to take off her mask, she did. And puke went everywhere. Everyone traveling was told that if they were sick or feeling under the weather, not to travel. So, when Jackie thought she was going to keep it pushing through the security after clearly showing signs that she was sick, she had to think again.

She was escorted right back to the security counter, and, fortunately, the airline changed her flight for the next day without penalty, all in the name of safety for other passengers. But unfortunately, by the time she arrived in the DR, the only room left was the one with the bunk beds. And the rest is history.

Well, that wasn't going to happen again. The girls already decided that since Honey was the new girl, if there were a room with bunk beds, it would be hers. Of course, they always tried their best to get a house where all the rooms were equally as nice, but every now and then, the pictures on the internet didn't match what they ended up with in real life.

But this time, Bae's room was everything and then some from what the internet said it was. When Bae entered her room, a huge smile covered her face as tears filled her eyes.

"Thank you, God. You did it." Bae's heart was full of gratitude. The day had come when she truly was making a living as an author. She was financially free and location free. She could make as much money as she set out to while doing the work she wanted. She could treat her girlfriends to luxurious trips and outings and was probably just two books away from having the same notoriety as James Patterson and Stephen King. Or more . . .

No, she hadn't been in the writing game as long as they had, but Bae always felt that God could and would promote her expediently if that's what He wanted. Well, she didn't know one-hundred percent if that's what God wanted for her, but it was undoubtedly her heart's desire. And growing up in the church, she was always taught that God wanted to give her the desires of her heart.

Bae dropped her vintage Chanel bag on the bed and headed straight for the private bath.

"Won't He do it?" Bae shouted, entering the beautiful bathroom. "Won't He do it?"

Bae didn't come up struggling, living in the hood, on food stamps, government assistance, or anything like that. She was that girl at school who most kids envied. The girls she invited to sleep over thought she was rich just because she had Cap'N Crunch and Fruity Pebbles cereal. And liquid hand soap instead of a bar of soap.

It wasn't until Bae got interested in pledging to a sorority at the University of Nevada-Las Vegas—one that was all about service—that she realized that for so many years, she'd taken the small things in life for granted. Things like name-brand cereal and liquid hand soap.

"Money won't change me," Bae promised God when she began praying for literary fame and fortune.

Again, money hadn't changed Bae. It only made her better . . . brought out the true giving heart inside her. She chalked it off as not just God wanting her to have more than enough but to have more than enough so that she could bless others with her overflow. And she was content doing just that, which was why, despite her not wanting a sixth wheel on their trip, she decided not to make Honey pay her back for the flight ticket or the rental. She'd just received a CashApp notification that Honey sent her money for her share of the trip with a note that read, "Let me know if I owe you more." Bae refunded it.

The other ladies screaming with excitement pulled Bae out of her thoughts. She smiled, knowing they were just as excited about their rooms as she was with hers.

"There ain't no booty room this time," Tyra stuck her head into Bae's bathroom and shouted. "All six rooms are amazeballs. They didn't trick us by only showing the foot of the bed of the booty room in the online pictures. Yes! There *is* a God." Her head disappeared as she retreated to her room.

"Indeed, there is," Bae said. She smiled as she heard Tyra's feet happily padding down the marble hall.

The driver managed to get all the girls' luggage to their respective rooms. They showered and changed into fresh clothes. After that, they met on the community indoor, covered patio/den area to discuss their plans for the next few days. Meanwhile, the house cook, Margaret, prepared their dinner in the kitchen.

"Well, we all agreed that tonight we would chill. Like we always do on day one," Tyra said, sipping on a cup of rum punch Margaret had mixed up for them.

"Oh, come on," Honey said. "After dinner and a couple more of these rum punches," she lifted her cup of the heavenly nectar, "we'll have a second wind. I know we didn't come all the way out of the country to stay in a house." Honey was feeling good and tipsy and ready to explore the town.

Bae shot Honey the side-eye. "Uh, excuse me, new girl, but this is a Fab Five tradition. There will be plenty of time to turn up, but on night one, we rest. We rejuvenate. We reset." Bae kicked her feet up on the table in front of her chair. "And *then* we set it off."

The other members of Fab Five cheered and high-fived one another.

"Set it off, we do," Gizelle confirmed.

"Okay," Honey said, trying her best not to sound like Debbie Downer. She leaned back in her chair, looking disappointed.

Jackie, Tyra, Angelina, and Gizelle looked at Honey and then at one another.

Bae stayed minding her own business, which was her cup of rum punch. She deliberately did not make eye contact with anyone. Queen Bae had spoken as far as she was concerned.

"I don't know. Maybe Honey is right," Angelina said. "We aren't the Golden Girls. We are the Fab Five. We don't need a nap. We can hang . . . right?" She looked to each of the girls to garner their support. "Besides, we slept on the plane."

"I don't know," Gizelle said. "I'm not trying to run out of gas at the beginning of the journey. We said we would get up in the morning and go on our first excursion. And doesn't the shuttle come at like nine o'clock in the morning?"

"Hold up." Tyra stood up. "Honey is right. We didn't come all this way to go to bed. We used to go to the club, dance, drink all night, hit the Waffle House, and then go straight to work in the same clothes we wore the night before."

A few of the ladies chuckled.

"Yeah, we had to go take catnaps in the bathroom stall every couple of hours," Gizelle said, "but we did that shit. We were champs. We ain't none of these new jack punks who gotta call off work the next morning."

The members of the Fab Five laughed and started reminiscing on the instances when they had pulled all-nighters, only to go into work the next day bright-eyed and bushy-tailed.

"So, I'm with Honey," Tyra said. "Let's start a *new* tradition." She held her cup in the air.

"But—" Bae started, but wasn't heard over all the cheering and celebrating and chatter of where they were going to go that evening.

All the other ladies were so geeked about heading out to kick it that they didn't even notice Bae slip out of the room and head upstairs to her bedroom.

"I'm keeping my black ass right here just like we always do on our first night," Bae complained as she walked over to the dresser and grabbed her laptop. That was her go-to when she was bothered. Writing. The one thing Bae could always control when she seemed like she was losing control of everything else was her pen and paper, a blank Word doc, and keyboard.

Bae was a hybrid writer. She typed her stories but always wrote notes and some of her thoughts and ideas on paper.

While her laptop booted up, she grabbed her notebook and favorite purple gel pen. She jotted down a few thoughts before retreating to her laptop.

As she pulled open her work in progress, Tyra sashayed by her bedroom door. Several seconds later, she backtracked and poked her head into Bae's room. "What the hell do you think you're doing? We're all sitting down there drinking, about to eat some authentic island food, and you up here on your laptop?" She walked closer to Bae's bed. "What are you working on that's so important that you aren't downstairs spending time with your girls?"

Bae kept her head down toward her laptop, only lifting her eyes up at Tyra. "Don't come in here fishing. You know you don't give a damn about what I'm working on. After all, you don't give a damn about breaking tradition." Bae pushed her laptop aside and looked up at Tyra. "As a matter of fact, are you coconspiring with Gizelle or something? You've been like her biggest cheerleader regarding this Honey situation."

"We still on that BS?" Tyra asked. "I thought we were past that. Here, we have traveled to this beautiful place, but no, you want to travel back to the past."

"As I said, you don't give a damn." Bae shook her head and turned her attention to her laptop.

"I may not give a damn about what you're writing or how you feel about Honey being on this trip," Tyra walked over to the French doors, "but I do give a damn about you." She stared out at the patio. "Nice view."

"Yeah, it's alright." Bae played it down. She had already been on that balcony doing the Holy Ghost dance because it was so mesmerizing.

Tyra turned and faced Bae. "Now I know you tripping for real. The queen of gratitude has a view that might as well be named God, and you talking about 'it's alright'? What's going on, Bae?" Tyra sat down on the edge of Bae's bed. She immediately hopped back up when Bae shot her a look that could cause serious bodily harm if it had power behind it. "Oh, my bad."

"Yeah, your bad, all right. Sitting on my bed in street clothes." Bae rolled her eyes as she tapped on her keyboard.

"Girl, you know I just took a shower and put on clean clothes. I ain't been nowhere . . . yet."

Bae looked at her. "So, y'all really are going to break tradition and go out tonight? Knowing we stay in, drink, eat, catch up, reminisce, and laugh it up every night on our first night?"

"And we can still do all that, except for the stay in part. Instead, we'll just do it out there." Tyra pointed to the outdoors. "Bae, I know you are a stickler for everything being decent and in order. For planning everything out to a T and not deviating from the plan. But are you sure this is just about breaking tradition? I'm sorry, but I don't see it as being that damn serious. And if it is to you, I'm really not trying to downplay it. But, sis, are you *sure* something else isn't going on with you?"

"Something like what?" Bae said defensively. "Why does everybody keep asking *me* that?"

"I don't know." Tyra threw her hands in the air and allowed them to fall lifelessly to her side. "Maybe it's because your birthday is coming up in a couple of weeks, and you're about to turn the big four-oh. The first one in our circle. I don't know." She shrugged. "Maybe you're feeling a certain way. Maybe hormones change at forty."

"Oh, so you think it's because I'm old and crabby?" Bae snapped.

"No, that's not what I'm trying to say. It's just that you've been acting differently the last few months. A little bit more on edge than your usual self. I mean, I know you are over the top. I just don't know . . . which is why I'm sincerely asking. We're your girls, yo. *I'm* your girl. Let me in." Tyra thought for a moment. "Do I need to call a tea party or something so that you only have to say it once?"

Bae leaned back against the soft, rose-gold headboard. "I appreciate you coming in here to check on me. But you wouldn't understand." Bae turned her attention back to her keyboard.

"Try me." Tyra perked up and hustled over to Bae's bedside. She wore a smile on her face . . . a contagious smile. When Bae looked up and saw it, she couldn't help but start smiling too.

"Oooh, I hate you." Bae tried to stop smiling.

"See, look at that smile," Tyra teased. "You know you want to bring your ass downstairs and chill with your girls. Eat some yum-yum, get your pretty ass dolled up, and let this country know that Boss Bae is in town."

Bae started laughing. She had to admit that of all the girls in her clique, even though she and Gizelle were the closest and Bae talked to her more than anyone else by default, Tyra was the most trustworthy one of the bunch. But even so, what Bae was really feeling, what *really* had her in her feelings . . . she would keep to herself.

But for now, she would play nice like Tyra had previously insisted.

Even though her clique usually rolled a certain way, there was now a spare, and all she could do was allow the sixth wheel to keep on rolling . . .

Until the sixth wheel falls off.

Chapter 5

Who's Coming with Me?

"Bae? Bae? Come on," Gizelle said as she stood at the end of Bae's bed, shaking her foot to wake her from her hangover. "Girl, I thought you were up already. Come on. The van is outside to take us to that forest trail thing. Get up!"

"Huh? What?" Bae rolled over and slightly pulled up her pink, satin sleep mask with the word "Queen" embroidered on it. "What time is it?" One eye peeked out as she grabbed her cell phone off the nightstand.

"Time to get in that van before it leaves us," Gizelle said.

"Shit, my phone is dead," Bae exclaimed. "My alarm." She sat straight up and pulled the mask off her face. Her matching satin scarf was wrapped around her head, leaving her bun sticking out at the top.

"Come on. I'll go stall the van," Gizelle said, hustling back to the door. "But hurry up."

Bae pulled the covers off and swung her legs off the edge of the bed. "Oh, hell no." She grabbed her forehead while closing her eyes. "You all go ahead without me."

"You can do it. You just got up too fast."

"Right. And I need to keep moving fast if I'm going to make it. And I'm not about to do that. I been done fell over and busted my head." She exhaled. "I can't. Just go." Bae fell backward onto the bed, her legs now straight out.

"I need more rest. I'll see y'all when y'all get back." She pulled the covers back over her body and her sleep mask down over her face. She was snoring before Gizelle could even further plead her case.

It was a no-win battle, so Gizelle simply sucked her teeth and closed the door behind her, deciding it was best to let sleeping Bae lie.

Bae slept for the next five hours, making her grand total of sleep since arriving in Saint Martin seven hours. She probably would have slept five more hours if she hadn't been awakened by all the laughter and chatter outside her window.

She pulled her satin mask off her face for the second time that day, threw the cover off her, and kicked her legs over the edge of the bed. This time, though, she stood, stretched, and yawned. After rubbing her eyes, she walked over to the window about three feet to the left of the French doors, which overlooked the backyard.

Bae pulled the curtains back, and there she saw the ladies having the time of their lives . . . without her.

Several were in the pool floating about. One sunbathed, while the others shared a covered lounge chair for two, sipping on drinks.

"Don't they look like just the perfect Fab Five," she seethed.

Not too long ago, Bae was in the mix, having the time of her life with the ladies. They found a club to hang out at last night just a few miles from their rental, where they spent the evening indulging in bottomless rum punch and popcorn while dancing to American tunes and local favorites. They danced with each other. They danced with strangers. And those who were tipsy enough danced with themselves, thinking they were dancing with someone else. Surprisingly enough, Bae even danced with Honey. Any negative feelings she had toward Honey were one-hundred percent gone after three rum punches and three top Billboard hits. Honey was officially one of the girls. Not one of the Fab Five, but definitely one of the girls.

Until . . .

Until Bae was standing in the window, on the inside looking out.

Until she now felt like the sixth wheel.

"Cannonball!" Honey yelled.

Bae watched as Honey ran toward the pool and jumped. Then in what seemed slow motion, she watched Honey pull her knees to her chest midair and drop into the pool, splashing the two ladies already in the water.

"Why are they cheering her on?" Bae asked. "I've done a cannonball a million times." She watched as Honey swam over to each floatie and high-fived its occupant. "And it wasn't even that great of a cannonball. She could have nailed her landing much better," Bae criticized. "What's she going to do next, yell 'Marco'?"

Marco Polo had been one of Bae's favorite games since she was young, on land or in water.

Bae shook her head before snatching the curtain closed. Unfortunately, she did it so hard that the rod came down.

"Oh well," she turned back and threw the words over her shoulder. "They can keep the damn security deposit to fix it."

Bae stomped off to the bathroom for her morning release. Early afternoon in this case. First, she lifted the toilet lid and flopped down on the toilet seat. Then, with legs spread apart, she placed her elbows on her knees and a fist under her chin—the modern-day Millie Jackson.

After flushing the toilet and washing her hands, Bae freshened up. Initially, she was going to shower, but since she planned on heading down to the pool to show the ladies how to do a *real* cannonball, she decided to wait until after swimming to shower.

Bae spread out her collection of ten or so swimsuits. She wanted to have at least two different suits to wear each day. She picked the Nike aerobic two-piece, figuring it would allow the best movement for her to drop a perfect cannonball into the water. After putting it on, along with a terry cloth coverup and some beach shoes, she was ready for war. Although she brought plenty of stunning sandals and slides for poolside, Bae was on a mission and needed the beach shoes to allow her the perfect grip for a perfect cannonball.

She retrieved a beach towel from the hall linen closet after grabbing her Dolce & Gabbana dark shades.

"Here she comes, Miss America," Tyra sang as Bae strutted down the stairs leading to the pool.

"You good now, sis?" Gizelle asked. "Let me make you a drink." Gizelle went to get up, but Bae put her hand out to stop her.

"No, thank you," Bae said as she approached a lounge chair. Without saying another word, she dropped her towel on the chair, took off her shades, and assumed "the position."

"Uh-oh, here it comes," Angelina said, clapping as she wobbled in her floatie.

Gizelle eyeballed Bae and shook her head. In her eyes, Bae looked like a bull seeing red and about to charge. That was a fair visualization. At least it matched perfectly the attitude Bae had.

A few seconds later, Bae performed the best cannonball of her life. She came up from the water smiling from ear to ear.

"See, Honey," Tyra shouted from the lounge chair next to Gizelle, where a table separated them. "Told you every trip, Bae kicks it off with a cannonball." Tyra turned her attention to Bae. "When we told Honey about your cannonball tradition, she mentioned that she always shied away from doing it because of her weight. She didn't want other people laughing or saying something smart. But we figured she's on her first girls' trip, so she might as well do her first cannonball."

"And so she did," Bae said with a sour face. "Yet another tradition Honey here has seemed to highjack."

"Whoa, wait a minute," Jackie said. She looked confused as her eyes darted from Bae to Gizelle. "I thought you said everything was squashed."

Gizelle shrugged and responded to Jackie, "I don't know. Last night she was good. You saw her."

"I am right here, you know," Bae said, "but then again, I've been invisible this entire trip, so maybe y'all don't see me here."

Gizelle rolled her eyes. "Here we go again."

"And just what the hell does that mean?" Bae asked.

"It means you're back on some bullshit, *that's* what." Gizelle shook her head, picked up her sunglasses from the table, and leaned back. "Are we going to have to keep you drunk to have fun with you on this trip?"

"I don't know because you haven't had any fun with me on this trip. Y'all have done whatever the hell y'all wanted to do. I missed a whole day because ole girl wanted to go out last night. And we *never* go out the night we arrive at our destination. And this is why. As I said, I missed a whole day and an excursion *I* paid for because we had to go out."

"I'm sorry," Honey said. "Maybe it wasn't a good idea that—"

"That you come on this trip with us?" Bae asked. "I agree."

"Actually, I was going to say that we went out last night," Honey said.

"I agree with you there as well, but we wouldn't have had to worry about all that if you hadn't come on the trip in the first place," Bae spat.

"Bae, you are being a straight-up bitch, and I don't even like calling females a bitch," Gizelle said.

Jackie looked at Gizelle with a puzzled face. "But you always call—"

"Not now, Jackie," Angelina said while shaking her head. "Don't do it."

Gizelle and Bae paid the other ladies no mind as their eyes stayed focused on each other.

"I'm acting like a bitch because I flipped the tab on a trip that I planned out and—"

"And we thank you," Gizelle interrupted. "We sincerely do. But just because you paid for this trip don't mean you gon' pimp us on it," she said. "As a matter of fact," she dug into her beach bag sitting next to her chair, "take this." She threw her credit card toward Bae. It didn't go far, landing at the foot of her chair. "Put the trip on my tab. 'Give us, us free.'" She looked at the other ladies. "Girls, y'all can do whatever you want to now. The trip is on me."

There were a few seconds of silence.

"Is *that* how you ladies feel?" Bae asked. "Is that how y'all *really* feel?" She looked around at them, giving them each the opportunity to speak.

Finally, Jackie spoke up. "Yeah, kinda, but—" She wiped the water from her eyes as a result of Angelina pushing water toward her to shut her up.

"Speak now or forever hold your peace," Bae dared them. "What, y'all scared?"

Silence until, once again, Jackie spoke up. "Kinda, yeah. You've been a little scary these—" Angelina splashing her silenced her again.

"No, let her talk," Bae demanded.

Silence.

Jackie went to open her mouth.

"You better not, or I'm gon' drown your ass next time," Angelina threatened.

At this point, Honey was too emotional to hide her feelings. "Look, I never . . ." She turned to Bae. "I promise you I never meant any harm. I wasn't trying to intrude, change tradition, or anything else."

Bae heard her but ignored her.

"So that you ladies enjoy one another and this vacation just like you have done all the others, I think it's best I try to book a flight back home."

"Honey, please—" Gizelle started.

"Say less," Bae said. "I'll text you the travel agent's information." Bae started swimming around the pool, living her best life—totally unbothered.

"Honey, please don't," Jackie said as Honey swam to the steps of the pool and climbed out.

"It's okay." Honey walked over to a lounge chair and picked up her towel. She wiped the water off her face that mixed in with her tears.

"Bae, if you were a book, I'd give you one fucking star," Gizelle said. "Why? Because I'm sure you'd be the main character, and whenever I hate the main character in a book, I hate the whole got darn book," Gizelle yelled, grabbing her towel and wrapping it around her waist. "Text me the travel agent's information as well. I'm out of this bitch too." Gizelle stormed off.

"Gizelle, come on," Tyra said.

"No, fuck this and fuck her," Gizelle said, her eyes filling with liquid anger. "You said the money wasn't going to change you."

"And you said we'd never get into a fight," Bae shot back.

"But y'all always . . ." This time, Jackie silenced herself.

"Not a real fight. And this feels real to me." Bae's lips trembled. She and Gizelle had several disagreements over the years. And they had back-and-forth banter that would have broken the average friendship apart. But, again, they didn't have the average friendship.

"Ladies, this is only day two of the trip, and we've done a few things we usually don't do on our trips," Tyra said, "but fighting and arguing is not one of them."

"But talking behind one another's back is?" Bae asked.

"What makes you think somebody—anybody—has been talking about you?" Tyra asked.

There was silence as all eyes went to Jackie.

"That's why I told you to shut up," Angelina mumbled to her.

"See?" Bae said.

"Not because I didn't want you to know we had been talking about you, because we haven't," Angelina explained. "But because I didn't want you to think we had. We know the rules. We spill the tea at the tea parties."

Bae let out a tsk. "Well, at least that's one tradition that didn't get broken on this trip."

Gizelle raised her arms and, in defeat, let them drop. "Always have to get in the last word, huh?" She shook her head. "I guess that's one thing about you that will never change." Gizelle began to rustle up her bag and drink.

"Bae!" Jackie called out.

When Bae turned her attention toward Jackie, no words were spoken. None had to be. Jackie's eyes pleaded with Bae not to do this. Not to ruin their trip. Not to let Gizelle leave.

Honey still stood with her towel in hand, watching the ladies interact. Although Kevin Costner stopped a 757 for Whitney Houston in *The Bodyguard*, Honey running away, for Bae, would have simply been Honey running away. She could run all the way back to Vegas as far as Bae cared. But it wasn't Honey running away. It was Gizelle.

Gizelle was halfway up the steps when Bae called out to her.

There was a slight hesitation from Gizelle as she contemplated on whether to acknowledge her friend. Just slight . . . as she continued up the steps.

"Gizzy," Bae yelled out as she swam toward the steps to climb out of the pool.

Gizelle could keep climbing those steps all she wanted, but Bae would be right behind her.

Figuring as much, Gizelle stopped at the top of the steps. "What, Bae?" She flung her body around, exasperated, to face Bae.

"Wait," Bae called out, not noticing that Gizelle stopped because she was too busy looking down, pushing herself out of the water. "I just want to apologize." Bae stood up and looked around at all the ladies. "To everybody." She took a couple of breaths and then padded over to get her towel. After drying off, she exhaled deeply, then allowed her shoulders to drop as if she were giving up.

However, Bae wasn't giving up. She never gave up on anything. But she was giving in. She was giving in to letting go. She had to let go of the foul energy she was carrying around that was making this one of the most memorable trips ever—but in an awful way.

"Ladies, this is not what this trip was supposed to be about," Bae said. "And I'm the reason why it's everything that it's not." She took several more breaths. "And I'm sorry. I have to stop and ask myself whether I'm likable or just tolerable. Because I don't want to be just tolerated. I don't want people going around saying, 'Oh, that's just Bae.'"

She continued looking from one girl to the next, making sure they knew her apology was truly directed at them.

"We have the best conversations in the world," Bae continued. "But I don't want to be heard just because I'm talking. I want to be listened to. I don't want y'all brushing off my words as just something Bae is saying because 'that's Bae.'" She looked at Jackie. "Yeah, the music was loud last night at the club, but not so loud that I didn't hear you tell Honey not to take the stuff out of my mouth personally or even seriously. To 'chew the meat and spit out the bones.'" The hurt in Bae's eyes was unmistakable. "From now on, don't just take my shit. If my trying to be cute and flip at the mouth is actually ugly, call me on my shit."

Jackie nodded. "I hear you, Bae, and I'm guilty as charged for what I said to Honey last night." She felt the need to defend herself. "I'm sorry, Bae. It's just that you and Gizelle have this thing y'all do where y'all shade each other and think nothing of it. And we all do a little bit of that in our circle. But sometimes, I think you use it to really say something negative and offensive. But because you say it to be funny-funny, jokey-jokey, it will not land and stick on someone."

"Stick and sting," Tyra chimed in.

"Why do you think we really call you Queen Bee?" Angelina asked.

Bae's eyes widened with surprise.

"I'm just kidding," Angelina said quickly. "It just seemed fitting. And besides, that's just how we do, right? So don't take it personally."

Bae's eyes softened as she understood the point Angelina was trying to make. "Touché, bitch, touché." Bae winked and smiled at Angelina. But her smile faded as she turned her attention to Gizelle. "Please stay. The one tradition I will fight to the death is you not being here on this trip. You are the nucleus of this group. I mean, I may be the light and the fire of the group," Bae bragged in a comedic manner as she patted her chest as if clearing her throat to let the words fall out. "But none of the Fab Five would have connected if it hadn't been you who connected us. We all met through you. So, as much as I hate saying it, and as much as I hate it being true, *you* are why Fab Five even exists." Bae clasped her hands in front of her and began swinging back and forth like a toddler. Then in a baby voice, she said, "So, please don't weave us."

She poked her lips out and continued swinging back and forth in a pouty manner. She even batted her eyes rapidly for added measure.

Gizelle stood for a moment in contemplation before looking over at Honey, who was also all set to leave.

Bae followed Gizelle's eyes to Honey, who turned her attention from Gizelle to Bae. Bae wanted to turn away, but she didn't. Instead, she allowed Honey to stare into her eyes, hoping to see the truth that she really was sorry. And quiet as it was kept, Bae wanted to read into Honey as well. What was her truth? Was she here to cause trouble, make trouble, or was she simply trouble? Or none of the above. Maybe she was just a girl going through a rough breakup and needed some sisterly love to help her heal.

Bae looked back at Gizelle. "Will you stop standing up there looking like Jerry Maguire?" Bae did her best impression when she called out, "Who's coming with me? The goldfish is coming with me. Is Honey coming with me?"

The girls started laughing.

Bae looked back at Honey. "And you can stay too," Bae said. Then she looked back at Gizelle. "Is that what you were waiting to hear? Jeez." With a smile, Bae reiterated to Honey that she'd love for her to stay.

"Yay," Jackie cheered.

No one else joined in when they realized Honey hadn't confirmed that she would.

"I know I can stay," Honey said to Bae. "Like yourself, I'm a grown woman. The question is, do *you* want me to stay? After all, you flipped the tab for this trip. And the last thing I want to do is stay somewhere I'm not wanted . . . for free."

This was the first time Honey had ever used such a serious tone with Bae. Like the girls had been telling her to do, she usually just brushed Bae's words off. But now, there seemed to be a new rule. Nobody had to take Bae's shit. They just had to call her on it. That was a rule Honey was ready to follow.

"I want you . . ." Bae cleared her throat.

Tyra looked at Bae, encouraging her with her eyes to continue.

Bae sighed. ". . . here . . . with us." She hacked up the courage to spit out the words, "Please stay and enjoy your first girls' trip and your first trip out of the country."

Honey thought for a moment, making Bae wait in anticipation. Her reply would seal the deal that the trip would go on as planned with Honey and Gizelle. "I would love to, Bae. Thank you."

Bae allowed her lips to do a quick smile with raised eyebrows before shouting, "Cannonball," and diving back into the pool.

And just like that, the girls were girls again. They spent the next few hours at the pool, had dinner, got dressed, then headed out to enjoy the evening on a double-decker party bus. Bae booked it to take them touring around town for four hours. It included an all-you-can-drink bar and was scheduled to make pit stops at some of the locals' evening hangouts and restaurants.

That adventure would be all the girls' first.

But that wouldn't be the last first of the night.

Chapter 6

I Kissed a Girl

"Turn down for what?" Gizelle shouted as she stood at the top of the double-decker bus with her hands in the air, each holding a cup of rum punch splashing and dripping down her arms.

The DJ was on the first level of the bus, but the music could be heard loud and clear due to the placement of a set of speakers on the open upper deck. Of course, the ladies weren't the only ones on the party bus. There were two other groups. But two hours in and countless rum punches later, they were all one big, happy family. Twerking. Dirty Dancing. Percolating. And Tyra swears she saw Angelina kiss a girl from another party.

"I didn't kiss her," Angelina said after so long of Tyra teasing her. "She had something stuck on her eyelash, and I was just getting it out."

No one made a big deal of it. For one, what went on during their trips out of the country stayed in that very country. And besides, come morning, even if Angelina had kissed a girl, she wouldn't remember. And even if Tyra saw her kiss a girl, she wouldn't remember it either, their memory loss being blamed on the alcohol.

The girls were worn out when they were dropped back off at the rental. Heads aching from drinking and bodies aching from dropping it like it was hot. They could barely make it to their respective bedrooms. So, they all decided to flop down right there in the living room and reminisce the night away.

"Man, y'all," Gizelle started, "I don't think we've ever turned up that hard in our whole, entire lives." Leaning back in her chair with her arms spread over each armrest of the chair, she looked over at Honey, who was sprawled out on the loveseat. "This is only day two, Honey. You gon' be able to hang? Or do you think you gon' need that travel agent's information after all?"

The other ladies started laughing.

"You gon' be able to hang with the famous Fab Five?" Tyra asked.

"Because, baby, last night was the Vegas Strip. That's rated R," Tyra said, sitting on the ottoman to the chair Gizelle was sprawled in, "That shit that just went down tonight was Fremont, Rated X."

"Word!" Bae laughed as she sat on the couch with Angelina and Jackie.

There were a few seconds of silence.

"I don't care what Snoop Doggy Dog says." Gizelle looked around the room. "I love y'all hoes."

Once again, the ladies laughed.

Honey's laughter faded. "Can I ask y'all something?"

"Not if you about to get serious," Bae said. "Save serious talk that you want us to remember for breakfast because tonight, everything is going in one ear and out the other."

Several of the girls chuckled.

"Go ahead, Honey," Gizelle insisted, "ask your question, boo."

"Okay." Honey took a deep breath.

"Well, damn, is it *that* serious?" Tyra asked. "Are we gon' have to jump you?"

Honey chuckled. "No, nothing like that. I just want to know how it is that none of you have ever gotten into real fights and arguments and stuff. I mean, earlier today, things got real. But still, no one put their paws on anyone. Because I've seen chicks in those groups on reality shows snatch another chick's edges for less. And y'all be going at it." She looked from Bae to Gizelle. "Especially you two."

Bae and Gizelle stared at each other.

"Those two have been playing the Dozen since I met them," Tyra said. "They're like a whole comedy show if you ask me. They would sell out shows every night if they got a residency here in Vegas. I mean, in Vegas," Tyra corrected, remembering they were out of the country.

"I know that's right," Angelina added.

"I don't know." Honey shook her head. "You have to have a special kind of humor. Y'all see what happened to that gospel artist, Kim Burrell, when she tried to be funny about broke friends."

"Oh yeah, I remember that," Angelina said. "They dragged her on the internet."

"Yeah, but I think that was about the setting and the atmosphere," Bae said.

"Perhaps. But I see where Honey is coming from," Gizelle said. "I swear when it comes to some of the conversations we have, if we were ever to be recorded, caught with a hot mic, stuff taken out of context—"

"Or even *in* context," Tyra interrupted.

"Right," Gizelle said, "we could be canceled as fuck."

"Hmmm, I guess you're right," Tyra said. "The Bae and Gizelle Show would be over before it started. Y'all would have folks crying in the audience—and not laughing from crying, but crying D. L. Hughley comedy-style crying. I refuse to sit in the front row of his shows. He will crack on an audience member so quick."

"And so bad," Gizelle added.

"Yeah, it's hard even to tell jokes anymore," Jackie contributed to the conversation.

"Keep my wife's name out your fucking mouth," Tyra yelled out.

There were a couple of chuckles.

"Hell, it's hard for artists to do almost anything anymore," Bae said. "It's hard to write sometimes. So many people walk around in offense now that the rest of us are walking on eggshells."

"True," Jackie agreed. She looked at Bae. "How can you even write books nowadays, Bae?"

Bae sighed. "Once upon a time, it was trying to write without getting hung up on if a comma goes here, italics there, etcetera," she said. A serious look came across her face. "It's rough. Because you know me, I just like to live life, have fun, say whatever, and do whatever. I know that I can't do half in real life what I do in my books," she continued. "But now, it's getting to the point where, hell, I might not even be able to do it in my books."

"Oh, you do even more in your books than in real life?" Honey asked. She did so jokingly, but there was a hint of fear in her eyes just imagining some of the stuff Bae writes in her books.

"Does she ever," Jackie proclaimed, turning red. "I'm getting embarrassed, and I didn't even write the books."

"Stop it. It is not that bad," Bae said in her defense.

The other ladies in Fab Five looked at Honey and said, "It's *that* bad."

They all laughed.

"But we have to admit that the stuff Bae writes be funny as hell," Gizelle added.

"Funny as hell to whom?" Angelina asked seriously. "Besides us? Because we know Bae."

"We know her heart." Gizelle put her hand over her chest and chuckled.

"Yeah, but back to Kim Burrell," Honey said. "She thought folks knew her heart as well."

"But what about the people who don't?" Angelina asked in serious mode. "The people who don't know Bae's heart and her intentions?"

"Well, it can't be too bad," Tyra said. "Look at how many books she sells. Film options. All of them paid speaking engagements." She looked at Bae. "Wasn't your last payment to speak at that university ridiculously obscene?"

"Well, let's just say people may call *me* full-figured, but they call my speaking engagement checks *five*-figure. Oweee!" Bae leaned forward and high-fived several of the girls.

"But, yeah, clearly, her books are funny to the people who read them," Tyra said.

Bae shook her head. "Not so much. I'd say they are funny to those who read the books and are my fans. Those who have been with me since I was just doing and saying stuff on my YouTube channel, IG, TikTok, and stuff."

"Like Cardi B," Tyra said. "And now you are getting those bags too."

"They aren't shocked by anything I write. It meets their expectations of my brand," Bae explained. "But I wake up every day making sure my books aren't on the banned book list." She laughed. "Because intentionally or not, words, let alone actions, can hurt other people. And ignorance is no longer an excuse because folks don't even give you a chance nowadays to get educated and get it right. They call you out instead of call you up."

"Ain't that the truth?" Gizelle asked while the other ladies nodded.

"Books aren't even a safe place anymore to just say whatever and do whatever in the name of fiction," Bae said. "Like, the world is so sensitive now that we must have sensitivity readers and sensitivity editors go behind our work to make sure no one is going to get offended by the words we write or how we describe people, places, and things. Not that, in some cases, books didn't already need this type of critique, because some of them did, and some of them still do. But now, it's like any little thing that hurts just one person's feelings out of millions must get dealt with."

"If God is concerned about just one sheep, the world we live in should be as well," Jackie said. "I mean, imagine the amazing world we could live in if everybody did take to heart just one person's feelings. And then corrected themselves for that one person."

"Someone is *always* going to get offended about *something,*" Gizelle said. "Some folks are good with the word 'minority,' while others aren't."

"Same with 'fat ass,'" Honey chimed in. She looked toward Bae. "Someone could call you a fat ass, and you'd take it as a compliment because you see fat ass as an asset. I, on the other hand, would be hurt by it."

"Damn right. Who wouldn't want to have a fat ass?" Bae asked.

"I know I would," Tyra said. "I'm jealous as fuck of Bae. I'm jealous of her curves. I'm jealous of her confidence when it comes to her curves. I'm jealous of her courage to show her curves."

Bae put her hand up to stop Tyra. "Hold up, sis. Let me play devil's advocate for a minute," she said. "What makes you think that what you just said isn't offensive? Why do people think I should have to muster up confidence and courage to show my curves?" Bae asked. "I could be offended by that concept alone. I mean, when Gizelle goes to the beach in her two-piece swimsuit, are people sitting around saying, 'I'm sure it took so much courage for her to put that on and come to the beach.'"

"Boom!" Tyra said, opening her palms as if dropping a bomb.

"That's society's doing," Honey said.

"Then it needs to be our *undoing*," Bae replied. "This is one reason why we play The Dozens with one another. Say whatever. Be flippant with one another. Deliberately see who can out-shade who. But all lighthearted fun. It's like we get immune to it in here . . . in our circle. That way, if we come into contact with it out there," Bae pointed aimlessly, "out in the world, it won't kill us. We're unbothered. You know?"

There was silence as the group took in Bae's reasoning.

"Nah, bitch," Gizelle said, "that's like Jay-Z and them other rappers using the word 'nigga' among themselves and in their music to make it normal and so-called lose its power when people outside our race call us that."

"Or like you using the word 'bitch' so that when men refer to us as that, it has no power," Bae shot back.

"Ooooh, double boom," Tyra said to Gizelle. "Bitch, she told yo' ass."

A few women in the group chuckled.

"I can't with y'all." Honey shook her head.

"And you can't without us," Gizelle smiled.

"True that," Bae said. She stood up and stretched. "I don't know about y'all, but this about-to-turn-forty-year-old bitch is about to turn in for the night."

"I know *that's* right."

"Same here."

"You don't have to tell me twice."

The ladies each headed to their rooms. They could pick up in the morning where they left off tonight.

Except there was still some unfinished business to be handled before the sun came up.

Chapter 7

Through the Fire

After taking a shower and sliding into her long, plum, satin gown, Bae grabbed her laptop, sat on the bed, and powered it up.

"Let me check a few emails. After that, I'm crashing," she said in hopes of encouraging herself not to get too caught up online.

After reading and replying to several emails, someone rapped lightly on the door. Before Bae could reply, the door slowly cracked open, and a voice asked, "Can I come in?"

Bae's mouth dropped open. Honey was the last person she expected to be at her door. After all, she hadn't been the most welcoming girl in the group. But she had her reasons. Reasons she very much felt justified her behavior. Some of them she'd already explained to the group and apologized for. And even though Honey accepted Bae's apology, and Bae had been on her best behavior since, Bae was not trying to get all buddy-buddy with Honey. And she definitely wasn't trying to have any one-on-one time with her for fear of what she might say or do around the girl with no eyewitness.

Bae neither admitted nor dismissed Honey. The girl had already let herself in. So what was left for Bae to do? Tell her to leave her room? That's what she wanted to say. But that wasn't nice. And since she couldn't say something nice, she said nothing.

After a few seconds, Honey invited herself deeper into Bae's room, pushing the door behind her.

Bae acted as though Honey wasn't even there as she cracked open another email.

"It got kind of serious out there, huh?" Honey asked.

"I guess." Bae shrugged. "Depending on what you call serious."

"You."

"Pardon me?" Bae said with an attitude, looking up from her laptop.

"I call *you* serious." Honey took a few steps closer, landing at the foot of Bae's bed. "For someone who claims to love and purposefully to be jokey-jokey, care-free, wanting to live life by doing and saying whatever in the name of fun and just living life unoffended, you sure do get serious . . . when it comes to me."

Bae froze for a moment, but the heat in her cheeks thawed her out quickly. She hastily deleted a spam email and proceeded to the next one.

Honey stood unmoved.

Sensing that Honey was demanding a response—as if she didn't plan on going anywhere until Bae gave her one—Bae looked up at her. "Don't flatter yourself, sweetie. I mean, Honey." She looked back at her laptop and began tapping away at the keys. A few seconds later, she looked up from her computer. "You still here?" She let out a harrumph and started typing again.

Bae was trying. She really was. But Honey was trying her. Why couldn't Honey just let Bae be? Enjoy their trip in Saint Martin, then return to Vegas and never have to see each other again.

Honey sat, staring at Bae with no intention of darting her eyes away if Bae caught her.

Finally, Bae exhaled and looked up at Honey. "Child, I have no idea what you are talking about. Therefore, if you're sitting there waiting for answers, you aren't going to get them. So, I advise you to keep it moving." She tapped a few keys on her computer.

"Come on, Bae, it's just you and me. You can keep it one hundred." Honey spoke in a soft, unagitated tone.

Why is she so fucking nice? Bae thought. *Why does she have to be sweet as honey, making it that much harder for me to be bitter toward her?*

Bae sucked her teeth. "As I said, I have no idea what you're talking about." She hit the button, and another spam email swooshed into Cyberland.

"Sure, you do," Honey said. "I think you know *exactly* what I mean." She slowly closed Bae's laptop, staring at Bae the entire time. Her action—her eyes—demanded some reaction from her.

Bae swallowed so loud that her saliva going down her throat sounded like a wave splashing against the shore. She looked up, her eyes locking with Honey's. She couldn't help but wonder if she was wearing her emotions on her face. *Had* she been wearing her emotions on her face? *All this time?*

If Bae were wearing her emotions on her face, Honey would see that she was nervous.

"I look at how you are with all the other women in the group," Honey said. "With other women, period. And it's different. It's different than it is with me. So, what I want to know is . . ." Honey turned her body, positioning it to face Bae, "What's different about the other women?"

Once again, Bae swallowed hard. If her saliva were a wave, she would want it to wash the look off her face. She couldn't describe the emotion she felt, which she was sure was being expressed on her face. But she sensed it made her look silly.

"I-I have no idea what you're talking about. I treat every woman's body the same." Bae's eyes bucked as she replayed the words in her head that just came out of her mouth. "Every woman the same. Everybody the same. Damn it. You *know* what I mean." Frustrated, Bae snatched the laptop from the bed and set it roughly on the nightstand.

Bae now had no problem describing the emotion she was currently feeling. It was one of frustration.

Honey stared at her for a few seconds before smiling and letting out a slight chuckle. Then she looked down while shaking her head.

"What? What's so funny?" Bae demanded to know.

Honey covered her mouth with her hand to stifle her laughter. "I'm sorry," she apologized . . . while still laughing. "It's just that this is the first time I-I have heard you stutter since I met you." She deliberately stuttered to mock Bae. "A woman usually so slick and smooth with her words . . . " She shrugged. "Just never thought I'd see the day is all."

Bae didn't see anything funny. This woman had put her through more emotions in the last few weeks than she'd experienced her entire life. Maybe Tyra was right. Maybe turning forty was messing with her mentally and emotionally. But unfortunately, Honey was going to get the brunt of it. She couldn't have picked a worse time to come into her life. Into her circle. Into her room.

"I don't know. It's funny to me. *You're* funny to me." Honey tilted her head to the left as she smiled into Bae's eyes. "But sometimes you confuse me. You know, with that sour-patch kid act of yours."

"Well, maybe it's because you haven't known me that long. Maybe *that's* why you're confused. Because this is no act. What you see is what you get."

"You could be right. I haven't known you that long," Honey agreed.

"And thank God we only have a couple more days on this trip because you can pretend like you don't know me at all after that, which is exactly what I'm going to do with you. Now, if you'll excuse me . . ." Bae shot her eyes toward the door in hopes that Honey would follow them, take the hint, and excuse herself from Bae's room.

Just as before, Honey sat. Unbothered. Unfazed. Unmoved.

Bae sucked her teeth and nodded toward the door. "Umm, if you'll excuse me, I was in here checking my emails before I was rudely interrupted." She snatched her laptop from the nightstand, opened it up, and went back to check her emails. She typed as she huffed, puffed, and rambled off a few choice words under her breath.

"She's got some damn nerve coming up in my room like she picked out and paid for this house." Bae shook her head and continued to huff and puff while going through emails.

Honey sat there for a moment, watching Bae carry on. "Uh, you *do* know I'm still sitting right here, don't you? I can hear everything you're saying . . . to yourself."

Bae stopped typing, allowed her tongue to roll over the back row of her upper teeth, wobbled her head, and then looked at Honey. "As a matter of fact, I didn't. Because you're already invisible to me."

"And that's precisely what you wish, huh? That I were invisible. That way, you wouldn't have to look at me. Look at me the way you do. Deliberately *not* look at me." She pushed Bae's laptop closed again. "Look at me."

When Bae felt Honey's index finger touch her chin, she became heated.

Heated with anger.

Angry that she was heated.

It was a vicious cycle.

That would burn Bae up if she didn't figure out how to put out the fire. Or how to get out of the fire.

But from the look in Honey's eyes when she lifted Bae's chin to face her, Honey was going to make her go through the fire.

"Would that be accurate?" Honey asked.

"Huh, what?" Bae stammered and quickly pulled herself from Honey's eyes. She started typing on her laptop.

If only it were still open.

It took a few seconds of Bae hearing her manicured nails hit the top of the laptop before she realized it was closed.

But she was the one open.

She was an open book.

And Honey was reading into her.

Bae looked down at her nails on the laptop.

"Look at me," Honey spoke. Her words, her tone, were like honey slithering down Bae's ears. "Bae?"

Hypnotized. Paralyzed. Tranquilized. Bae was *ized* by Honey's eyes.

"Bae." Honey softly laid her hand on top of Bae's.

For Bae, it was like being tased. She snapped out of her euphoric-like fog, quickly snatching her hand away.

"I'm sorry," Honey said sincerely. "I'm sorry for whatever it is about me that makes you—"

"Me," Bae spoke as if a lightbulb were going off.

"Pardon me?" Honey asked, confused.

Bae blinked, bringing herself fully out of her trance. "Uh, it's, uh, me, Honey." She pulled her face away from Honey and shook it off. Again, "it" being her emotions, her facial expression. "I just, uh, you know. It's just been Gizelle . . . the girls. Uh, you know, just me. And them. You know? So, again, it's all me. I've always said I'm too old to be making new friends. Especially now that I'm about to turn forty. And besides, even if we were accepting new members into Fab Five, it wouldn't be you."

"Come again?" Honey gave Bae the side-eye. "Just when I thought we were making progress, here comes the sour side." Honey shook her head and let out a tsk.

"No, that's not what I mean. I mean, there's no room for you. You're big," Bae said, genuinely struggling to piece her words together.

"Before I get offended, do you want to explain what that means?" Honey asked. After the ladies' conversation earlier that evening, she thought it best not to call Bae out automatically.

Bae thumped herself on her head. "Ugh." She closed her eyes, breathed deeply, and counted to three in her head. "Look, it's no secret that I command and demand attention. I lead the pack, which means can't nobody see them skinny heifers behind me."

Honey put her head down and let out a laugh.

"Seriously. I'm not the big girl at the club who sits at the table and watches the purses and coats," Bae said. "I'm the girl with the big personality who *lets* those skinny bitches hold *my* purse and coat like the skinny-ass coatracks they are."

"Bae, that is *not* nice," Honey said, her mouth wide open.

"What?" Bae didn't see—or hear, for that matter—the problem with what she said.

"What do you mean, what? If they were talking about us being big in the other room, we'd be fit to be tied."

"Not me. Have you seen me and Gizelle go at it?"

Honey thought for a moment. "Yeah, you're right." She nodded but then looked back at Bae with a shameful look. "But still."

"No, fuck that," Bae said. "Skinny bitches and them self-proclaimed 'big-boned' bitches who are only two chicken wings from being full-figured like us, been labeling us for years." Bae used her fingers to form air quotations. "The big one in the group." She sucked her teeth. "And even if they don't say it, they think it." She used her fingers to make air quotations again. "There's always a big girl in the clique." She shook her head. "So, what I'm saying right now is just balancing out the universe, baby. Period." Bae dotted the air in front of her.

Honey shook her head and exhaled. "Well, at least I know now that if I ever want to join the clique, I have to lose at least seventy-five pounds."

The ladies chuckled.

"No, you look good just like that." Bae looked Honey up and down. Subconsciously. Then her roaming eyes landed on Honey's. "Don't change a thing."

Honey dropped her head and blushed. "I won't," she said, looking up at Bae.

"Good." Bae smiled.

The two shared a smile for a few seconds. Honey's eyes slowly but surely melted away the hard exterior Bae was trying to maintain to keep Honey at bay.

"And I'm, uh," Bae stuttered, "sorry about, you know, how I've been acting. We're in fucking Saint Martin. I don't want to be like the women on those housewives shows when they go on trips and waste precious time fighting and acting ugly. That's not even me. Life's too short."

"Yes, it is," Honey agreed. "So, we should absolutely make the most of it, starting with the last days of this trip."

Bae breathed a sigh of relief. She was so glad to have finally gotten that off her chest. "Good."

"Good," Honey repeated. "So, what do you say we hug it out before I head back to my room?" She stood.

Bae thought for a moment. "Well, I'm usually not the hugging type, but what the heck. I'll make an exception. Nobody needs to know. Plus, we're doing all types of new stuff on this trip." She spread her arms wide. "To new traditions." Honey walked around the bed, bent down, and hugged Bae.

While hugging her, Honey inhaled. "Mmmm." She pulled back, her arms still around Bae but looking Bae in the eyes. "Cherry Blossom?"

Bae nodded.

Honey leaned back into Bae, her nose grazing Bae's neck. She sniffed. "Smells *so* good."

Internally, Bae was screaming at herself for enjoying Honey's touch so much. She was screaming at herself even louder for giving in to the touch, for giving in to this feeling. For *finally* giving in . . . and letting go.

"Thank you." Bae blushed.

Honey pulled back again. "You're welcome."

After a moment, Bae stood, forcing Honey to step back. "Well, I think we should get to bed."

Standing in her tracks, Honey replied, "Yeah, we should."

The two women stood there, neither of them speaking. At least not with their mouths.

"Bae," Honey placed her hand on Bae's shoulder, "I like you."

Now, Bae wasn't just open like an open book. She was *wide* open. "I like you too."

"So, no more pulling my hair on the playground pretending you hate me because you secretly like me so much?" Honey asked.

Bae chuckled like a schoolgirl with a crush. "No more of that," she agreed.

The two women stood there for several more seconds.

"So, what do you think we should do about this mutual like we have for each other?" Honey asked.

Bae looked down, five shades of sadness washing away the joy she momentarily felt just a few seconds ago. "If I knew, do you think I'd act the way I do?"

"Wait, I don't get it," Honey said, clueless about how Bae's energy could suddenly change. "Now, I'm more confused than before."

Bae looked up at her. "*You're* confused? I've been confused my entire life," she admitted.

Honey listened. She waited for Bae to say more, but Bae said nothing, leaving her standing there, soaking wet in her puddle of confusion.

Bae detected Honey's bewilderment and became frustrated. "So, are you *really* going to make me say it?" she asked. "Is this like payback for me being such a big bitch toward you?"

"Bae, baby, I'm not trying to pay you back or anything like that. I genuinely don't know what's going on here."

Bae read Honey's eyes. She could see that Honey, indeed, was at a loss.

"Just say it," Honey demanded. "Whatever it is you're trying to say here. Please just say it. Don't start talking in circles now. You've shot it straight from the moment I met you, so don't start swerving."

Bae took a deep breath, held it for a few seconds, then spoke. "I don't know how." She exhaled as if she'd been holding in a secret her entire life and was finally free to tell it.

Some good it did Honey, though. She was still just as confused as ever. And Bae could tell by the look still hanging on Honey's face. Finally, Bae stomped her foot in total frustration.

"To be gay. I don't know how to be gay," Bae blurted quickly and in a hurry so that the words would travel far. Too far. So far into Honey's ear gates that she could never retrieve them.

Honey stared at Bae for a moment before bursting out laughing.

At first, her laughter upset Bae, but it became so contagious that before she knew it, both women were bent over laughing. Tears poured from their eyes.

"I'm weak," Bae said, falling on the bed.

"Me too." Honey joined her.

The two women sat on the bed, still laughing hard. Honey threw her arm around Bae as they laughed. This went on for a few minutes until they regained their composure.

"Oh my goodness," Bae said. "That was too much."

"Right," Honey agreed.

Bae took a deep breath and then turned and looked at Honey. "What the hell were we laughing at anyway?"

Her question only set off Honey's laughing spell again.

"Stop it," Bae pleaded as she started laughing again. "My stomach hurts."

They laughed for a few more seconds before Bae turned the conversation back to the question at hand.

"So, tell me," Bae said, "what was so funny?"

"As I said before, *you're* funny," Honey said. "Talking about you don't know how to be gay."

"But I don't," Bae admitted.

Honey looked at her and noted in her spirit how serious she was. "Sweetheart, look at me." Honey turned her body toward Bae and rested her hand on Bae's cheek while Bae stared into her eyes. "I'm about to say something to you, and I want you to hear me and hear me well. And I wish to God this was something someone told you a long time ago." Honey rubbed Bae's cheek with her thumb. "You listening? You hearing me right now?" she asked.

Bae nodded.

"You don't have to know *how* to be gay. It's not something you need to know how to do. Being gay isn't something you are taught or something you learn how to do," Honey told her.

"I know, I know." Bae rolled her eyes. "You're born that way." Bae went to turn away from Honey. "I've heard that, but it still hasn't helped."

Honey was quick to gently grab Bae by the face again and turn her toward her. "Let me finish," she said. "What I was going to say is that you don't have to know *how* to be gay. It's not something you learn or that someone teaches you how to be. The only thing you need to know is how to love. And with that love, you can give it to whoever you want. Got that?"

With eyes filled with tears, Bae nodded. "Got it." She exhaled. A breath that she'd been holding inside for far too long.

Honey wiped away the tears that now streamed down Bae's face. "You okay? You good?"

Bae sniffed and nodded. "Yes, I am now. I really am okay." She nodded and smiled. She unquestionably was okay. With who she was. With herself.

"Good," Honey said. "Now, if you'll let me, there is something I can teach you."

Honey leaned in and placed a kiss on Bae's lips. Then she pulled back to get Bae's reaction, and when she realized the kiss was welcomed, she kissed her again . . . and again. And then here. And then there. And, as promised, Honey did teach Bae something. She taught her that she could not only love whomever she wanted to, but she could also kiss them too.

And so much more . . .

Chapter 8

A Taste of Honey

"The dead has arisen," Gizelle said as Bae walked out to the enclosed den where the other ladies were enjoying the breakfast Margaret had prepared.

Wrapped in her thick white cotton spa robe, Bae walked over to the table, grabbed a strawberry from the bowl of freshly cut fruit, and then sat down in one of the comfy chairs that stood separate from the dining table and chairs.

The other girls had been at the table for at least half an hour, devouring the spread.

"Not going to join us at the table and eat?" Tyra asked Bae.

"Oh, she's probably full," Gizelle said without looking up from her plate as she bit a piece of cantaloupe she had in her hands.

"From what?" Jackie asked. "We haven't eaten yet."

"Oh, I'm sure Bae had a late-night snack." Gizelle looked over her shoulder at Bae. "Those scrumptious meat pies Margaret prepared before she left last evening for us to snack on, I know they were calling your name. And there's nothing like having your name called out. Right, Bae?" Gizelle popped the remainder of the cantaloupe into her mouth, turned back around, and picked up a piece of toast. "I know it called my name. Like literally pulled me out of my sleep. I ate two of those bad buddies in the middle of the night." She bit into her toast. "Oh my God! And it was just as good as this toast." She pulled the toast back and began examining it. "This ain't no regular ole toast."

"Okayyy," Tyra said. "I thought it was just me."

"Me too," Jackie added. "Maybe the bread tastes different when you're out of the country."

"Maybe *everything* tastes different." Gizelle took another bite of her toast.

"Or maybe just everything Margaret makes," Angelina added. "I know what goes on during our vacation is supposed to stay, but can we take Margaret with us, please?"

The girls chuckled.

"Or at least this toast," Tyra said.

Honey laughed. "I was trying to stay away from carbs." She stood and bent over to grab a piece of toast, "but damn. If y'all raving over a piece of bread like that . . ." Her words trailed off.

"Oh, by all means, Honey, go for it," Gizelle said mockingly. "Life is short," she continued. "A little carb ain't gon' kill ya. Now eating someone out a lot, that just might."

All eyes shot toward Gizelle.

"Oopsie." Gizelle covered her smile with her hand. "I meant eating out a lot. My bad." She bit into her toast again.

Honey let out a confused chuckle but proceeded to butter her bread.

The girls had been in each other's lives for quite some time and practically spoke their own language. It was one Honey didn't always understand, but it often amused her. And she liked the challenge of putting the puzzle pieces together that made up the Fab Five. And it helped that whenever Jackie noticed the confused look on her face, she was quick to translate or explain. Only this time, Jackie looked just as confused as Honey.

"Bae, here, you have to try it." Gizelle grabbed a saucer, placed a slice of toast on it, and handed it to Bae.

"Thank you," Bae said. She went to take a bite but paused when Gizelle spoke up.

"Don't you want some butter or something on it?" she asked.

"No, thank you. I'm good," she replied.

"Wait, hold up." Gizelle quickly picked up a small glass condiment bowl and pushed it toward Bae. "How about a taste of honey? I'm sure that's more your style anyway nowadays."

Bae wore a puzzled look as she rejected Gizelle's offer. "No, thank you." She let out a confused chuckle and then looked at the other girls, who were busy eating their food.

"So, what's on our agenda for the day?" Honey asked. "I'm ready to shake a tail feather like we did last night. I haven't danced so much and had this much fun since I can remember." Honey started rocking back and forth while snapping her fingers.

"Now you're out of jail and in a circle," Angelina said, "so get used to it."

Realizing what she just said, Angelina waited for Bae to cop an attitude. Like she did whenever she felt someone was trying to infiltrate their circle. But instead, she was surprised to see Bae unfazed by her comment as she sat in her chair eating the toast Gizelle had given her.

Angelina looked at the other girls, who were bracing themselves as well.

"Wasn't that the best time?" Jackie said, quickly moving things on before what Angelina said registered with Bae.

"Agreed," Angelina said. "I love vacations with my boo-thang, but ain't nothing like a trip with my girls." She and Jackie, who were sitting next to each other, high-fived.

Gizelle looked at Honey. "So, Honey, how are you enjoying your first time out of the country?"

"I'm having a blast." Honey's eyes lit up. "As I said before, you all have been so welcoming. I'm not used to this from other women."

"Could have fooled me," Gizelle said almost under her breath as she grabbed her glass of orange juice and took a sip.

There was an apparent shift that took place somewhere between last night and this morning. The foul air Bae was once blowing out now seemed to be coming from Gizelle's direction.

"Anyway, I could get used to this." Honey smiled.

"I bet you could." Again, Gizelle spoke under her breath.

Tyra clasped her hands together. "So, what's on the agenda today, again?" She looked at her watch. "What time do we plan on heading out?"

"Shopping, shopping, and more shopping," Bae informed the girls. "Our transportation will be here in a couple of hours. After that, I figured we come back home and wind down at the pool. I have a mobile spa coming. It's a full team, which means we can get massages, manis, pedis, get our hair did, and a wax." She put her hands together in prayer mode and bowed her head. "Whatever you like." She mocked Eddie Murphy's movie *Coming to America*.

The girls chuckled.

"Sounds divine," Jackie said. She got up from the table. "Well, I'm going to call the hubby and kids, get myself together, and meet you ladies back down here in two hours."

"I'm right behind you," Tyra said, taking one last bite of toast. "I'll have to stuff myself into my swimsuit this afternoon if I don't stop."

"Sista girlfriend, I'm on vacation." Angelina stuffed the last of her toast in her mouth and started singing as she stood up, raised her arms, and bounced her butt up and down. "*I thought I told ya that we won't stop.*"

"*Don't stop, get it, get it. Don't stop, get it, get it,*" Tyra sang as she, Jackie, and Angelina bounced out of the room.

"So, Honey, tell me more about your ex," Gizelle said. "I know you've shared some things with me about him when we've gone out to lunch a couple of times. But how are you doing? Are you good? Has he reached out to you? Do you think about getting back with him? I mean, maybe your leaving the country is an eye-opener for him, and he'll change. This could be just the phase that brings you two back together and closer than ever."

"You Iyanla now?" Bae jumped in with an attitude. "I'm sure she didn't come on a girls' trip to talk about a man." She sucked her teeth. "As a matter of fact, she came on this trip to get *away* from him."

Gizelle whipped around in her chair to face Bae. "And what makes you so sure? You hardly even talk to her, and when you do, you a crab-ass bitch toward her."

"You don't know what I am toward her." Bae stood up. "And besides, I've apologized for my actions. We've had a great time since. So, why are you trying to go backward when everybody else is moving forward?" Bae leaned toward Gizelle and pointed in her face. "Now *you're* the one acting like a crab."

Honey got up and stood between them. "Whoa, whoa, whoa. Hold up, ladies." She looked at Gizelle. "I don't mind you asking me about my ex. It feels good that somebody cares and wants to know what's going on inside my head and heart."

"Thank you," Gizelle said to Honey while shooting Bae an I-told-you-so look.

Next, Honey turned her attention toward Bae. "And thank you for being concerned, Bae." Honey gave her a soft smile.

When Bae returned the smile, Honey hurried to pull her eyes away from Bae's because she would have gotten stuck in them in a few more seconds like she did last night. "But right now, like the other girls, I just want to get myself together, go shopping, and have fun hanging out with you ladies. Does that sound like a plan?" She looked back and forth between Bae and Gizelle. When neither responded, she repeated her question.

After a few seconds, Gizelle let out a hot gush of wind. "Yeah, sounds like a plan for sure." She turned back around to the table, picked up a strawberry from the fruit bowl, and tossed it into her mouth.

"Cool, I'll see you ladies in a bit." Honey exited the room and headed up the stairs to her bedroom, winking at Bae on her way out.

Bae and Gizelle remained in the room, where nothing but silence joined them. Finally, after a moment or so, Bae spoke. "Well, I'm going to do a little meditating and yoga on my balcony. I'll catch up with y'all back down here when our ride gets here."

"Yep," Gizelle said, staring straight ahead.

Bae stood there for a moment. She opened her mouth to say one last thing, but for the first time since she met Gizelle, she decided against it. Twelve in a Dozen was enough this time.

The girls had the most amazing time shopping for souvenirs and exploring Saint Martin. And after a few hours of doing so, they were glad to head back to their rental and hang out at the pool. Even though Bae and Gizelle seemed cool, there was something in the air that none of the other girls could cohesively put their finger on. But it didn't stop them from having the time of their lives splashing around in the pool, floating on floaties, some equipped with everything but a television. That is when they weren't getting a mani, pedi, massage, or their hair braided. This was the ultimate girls' trip. The ladies couldn't stop thanking Bae for providing them with such a fantastic experience.

"Bae, I promise you when I make a million-dollar commission for selling one of them houses out there in Red Rock, I got you," Tyra promised her. She looked around at the other girls doing their own thing in the pool or poolside. "I got all of y'all. That's my word." She pumped her fist to her chest and pretended as if she were going to cry.

"We know you do, Tyra, and we're going to hold you to it," Jackie said.

As a real estate agent, Tyra swore up and down that her vision boarding and manifestation practice was why she sold at least half of all the homes she showed in a month. And she didn't sell no punk houses either. Half a million and up. The firm she worked for had agents to handle the sale of homes under half a million. Tyra graduated from the low-tier showings to the middle tier but was hell-bent on manifesting to three-tier showings, which was a million and a half upward. And her girls knew she could do it. Therefore, they knew it wouldn't be long until Tyra made good on her word.

"This is the fucking life," a tipsy Tyra shouted.

"Quiet down, Tyra." Jackie put her index finger over her mouth. "We have guests." She was referring to the spa staff.

"Oh, my fucking bad," Tyra said and then stuck her tongue out at Jackie, who pulled the brim of her over-sized floppy sunhat to cover her embarrassed flushed face.

"I done told you that you gon' have to cut out all that cussing," Bae told Tyra as she raised her upper body from the lounge chair where she was getting a pedicure. "Bitch, I'm saved."

The girls chuckled except for Jackie, who was that much more embarrassed.

"No, but seriously," Bae said, "it's my pleasure. Y'all my girls. Y'all been down with me from day one."

"Speaking of going down on you . . . I mean being down *with* you," Gizelle said, "Honey hasn't. That is, Honey hasn't been down with you, unlike the rest of us. And yet you decided to pay her share as well."

"For real?" Tyra asked.

"Yeah. I mean, Honey CashApped Bae the money, but Bae refunded it. Go figure." Gizelle shrugged her shoulders and said sarcastically, "Look at Bae, turning over a new leaf. I'm so proud of you."

"Yeah, well," Bae said smugly, "I didn't want to come across as petty and make Honey be the only one paying for the trip."

"Huh, Miss Petty Betty herself," Gizelle shot back.

"Anyway, Honey, you're welcome," Bae said, not in the mood to go back and forth with Gizelle. But that didn't stop Gizelle.

"And I'm sure there are a million ways you'll be able to thank her," Gizelle said to Honey and let out a tsk.

Bae was good and tired of how Gizelle had been acting all day.

And so was Tyra.

"Look, I don't know what's going on, but you hoes better get over it," Tyra said.

"I know what's going on," Jackie said. "It's so obvious. It's about Honey."

Bae's eyes got larger than the round donut ring Jackie was floating on. "What-What are you talking about?"

"You're jealous that because Honey and Gizelle spend every day at work, they are going to become besties," Jackie said. "You think we don't know how you really feel about Gizelle?"

Just when Bae thought her eyes couldn't get any bigger, there she sat with eyes as big as the cartoon character Garfield, the cat.

"We know she's your bestie. I mean, sure, me and the other ladies are your best friends, but Gizelle is your bestie. After all, she was right behind you when you moved to Vegas from Michigan. You two have been friends longer than the rest of us, so it's cool. We get it. And we understand. And even though you basically admitted such and apologized," Jackie now addressed Gizelle, "you're feeling a way because you can't believe Bae would think you would ever replace her for one minute. You thought you two were better than that. Am I right?" She looked back and forth between Gizelle and Bae. "That's it, right?"

"Yeah, Jackie, you're right," Gizelle said. "I did think we were better than that. But I guess I was wrong." She gathered her things and headed up the stairs.

And this time, Kevin let Whitney go.

Chapter 9

So, Now What?

Bae sat at the bar in her penthouse, stirring her drink as she stared out the window. The ladies returned from Saint Martin the night before, and ever since, all Bae kept asking herself was . . . "Now what?"

Now what, when it came to her and Honey's relationship, as she and Honey hadn't even exchange phone numbers? After their night of intimacy in Saint Martin, nothing else happened between them. Nothing sexual, anyway. They continued the remainder of the trip like nothing had even happened between them. And the great thing about it waas that there wasn't even any weird awkwardness between them.

However, speaking of Gizelle . . .

Now what, when it came to her and Gizelle's relationship? She and Gizelle had far too much history, so that one was a bit more complicated to figure out than the one she had with Honey.

Honey and Bae may not have acted weird on the rest of the trip, but that didn't stop Gizelle from acting funny. But not even Gizelle stopped it from being one of the best girls' trips of their lives. Still, it left a sour taste in Bae's mouth because, once again, a twenty-four-hour period had lapsed where the two besties hadn't talked to each other, which was not sitting well with Bae.

Now what, when it came to the most important relationship in her life other than the one she had with God,
which was her relationship with herself?

As Bae took a sip from her drink, she decided she
would tackle her relationship with Honey first. That was
easy. There wouldn't be one. Yes, Honey had brought
something out in Bae that had been lying dormant for
years. And Bae was grateful for that. Otherwise, she
would have continued living her life as a lie. But Honey
wasn't her truth.

Next, she tackled her relationship with Gizelle. It took
her dialing Gizelle's number a thousand times, but she
finally let the call go through. But she punked out on
having a one-on-one with Gizelle and invited the rest of
the Fab Five on the FaceTime call. And as a result, they
scheduled an in-person tea party for that upcoming
weekend.

As far as her relationship with herself and God, that
was a no-brainer for Bae. She loved the hell out of herself.
The only person she loved more than herself was God. So,
even though she was mad at herself for not being honest
with herself for so long, even though she was angry at
herself for all the lies she told herself, she forgave herself.

And her relationship with God? Well, she prayed He
would forgive her as well. Not for who she was. But for
thinking He would forsake her for the lies she'd told
herself about who she was . . . and who she wasn't.

Hey, Narrator, I'ma let you finish, but this is the
novella of the year, so there is something I want to say.

I know what people are thinking. They're thinking
Gizelle, Honey, and I, Bae Bee Anthony, will have some
kind of threesome. We'll be fuck buddies, bumping
coochies before we head out to the club to take some

dick home or let dick take us home. Because that's what lesbians are, right? That's what lesbians do, right? We're not people who fall in love and want a monogamous relationship with one woman, right? We just want to lust after and fuck other women. Not love a woman. Not be loved by a woman. Not make a family with a woman. Right?

Answer me, damn it!

Somebody who knows all the answers, please answer me because I'm seriously asking this question for a friend because I honestly don't have the answer myself. How the hell am I supposed to know how to be gay, bitch? I'm saved. Isn't that one of the big sins in the Bible? At least the main one society seems to focus on constantly. I mean, I really must have missed the memo that we only care about whether gay people go to hell.

The bitch at the bakery will make my fat ass a cake because she doesn't care if I go to hell for gluttony, greed, or what the fuck ever. But she cares if I go to hell for being homosexual so that she won't make me a cake? Now you see why the fuck I was so confused in middle school. And two decades later, a bitch still confused.

And not knowing these answers could be why I've had so many screwed-up relationships in my life. I'm not saying it is, and I'm not saying it isn't. I'm just saying that I don't know.

But what I *do* know is that people look at me and automatically think I have fat-girl issues. Hell, I got *girl* issues. I wish I could be in Jay-Z mode versus Kanye mode and say I got ninety-nine problems, but a bitch ain't one. A bitch is ninety-nine of them motherfuckers.

It goes beyond Gizelle and Honey. There was my first editor in New York. Then Sophie in college. Next, my brother's wife, Rebecca (that's a whole other book). And the ninety-five other females I pretended to hate, using that anger as a weapon to, perhaps, keep from getting the answers from within myself. And just in case you're wondering, Flower is not among those other ninety-five. I really did feel threatened that she would try to infiltrate the tribe.

I know, I know. It's time for Kanye to give Taylor the mic back.

I hope this little interruption didn't take away from the great job the Narrator has been doing so far in giving you the tea. I just could no longer keep quiet. As in the past, silence had gotten me nowhere, but everywhere I *didn't* want to be.

But now that I know where I *do* want to be, will I go there?

Bae drops mic.

Narrator picks mic back up.

"Am I the first one here?" Tyra walked into Bae's penthouse. "What? Gizelle's not here yet?" Tyra started looking around. She jokingly looked under the couch.

"Girl, cut it out." Bae chuckled.

"Let's just hope she doesn't walk in late with Honey," Tyra said.

Bae tilted her head and rolled her eyes at her. "Stop it for real." She walked to the bar, asking, "Can I fix you a drink?"

"Nah, I haven't eaten yet," Tyra said. "Do you have something I can snack on first?"

"Yeah, hold up a sec." Bae fixed herself a drink and then joined Tyra over at the couch, her glass in one hand and a bowl of lime-flavored tortilla chips in the other. "Here you go."

"Thank you." Tyra accepted the bowl from Bae and started eating some of the chips.

"Bae, I know I've said it a thousand times," Tyra started, "but thank you again for our trip. Ever since we landed, I've had a smile on my face, thinking about what a blast we had."

"You're welcome." Bae smiled, glad she could put that kind of smile on her friend's face. She went to take a sip of her drink when the door buzzed. She paused, the glass at her lips.

"Go 'head," Tyra said, setting the bowl on the table. "I'll get it."

She got up and answered the door, where she found the remaining members of Fab Five. "What up, chicks?" Tyra said.

The women greeted one another, fixed drinks, and gathered around the coffee table, discussing some of the highlights of their trip the entire time.

And although both Gizelle and Bae were their usual engaging selves, they seemed to avoid interacting with each other. This didn't go unnoticed by the other women . . . to the point that after two drinks, Jackie had the liquid courage to speak on it.

"So, what's up with this weird energy between the besties?" Jackie waved an accusing finger from Gizelle to Bae. "And don't pull that ole 'I don't know what you're talking about' bullshit," she slurred.

"Uh-oh. Who invited Jacqué?" Angelina laughed.

"No, no," Jackie said, shaking her head. "This is Jackie. This is *me* wanting to know what this . . ." Then she stirred the air with her hands, ". . . is."

Gizelle chuckled. She looked at Bae. "Come on, let's entertain her." She winked at Bae before turning her attention to Jackie. "And do tell me, Jackie, what this *is*."

With her drink in hand, Jackie leaned forward and stared at Gizelle. "The same *this* that was in Saint Martin with us the last couple of days. The same *this* we all pretended wasn't there because we wanted to end our trip with a bang and not a boom from you two blowing up at each other."

Gizelle replied first. "There is no angry tension between Bae and me, Jackie, so I hate to say it, but I don't know what you're talking about." She looked at her bestie. "Bae, what say you?"

"I say there is no angry tension between us either," Bae said.

"And I agree as well," Jackie said. "What I'm sensing isn't anger but tension." She glared between the two women. "I just can't seem to put my little finger on it." She licked her index finger and dotted the air. "Can you, ladies?" She looked toward Tyra and Angelina. "Do you feel it too?"

Tyra cleared her throat. "Well, now that you mention it, Jackie, yeah, I sense a little something-something going on. But I just figured it was some lingering feelings about the whole Honey issue."

Gizelle let out a knowing harrumph.

"See? See what I'm talking about?" Jackie pointed an accusing finger at Gizelle.

"And what's that supposed to mean?" Bae asked Gizelle.

"What?" Gizelle feigned ignorance and innocence.

"That little harrumph you just let out when she mentioned Honey," Bae said. "It's not the first time you've done that or made slick, little comments, particularly regarding Honey." Bae leaned back on the couch with her drink in hand, crossing her legs while staring at Gizelle. "So, instead of doing the two-step and dancing around stuff, why don't you just say whatever is on your mind? After all, with your dad being white and all, you know you took after his side of the family, and you don't have the good ol' rhythm."

Jackie frowned. "Hey, my dad and momma are white. So, what's that supposed to mean?" She looked at Bae with pouty lips.

"It means that it's a shame that both your parents are white, and you *still* have more rhythm than Gizelle." She turned to face Gizelle. "At least right now when it comes to dancing around words." She leaned in again toward Gizelle. "So, come on, Gizelle, stop dancing or catch the beat. One or the other." She leaned back again.

This wasn't necessarily how Bae envisioned talking things out with Gizelle, but it went without saying that this was their love language. One they both spoke and understood. So, it only makes sense that this wouldn't go down any other way.

Gizelle bit her bottom lip and let out a wicked laugh while she shook her head. "Bae Bee, you *don't* want to do this." She leaned in to meet Bae's stance and demeanor. "Not here. Not now. Trust me." And now it was Gizelle who leaned back and crossed *her* legs.

"Trust me, I do," Bae said, "because like Jackie said, whatever *this* is, we need to handle it so we can move on."

"Whatever *it* is, huh?" Gizelle said sarcastically. "It has a name. Its name is Honey."

"I knew it, damn it. I knew it," Tyra said as she jumped up and began doing a victory dance. "I knew some shit went down with Honey." She pointed between Bae and Gizelle. "I couldn't figure out with whom, though. But that morning at breakfast in Saint Martin, the stuff Gizelle was saying, I knew something was up."

Bae and Gizelle remained silent as they stared intensely into each other's eyes.

Tyra waited impatiently for some response as she looked back and forth between the two. "Oh, so now you bitches wanna exercise your right to remain silent? Any other time we can't shut y'all up, and now the cat's got your tongues?"

"Or maybe Bae's tongue got a cat," Gizelle laughed.

"Laughing to keep from crying, Gizelle?" Bae asked. "Since, of course, you'd rather it had been *your* cat that the tongue got?"

Tyra's, Angelina's, and Jackie's mouths dropped *wide* open.

"Wait a minute," Tyra said in shock. "So, it was you and Honey something happened between?" she asked Bae. "But *you* wanted to be with Honey?" she asked Gizelle. "So, at the end of the day, all of that crazy-ass energy on the trip was because of Honey's honey?" Tyra burst out laughing. She looked at Jackie, offering her a high five.

"Not now." Jackie shook her head at Tyra. "Not now."

Tyra's laughter faded.

Meanwhile, Gizelle and Bae sat there, having a visual standoff.

Angelina placed her glass on the table and sat up straight with a serious look on her face. "Uh, ladies, I think we may want to let Gizelle and Bae be alone."

"That might be a good idea," Bae suggested after having second thoughts about having this conversation among the Fab Five.

"Yeah, ladies, run along." Gizelle shooed her hand. "Because I'm sure Bae is terrified right now."

"Terrified?" Bae snapped. "Of what? Of whom? Of *you?*" She let out a tsk. "Child, please. Since when have I ever been terrified of the words that come out of *your* mouth?"

"Since you don't want the other girls to find out that you want Honey," Gizelle spat.

"'Spite popular opinion," Bae said, "no, I'm not terrified at all. I'm not terrified that you all will find out that I want Honey. Because that's not true."

Gizelle threw her hands up and let out a sarcastic chuckle. "Oh, so now you want to call me a liar?" She threw her hands on her hips. "You're the biggest lie in the room. How much longer are you going to live a lie, Bae? Huh, how much longer?" Gizelle was all up in Bae's face at this point. "You don't want Honey, huh? Is it because you *already* had her?" Gizelle asked. "I saw you two that night. Yeah, those meat pies were calling my name, so when I got up in the middle of the night to go grab one, I walked by your room and just happened to hear you calling out Honey's name." Gizelle shook her head. "The next time you want to screw my coworker, at least have the decency to close your bedroom door all the way."

The girls remained paralyzed, thinking that Gizelle and Bae's verbal assaults on each other would finally turn physical after all these years.

"Take all the shots you want at me, Gizelle, but I'm not living a lie," Bae said, standing her ground. "Me wanting Honey is the lie. Because the truth is, it's not Honey I want. It's *you*, damn it!" Bae took in the deepest cleansing breath she could ever recall taking, including the ones in all those tons of YouTube meditation and manifestation videos she watched. And then she did it. She did something she had wanted to do since middle school. She placed her hands on Gizelle's cheeks, pulled her lips to hers, and kissed her gently. Afterward, she pulled back to get Gizelle's reaction. And since it wasn't one of disgust or even regret, she pulled her in and kissed her again . . . and again, until this time, she slid her tongue into Gizelle's mouth, and their tongues did a song and dance other than the ones of years past.

And it didn't matter what color Gizelle's daddy was. This girl's tongue *had* rhythm. It found the beat. And she found the beat . . . to Bae's heart.

Jackie's, Tyra's, and Angelina's mouths went from being wide open in shock to being open in awe, adoration, and admiration of what they were witnessing between two of their friends they loved dearly.

"Do you think I didn't know what this was all these years, Bae?" Gizelle said once their lips parted. Not even her rapid blinking could hold back the tears in her eyes. "You think I don't recognize this little routine and act of yours you've been doing since middle school?"

"You mean that *we've* been doing?" Bae corrected. "If I recall correctly, I haven't been on the dance floor alone."

"No, you haven't, have you?" Gizelle admitted. "And I recognized the melody when you started playing it with Honey."

Bae stepped back, although everything in her being wanted to step closer to Gizelle. She wanted to step inside her. Be one with her. Closer to the person she'd been the closest to her entire life. But like she'd done from the start, like she'd done the moment she first saw Gizelle walking down the hallway with Richard—not the captain of the basketball or football team or anything like that, but still the most beautiful boy in the school. So, one would think it would have been him whose Bae's eyes were glued to . . . but it wasn't.

It was her.

It was Gizelle.

It had always been Gizelle.

At the time, Bae didn't understand why she had the feelings she was having. She didn't know what they were. How to describe them. What they meant. If she should act on them. How to act on them.

And that made her angry. And so she took her anger out on the source.

"What you looking at, fatso?" Gizelle had said to the staring new girl at the school.

"Oh, my bad. I thought I saw an actual pencil walking down the hallway and thought I was going crazy," Bae shot back.

"My grandma is always saying to people, 'Your eyes are bigger than your belly,' so I'm assuming with that big-ass belly of yours, your eyes should have figured it out when I was long back down the hall."

By now, a crowd gathered around as Gizelle and Bae went head-to-head, firing off verbal shots. Finally, after six rounds each, the bell rang, allowing Bae to get that last blow in, which became the norm.

Although the two girls weren't in the same English class, they had the same assignment, and a week later, at the public library, while searching for the same book they each needed, they just happened to be reaching for it at the same time.

"You go ahead and take it," Gizelle said, "because I'm sure you'd rather spend your money on a supersized meal versus a book."

And so The Dozens began. After Bae's thirteenth shot, the two decided to share the book, allowing both to keep the money they would have otherwise had to use to purchase the book, then headed to the library café for snacks.

For the next few days, they met at the library after school. Each took turns reading a few chapters at a time until they finished reading the book. They both received an A on their book reports.

So now what? was the unspoken question each of their eyes asked once they no longer had a reason to meet up each day.

And without even setting a date, they both continued showing up at the library at the same time as they'd done when they needed to share the book.

Then it was the park.

Then it was the rec.
Then it was each other's houses.
The mall.
High school.
College.
All the way to Vegas, and now in the living room of
Bae's penthouse.

"So, now what?" Bae asked.

Gizelle blinked, tears falling. "Now, it is what I should have done years ago, back in junior high . . . to you instead of Richard." She exhaled as she went to take a step toward Bae, as she quickly wiped away her tears.

Bae stared at Gizelle, holding her tears back. What were the tears for? What were they about? She didn't know that answer any more than she knew the answer to why she felt the way she did about Gizelle when she first laid eyes on her. But this time, it didn't make her angry. It made her sad. Maybe that's what the tears were for . . . because she was sad.

Sad that so much time had been wasted living a lie.

But as had been hammered into Bae's spirit so much for the last few weeks, life was too short . . . too short to live a lie. And at that moment, she decided that was something she would no longer do.

"Gizelle, you are more than my bestie. You are my truth." And she kissed Gizelle like the entire world was watching, and she didn't care.

Gizelle was her truth.

The whole truth.

And nothing but.

The End.

P. S. Sorry for interrupting, but it's me again, Bae. If there were another chapter to this story, it would be titled "Girl Gets Girl." ☺